THE HATCHER

AND OTHER STORIES

BY IZAAK DAVID DIGGS

1	THE HATCHER
31	THE CORRIDOR
81	GREEN BOX TIME
109	TWELVE MILES
135	ALL THAT WAS BECOMES AGAIN
164	RESET

© 2022 Izaak David Diggs

ISBN 979-8-9864828-2-8

Cover art by Ike James

Official release 27Sep22

THE HATCHER THE HATCHER THE HATCHER THE HATCHER
HATCHER THE HATCHER THE HATCHER THE HATCHER THE
HATCHER THE HATCHER THE HATCHER THE HATCHER THE
HATCHER THE HATCHER THE HATCHER THE HATCHER THE

HATCHER **THE HATCHER** THE HATCHER

THE HATCHER THE HATCHER THE HATCHER THE HATCHER THE
HATCHER THE HATCHER THE HATCHER THE HATCHER THE
HATCHER THE HATCHER THE HATCHER THE HATCHER THE
HATCHER THE HATCHER THE HATCHER THE HATCHER THE
HATCHER THE HATCHER THE HATCHER THE HATCHER THE
HATCHER THE HATCHER THE HATCHER THE HATCHER THE
HATCHER THE HATCHER THE HATCHER THE HATCHER THE
HATCHER THE HATCHER THE HATCHER THE HATCHER THE
HATCHER THE HATCHER THE HATCHER THE HATCHER THE
HATCHER THE HATCHER THE HATCHER THE HATCHER THE
HATCHER THE HATCHER THE HATCHER THE HATCHER THE
HATCHER THE HATCHER THE HATCHER THE HATCHER THE
HATCHER THE HATCHER THE HATCHER THE HATCHER THE
HATCHER THE HATCHER THE HATCHER THE HATCHER THE
HATCHER THE HATCHER THE HATCHER THE HATCHER THE
HATCHER THE HATCHER THE HATCHER THE HATCHER THE
HATCHER THE HATCHER THE HATCHER THE HATCHER THE
HATCHER THE HATCHER THE HATCHER THE HATCHER THE
HATCHER THE HATCHER THE HATCHER THE HATCHER THE
HATCHER THE HATCHER THE HATCHER THE HATCHER THE
HATCHER THE HATCHER THE HATCHER THE HATCHER THE
HATCHER THE HATCHER THE HATCHER THE HATCHER THE
HATCHER THE HATCHER THE HATCHER THE HATCHER THE
HATCHER THE HATCHER THE HATCHER THE HATCHER THE
HATCHER THE HATCHER THE HATCHER THE HATCHER THE
HATCHER THE HATCHER THE HATCHER THE HATCHER THE
HATCHER THE HATCHER THE HATCHER THE HATCHER THE
HATCHER THE HATCHER THE HATCHER THE HATCHER THE
HATCHER THE HATCHER THE HATCHER THE HATCHER THE
HATCHER

She was surrounded. Being concerned about that fact was acceptable but being anxious about it was not; anxiety was weakness and weakness could get her killed. The town was well kept, every lawn deep green, every house and business tended to, but everything good was on the surface—below the surface were armed men and women who wanted to kill the stranger in the car with the out of state plates. The woman understood her concern was transforming into anxiety and drew a deep breath—

A police SUV pulled out of a McDonald's parking lot. Was it following her? The woman made a right turn and a few seconds later the police SUV did the same: Yes, it was following her. That realization and then the lights on the upper windshield of the cop car came on. The woman thought of the guns tucked within reach but they were useless; you shoot one cop and a dozen other cops take their place bent on killing you.

This is not helping—the tags are current as is my license. The title is in my name and I have no warrants. Everything is okay.

She pulled over, rolled down the front windows, and placed her hands on the steering wheel. Her plates were out of state but Kansas was seen as a friendly state to the state she was driving through. The cop emerged from his SUV. Bulky man, thirties, goatee beginning to go gray. Sunglasses. Expressionless face. As he walked towards the car the woman willed herself not to grip the steering wheel, not to give away the anxiety she was struggling to contain.

"Good afternoon," The cop said through a tight smile, drawling in the manner she expected. "Do you know why I pulled you over, this afternoon?"

He could be one of them...shoots me and plants a gun, well, another gun, in the car—
Stop that shit. Not helping, not helping at all.

"Nope, officer. I'm pretty sure I wasn't speeding."

"Pretty sure?" He leaned forward to look in the car. "You've got a certified speedometer..."

"Completely sure," she managed a smile.

Something is off, there is something off about this cop...
He's one of them, getting you to let your guard...

No. Stop, just…stop.

"We saw you come into town," the cop continued. "Don't see too many Crown Victorias any more. Another officer ran your plates and they came back clean as you intended."

As you intended?! Not good, not good at all.

The woman struggled to keep her hands relaxed, not gripping the wheel and kneading it.

"What do you mean, officer?" She asked.

This is it, The Moment.

The closest gun was in a secret panel in the dash—could she grab it before the cop drew his service weapon?

Stupid: You kill a cop and then you have all the cops in the world on you.

The cop looked up and down the street and around at all the houses. Was his arm closer to his sidearm?

"I mean," he said without looking at her. "You shouldn't be in a car that stands out."

That said, he looked in her face and nodded.

"The water is deep and fast," the cop whispered, a hint of a smile changing his mouth.

Those words, how could so much relief be released with those five words?

"But we know where to cross." She finished for him.

"How long do you need?" He asked.

"Fifteen minutes depending on the pickup. She's at 4317 Davis and then I take the highway east."

"Solid estimate," he said with another nod before tapping the door with his right palm. "Travel safe."

The Driver just nodded, too shaky to form words.

4317 Davis was a large house, single story with brick facades. Older neighborhood, posh but established posh, old money posh. There was no one out front.

"Where the fuck are you?" The driver hissed.

She drove on, picked up her phone, and texted a message along those lines.

"Sorry, overslept," came the response followed by. "B right out."

The driver circled the block, watching for oversized pickups and SUVs with US flag stickers. Sometimes they were obvious like that but sometimes they came at you in a Tesla or a Prius—preconceptions, like anxiety, could get you killed. On the second pass of the house, a woman in her mid 20s with light brown hair was walking down the path from the house to the sidewalk. She was tall for a woman, thin but with breasts that may or may not have been fake. An expensive looking bag was carelessly slung over her shoulder. She frowned when dropping into the Crown Victoria.

"This car is old," the younger woman said.

"But, unlike you, it is on time."

"No need to be a bitch," the passenger said as she settled in the back seat. The driver turned to look back at her.

"I have to be a bitch," she said to her passenger. "This is very serious business, there are people who will try and stop us with any means at their disposal."

The passenger lost her insolence, looked scared. This made her more human to the driver, something she wasn't sure that she wanted.

"Really?" There was doubt in the passenger's voice and on her face. "I thought the Libs just said that to scare people."

"No, it is as dangerous as they say, but I will get you there safe."

The driver faced forward again, reaching down for the stick shift.

"Please fasten your safety belt," she added.

Because the woman hadn't been ready, it was nearly twenty minutes before they were on the highway east and leaving the small town behind.

"Do I have to be Jane?" The woman in the backseat asked.

"Pardon?"

"Jane, the name they gave me when I made arrangements. I asked for another name but the last message I couldn't reply to."

"It's just a temporary name—"

"Yeah, I know, but—"

"Okay, what would you like to be called?" She saw a familiar expression on the passenger's face and added. "And it can't be your own name."

"Abigail," the passenger said brightly.

"Abigail?"

4

"Yeah."

"Okay, we don't have an Abigail on this trip so, sure…why not."

"What about you? What do we call you?"

The driver felt a familiarity growing between them and familiarity could lead to friendliness which could lead to bad decisions based on emotion.

"Just the Driver," she said firmly.

"The Driver?" Abigail sounded unsure.

"Yeah."

TWO

The Driver watched the fuel gauge which claimed a little less than half a tank. All fuel stops had been planned, it was all part of the choreography, but she still didn't like being below half a tank. After forty-five minutes of driving they came to a large city. The Driver hated traffic, all the vehicles in a big rush; she allowed herself the luxury of kneading the steering wheel and cursing under her breath. After fifteen minutes, they came to the exit she sought. It led to a busy area full of box stores and fast food restaurants. Suburbia. In the beginning, the Driver had the preconception that the danger she faced would mostly be in rural areas or small towns like one she had picked Abigail up in. When she voiced that opinion, her trainer had looked at her like she was an idiot.

"That is a preconception," he had said. "And preconceptions will get you and your charges killed."

The driver followed the surface streets until she came to a gated community. The gate was a problem, a guard in a booth scrutinizing her, the car, and the woman in the backseat. Maybe they were trained to see things, maybe they weren't. Maybe they were benign or maybe they were part of the groups that wanted to neutralize people like the Driver.

"Good afternoon," a blonde woman in her late forties smiled from the booth. Her teeth were perfectly white and her polo shirt ironed.

"I am here to see the Blitzens," the driver smiled. "My name is Ruth Jacoby, should be on the list."

"Let me look that up, Ruth," the woman smiled before picking up a tablet.

There was a moment...the guard was smiling but she looked at the car and her eyes changed...

Paranoid. You are totally fucking paranoid.

"You are good to go," the guard said after a few moments, turning back to "Ruth" with a smile but—

The smile is different, and it's a billion miles from her eyes. This is not paranoia, we've been made.

"Thank you," the Driver struggled to keep the tension she was feeling invisible and smiled up at the guard before driving on.

"Something's up," Abigail said from the back seat.

"Pardon?"

"Your energy changed," the passenger explained. "Don't worry, I pick up things like that, I'm kinda psychic."

The driver rolled her eyes and listened as her phone gave directions to the address she sought.

The house was two stories high, newer, pale red stucco. Not pink, pale red. Tidy lawn in the small front yard. Newer SUV parked in the driveway with a US flag sticker in the back window. A large, cloth US flag fluttering on a pole mounted to the front of the house. The Driver stared at the flag and thought back to her orientation.

"Keep in mind there will be plants," her trainer had told them. "Women looking for our help who will set you up and compromise your situation." A tapping on the passenger window, the Driver jolted back into the present, her hand automatically going to the gun in the pocket built into her door. It was a woman around forty, bland but attractive, maybe thirty pounds overweight but making the most of it with a well chosen, dark blue blouse and matching skirt. The driver motioned for her to get in. The woman smiled pleasantly to both the driver and Abigail.

"I'm Mary, I guess," she said to the other passenger.

"Abigail," the younger woman smiled back.

The smile left Mary's face and she looked at the woman behind the wheel for help.

"She wanted to change her name," the Driver sighed. "Please…fasten your seat belt."

As Mary got situated, the Driver sent a coded text about her suspicions about the woman in the guard booth. A few moments later a coded text came back: *Stay the course.*

"How long of a drive is it?" Mary asked.

Something about the tone of her voice made the Driver suspicious— *You're seeing saboteurs everywhere, this is not helping the situation.*

"Fifteen hours," the driver replied. "We have one more passenger to pick up."

THREE

Yes, the white Tesla was definitely following them. The driver wanted to change the route and evade their tail but she had been told to stay the course. They got on another interstate, this one heading north. The three women passed a billboard for a local megachurch, another reminding them that Jesus had died for their sins, and a third billboard advertising a new housing community. The fuel gauge was now at a third. The white Tesla was staying back but keeping them in sight. They knew how to tail, this was a bad thing, it indicated skills and knowledge the Driver didn't want to confront. There were many large pickups and SUVs with US flag stickers but not everyone of them was a potential danger—right? The air conditioner struggled against the humidity. Abigail mentioned it and the Driver turned the air conditioning up.

After an hour they got off the interstate and traveled east on a local road winding through farmland and small towns. It made the Driver uneasy, dug out all her preconceptions, she forced them back down.
"Why do they call you guys *Hatchers*?" Abigail asked brightly.
"Please, we don't talk about that—"
"Why? It's just *us;* we're all in this situation."
"We need you to follow the rules, Abigail. Please understand the rules are there for a reason."
The woman in the back seat allowed herself a bit of a pout.
What's her story, anyway? A good time girl who got careless? Drunk mistake?
Speaking of rules, what about the one about becoming familiar with the passengers?
"Can we have some music, at least?" Abigail asked. "The silence is murder."
The Driver cringed at that word but turned on the radio. Mary was quiet, too quiet, she seemed a friendly chatty sort but she was really quiet and that made the Driver suspicious.

The Crown Victoria came to a college town, older brick buildings, lots of trees. Students on bicycles, men with beards and messenger bags. The Driver found the apartment building they sought. A woman in her mid twenties with an eyebrow piercing and cropped hair saw the car and walked towards it. She was dressed all in black and wearing Chuck Taylors. The young woman climbed in next to Abigail.

"Sweet ride," she said to the Driver. "Didn't know these came in a stick."

"They don't," the Driver replied. "I had it done custom."

She found herself liking the third passenger but quickly shut those emotions down—

Don't get attached, don't get attached, how many times did Larry drill that into us?

"You must be Rose," Mary smiled from the front seat.

"Yeah, and you guys are Mary and Jane."

"She changed her name to Abigail," Mary's smile wavered a little before she forced it back into place.

"Abigail is a good name," Rose smiled agreeably.

The Driver wasn't listening to their soft greetings, the Tesla was still there.

They backtracked to the interstate. The gas gauge was at a quarter tank and the fuel stop was roughly an hour and a half north. Everything was planned, everything was calculated for as few stops as possible—stops could be dangerous. Who knows what the Tesla would do when they stopped for fuel and the bathroom? Scheduling bathroom breaks was impossible, considering the condition her passengers were in.

"I'm sorry," Abigail said. "But I need to use the ladies room."

It was unfortunate but things like that came up.

"There's a rest area eight miles ahead," the Driver said. "Why don't we make it a group stop?"

The others voiced their agreement.

FOUR

A Tesla held, what, four people at most? Worst case scenario, four people with guns who could be amateurs or they could be ex-military. The Driver tucked her favorite gun, a Smith and Wesson .357, into the back of jeans and leaned against the hood as the passengers went to relieve themselves. The Tesla parked a few spots down, only one shape inside. One shape, one shooter, that was workable…the last thing she needed but workable. A man got out, he looked eighty with white hair and a matching full beard. Stooped from age. Long sleeve button down shirt, khakis, and sneakers the Driver associated with aging mall walkers. The stranger was smiling, not at people, just smiling. He walked over towards the Crown Victoria and the woman with the gun like a jawbone down the back of her jeans.

"Lovely day, isn't it?" He laughed lightly.

The man seemed harmless but he had been following them since the second stop so he wasn't harmless, he was one of Them.

"Yep," the Driver replied flatly.

The old man looked around and nodded his head in appreciation.

"We are truly blessed with days like this, aren't we?" His smile thinned and something lit up in his eyes as he continued. *"Mara."*

The Driver kept any discomfort at the old man knowing her name buried.

"You need to take your little game elsewhere, mister," she hard stared the stranger.

He didn't flinch, if anything he took a step closer.

"This woman," he announced loudly, turning to address the others at the rest stop. "Is doing something illegal! More importantly, she is doing something *wrong*!"

People were looking over, some frowning—were the frowns about being annoyed by the loud, old man or because the Driver was "doing something wrong"?

"She is taking three women," the old man proclaimed. "Three poor, misguided souls, to have their babies murdered!"

"Shut up you old fucktard!" Rose had come out first and was stepping up to the old man. "You may be a thousand years old but I will beat your ass, you Trump loving shitheel!"

The old man looked startled than pleased at that; he let Rose see that she had played *his* game for a moment before becoming the voice of righteous reason again.

"Poor girl! So misled!" He cried, his voice cracking meaningfully, shaking his head to bring it home.

"I am so warning you," Rose snarled.

Mary was at her side, taking an arm.

"Rose, he's an old man!" The oldest of the women said. "I'm sure he has a good heart and has good intentions."

Rose shook her hand off and got in the car. The Driver half heard them but was focused on the other people in the parking lot. There were large pickups, one with a big US flag in the bed, probably with guns in the cab. She motioned everyone back into the car and once everyone had their safety belts on, drove them out of the rest stop. No one followed, not even the old man in the Tesla.

FIVE

"You didn't need to say those things," Mary chided, looking through the windshield with a minute frown. "You didn't need to use such language."

"It's backwards assholes like that who voted for you know who and created this situation," Rose muttered, gesturing around the car at her fellow passengers and their driver.

"So…everyone who voted for Trump is a backwards asshole?" Abigail asked.

"I don't like this conversation," the Driver said firmly. "We have to be unified, there are still many miles between here and where we're going."

"Sorry," Mary mumbled.

"Biden was a joke," Abigail muttered under her breath.

"Abigail…*no*," the Driver said strictly.

"I apologize for swearing," Rose sighed. "I'm just frustrated."

No one said anything in response. The Driver texted her handlers to keep them in the loop about the situation at the rest stop.

The Driver had contemplated wearing an adult diaper for the trip but when she had done so in the past it had been uncomfortable and she had developed a rash. Reluctantly, she locked the car and followed the others into the bathroom after filling the car. Her passengers had urinated quickly but the Driver realized she had to do something more.

"We're going outside for some air," Mary said to the stall of the door the Driver was in.

"Keep your eyes open. If there is a problem, come get me."

"Just," Mary paused, the Driver could hear a cringe in her voice. "Do what you need to do."

She did. *Mara*. The old man knew her real name, probably the surname as well. It didn't matter, the Driver didn't have a house to bomb or loved ones to be terrorized. The Driver cleaned up and flushed. Two women were in the bathroom, one white and blonde and the other black with long,straightened hair. They were looking right at the stall door, waiting—

And the blonde one was moving her arm and something was at the end of the arm, something bad. The dark haired one was reaching for something, something probably worse—

But the blonde was closer. If only one of them had combat training the situation was fucked but the blonde was easily disarmed, the knife clattering onto the floor.

"Pick that shit up," the dark haired one said firmly.

But she made the mistake of looking over at her companion and that was the opening the Driver needed. She disarmed the second one who struggled which led to a bone in her forearm being snapped.

"Ah, fuck!" She cried, dropping to her knees and drawing her injured arm to her chest.

Now the Driver had her own gun leveled at the blonde.

"We know you, Mara," the blonde said. "This doesn't stop—"

Anger rose in the Driver and she was helpless against it, pistol whipping the blonde to the tile and then hating herself for giving into emotion—when you gave into emotion you were playing *Their* game.

The Driver walked out quickly. The others were waiting at the front of the car. The Driver unlocked the Crown Victoria with the fob.

"Get in," she said firmly.

The other three women did. The Driver got behind the wheel, anxiety—like the urge to pistol whip the blonde—rising with such vigor she wasn't sure that she could force it back down.

They attacked me, but if the cops in this area are with Them the only part of the story that will become official record is that I drew an illegal weapon and assaulted both women.

Two women were approaching the Crown Victoria, both were soft looking and in their mid-fifties. One had moved into the path of the Crown Victoria—

Do I run her down? How far do I take this?

The other older woman was motioning for the Driver to roll down her window which was done reluctantly.

"The water is deep and fast," she said carefully after looking around the parking lot.

13

"But we know where to cross," the Driver replied. "There are two of them in the bathroom."

"Okay, okay," the older woman was thinking and then looking at the women in the car with a kind smile. "Don't y'all worry, you got friends around here."

"Thank you," the Driver said.

SIX

"Who were those women?" Abigail asked as they got back on the interstate.

"Rules, Abigail, rules," the Driver sighed, getting up to eighty-five.

The women in the parking lot didn't appear to be trained in situations like "cleaning" the bathroom, had someone else got in there before the women? Maybe someone aligned with Them?

"We're part of this, too," Abigail continued.

"You're part of it for sixteen hours," the Driver corrected her. "Those women, me, this is our *life* now."

"But, we're doing something illegal, too—"

"None of us are doing anything illegal," the Driver said firmly. "I am driving three women for an unspecified medical procedure in Denver."

"What's with you, Mary?" Abigail leaned forward. "You seem like the last person in the world who'd be doing something like this...."

The older woman looked uncomfortable, her hands fidgeting in her lap.

"Abigail!" The Driver said more firmly, raising her voice.

But then the woman in the backseat and her rule breaking had become unimportant—two large, black pickups were closing on them. They had the same front license plate brackets, US flags set into chrome; the Driver recognized the brackets and understood who was closing on them.

"Okay," she sighed. "We're gonna go fast now but everything is going to be okay."

"We're already going 85," Mary leaned over to see the speedometer, concern in her voice.

"It's okay," the Driver said, softer.

Seeing a gap, she dropped into fourth and floored the accelerator quickly reaching a hundred before going back into fifth gear. The trucks were, surprisingly, keeping up, clearly modified. How fast would she need to go? One-twenty? One-thirty?

"Shit, this is fast," Rose said through clenched teeth.

"Please don't swear," Mary said weakly.

Traffic was moderate, and the Driver struggled to weave through it, feeling a sheen of sweat in her armpits and on her hands. The trucks were struggling more, their center of gravity working against them.

They're not trained drivers, that gives us a chance.
They were now at 115. One of the trucks overcorrected changing lanes and lost control, swerving and then doing a barrel roll into the opposite lanes, colliding with a few cars.

"Oh, Lord,"Mary moaned. "Those poor people!"

The Driver got up to 120. The remaining truck couldn't keep up and was finally lost when the Driver jerked over onto the shoulder to pass slower moving cars.

SEVEN

"That was literally insane."

The car had been silent for a few minutes before Abigail said that.

"If you hadn't voted for that asshole, this situation wouldn't exist," Rose said, anger clear in her voice.

"Are you really blaming us?" Mary asked, she sounded hurt.

"Ladies!" The Driver said firmly. "We don't need this now, we have many hours left, we can't be fighting each other."

"That *was* nuts," Rose said quietly. "I didn't expect that."

"That wasn't the end of it? Is it?" Abigail asked.

"No," the Driver sighed. "We're still in an Anti state."

But that wasn't it, the Driver understood why *her car* was being targeted but also understood that suspicion was not to be shared with her passengers.

An hour passed. The radio was playing pop music that none of them were enjoying so the Driver switched it off. As her hand left the controls, she realized a familiar sort of vehicle was coming up fast behind them: A state trooper SUV. The Driver grabbed her phone and sent a coded text. Was she going the speed limit? Yes...not that it mattered. The state trooper could be benign, responding to reports of the chase, or the driver could be one of Them. The Driver got in the slow lane. The trooper got behind the Crown Victoria and turned his lights and siren on.

"Fuck, I mean, *crap*," Rose said.

"This is one occasion where the first word fits," Mary said softly.

"It's okay," the Driver said. "Worse case scenario, they arrest me and deliver the three of you home——"

Mary leaned forward and started sobbing, Rose moved to comfort her and the older woman didn't resist.

"Sorry," Mary said, composing herself. "That snuck up on me."

"We're going to get through this," the Driver said firmly.

"I'm almost out of time," Mary shook her head.

"I'm not the only one, Mary. We can have another driver pick you up tomorrow——"

"You don't understand," the older woman smiled bitterly.

And the cop was rapping on the driver's side window. The Driver rolled it down.

"Please shut your engine off, ma'am," the trooper said grimly. He appeared Hispanic and roughly forty, clean shaven.

The Driver did as instructed and put her hands on the steering wheel. "What is this about, officer?"

The trooper laughed at that, a cold mechanical laugh.

"I have had many reports of a vehicle matching this description driving erratically at a high rate of speed—"

"We are a car full of women, officer," the Driver said. "The men in those pickups made obscene remarks and were chasing us."

"You're already going to Hell, Mara," the officer put his hand over his service weapon. "What's adding lying to a long, long list?"

A minivan pulled up behind the trooper's SUV, the cop motioned for it to drive on but a white woman climbed out as did her four passengers, all of whom were filming the cop with their phones.

"Why did you pull them over, officer?" The minivan driver asked.

"Ma'am," the trooper said firmly. "I need you to get back into your vehicle and get back on the highway!"

An SUV pulled up behind the minivan. It was driven by a black man somewhere around forty wearing a blue suit. His three passengers got out and began filming the officer with their phones.

"Please explain why you are detaining these women, officer," the SUV driver requested politely.

The cop's hand was hovering over his sidearm, the Driver could tell he was weighing his options.

"Enjoy your momentary victory, Mara," the trooper said without taking his eyes off the people surrounding the minivan and the SUV. "This is a big state and there are a lot of miles between here and the border."

The trooper climbed back into his SUV and drove off. The Driver climbed out of the Crown Victoria, made eye contact with the drivers of the SUV and minivan and nodded to both in turn.

EIGHT

"So…your name is Mara?" Abigail asked a mile down the road.

"If she wanted us to call her that, she would have given us her name," Mary interjected timidly.

"And what about you?" Abigail continued. "You seemed extremely upset about the idea of going home."

"Maybe we should drop both things," Rose muttered.

Abigail turned on the other woman on the back seat sharply but Mary leaned back and put her arm between them.

"I can't have another baby with my husband," she said. "I can't bring another child into that world."

"What world is that?" Rose asked gently.

Mary just shook her head and sat facing forward again.

"His family is always watching," she continued. "They saw me being picked up by a car with out of state plates, this is my one chance, once I am back there I will be even more tightly controlled."

"What about when you go back after the procedure?" Abigail asked.

"What—"

"I don't know," Mary snapped. "I can't…I can't think that far ahead, I'm scared to, all I know is I can't bring someone else into that world."

The other passengers slipped into a respectful silence.

"Can I ask one question, driver?" Rose asked.

"I guess."

"Do you do this because you're a woman?"

A long pause, the Driver moved into the fast lane to pass a fuel truck.

"No, I do this because I'm a human being."

The Driver stayed at five over the limit. *They* had other cops in their ranks, more yelling old men in Teslas, other people in oversized pickups that would chase them. It was the same on every delivery and she had always made her deliveries, all thirty-three of them but—

How long would her luck hold out? This time she had broken an arm, pistol whipped one of Their ranks, embarrassed one of Their cops—surely They would not let that stand.

"You seem tense, driver," Abigail said.

"It doesn't take a psychic to see that," the Driver grunted.

"You're good at this," Abigail continued. "I'm guessing you've done this a lot."

"This is my thirty-fourth delivery."

"Delivery?" Rose asked. "Is that term supposed to be ironic or clinical?"
The Driver didn't get what she meant, maybe that it sounded like a cold term for transporting other human beings.

"We can't look at you as human beings," the Driver said. "We have to remain completely removed from this emotionally."

"That's weird," Rose replied. "What's so bad about emotional attachment?"
The Driver just shook her head and they drove on in silence.

NINE

"I think we need to change up with route, they keep locating me," the Driver sent an encoded text.

The response came three minutes and eight seconds later:

"Copy that and agreed. New route is attached. It will take you out of the way, hopefully They won't expect that."

The passengers were using the restroom. The Driver hadn't needed it; she was drinking as little as possible so she wouldn't have to leave the car unattended; They kept finding her, They were capable of sabotaging the car. The pursuers had her marked as she had made the most deliveries and, as others had pointed out, the Crown Victoria stood out, but the Driver's instincts were telling there was something else—

A tracker. One of the people in the car has a tracker...but which one? I would bet against Mary, her fear of returning home without the procedure was palpable....

"Nice, hadn't noticed this before," Rose was smiling and pointing at the trunk lid where a white sticker with red numbers was attached to the painted metal: 062422.

The Driver just mumbled something, craving a cigarette, craving many escapes from the stress that kept climbing up from the murk.

"My sister is in a wheelchair," Rose continued quietly. "She got beaten during the protests in Portland...do you remember—"

"I'm sorry, but I can't," the Driver said firmly. *It could be her*

Rose looked confused so the Driver continued.

"This personal shit, I can't do it, it's just how this works—okay?"

The passenger looked hurt but was working to push it back down, she nodded and got in the back seat. Across the parking lot Abigail was flirting with a couple of guys in their 20s. When she looked over, the Driver gestured towards her. The younger woman touched one of the guys on the shoulder and then walked back to the Crown Victoria. She was getting in as Mary approached from the truck stop and they were off.

"Why are we going the opposite direction?" Abigail asked as they merged back onto the highway.

"They keep finding us," the Driver explained. *Is it you, Abigail?* "Need to mix things up a bit."

Four miles down the highway, she turned onto a secondary road heading south and then west on a road so narrow there wasn't a yellow line. The Driver got up to eighty. When Mary sucked air through her teeth the Driver automatically smiled.

"You have nothing to worry about; this car may be twenty years old but I take really good care of it…it's my partner."

"That's an interesting way to put it," Rose said.

"That seat folds down into a bed," the Driver explained. "Everything I own is in the trunk."

"Where do you go to the bathroom?" Abigail asked, doubt in her voice.

"Truck stops, side of the road…"

What are you doing? What is one of the top rules? Don't make friends. I know you want to, fuck, it's a human need, but it one of the big rules.

The internal chiding was broken by a dot in the rear view mirror. A car? The Driver looked down at the speedometer, she was at 75 after slowing for a curve. If someone was approaching like that they had to be going 90.

"Everyone's seatbelt on good?" She asked firmly.

"I hate it when you ask that," Abigail pouted.

The Driver got up to 90. Narrow as the road was, the asphalt was in good condition. On one side was a sparse wood with trees she couldn't identify, on the left some sort of field with crops, maybe sorghum. The dot was still closing.

How? They would have be pushing 110.

It had to be Them which confirmed the tracker which made keeping her distance from the passengers a little easier.

Fucking tracker; there is no doubt now.

How long was the road? Twenty miles? That gave her ten minutes or so alone with the vehicle, hopefully it was just one. Smooth as the road was, there were curves; they were gentle but even gentle ones at 90 made the car lean and the tires resist a little. And the dot was not longer a dot, it was a big truck, maybe a Ford F550, with a big, metal push bar on the front, the kind for moving stalled cars off the highway—

Or ramming a Crown Victoria off the road.

She didn't like the truck but more so the Driver didn't like how the driver was able to keep it under control at such a high rate of speed. It was—
*It's not a truck, it is **the** Truck.*
After all her deliveries the Driver was finally face to mirror with the Truck, the legendary vehicle that had forced four Hatchers off the road, killing a total of eight people. All three passengers were looking in the rear view mirror.

"How can a truck like that go so fast?" Mary asked, openly fearful.

"Probably custom engine and suspension," Rose replied. "It's actually kinda cool."

"Shhh," the Driver admonished them. "I need to concentrate."

The Truck closed the distance until it was one car length behind them at 105 miles per hour. The Driver had been forced to look—along with other Hatchers—at photographs of the Truck's victims, mangled cars and bodies. "This is what we are up against!" The trainer had yelled, jabbing each photo with an angry finger. "This is the evil we are working against!"

And now it was on her rear bumper.

"Okay, God," the Driver said softly in the present. "If there was one time I could use a hand, this is it."

"Are you okay with us praying?" Mary asked.

"Yeah, but silent prayers."

The Driver got up to 120. Now the graceful curves were tests of her nerves and skill; if she dropped off the Truck would be on them. The car leaned and the tires chirped, when they did Mary's lips began moving frantically as she colored her prayers with fear. The Truck was several car lengths behind them, obviously even its driver had limits—

But a long straightaway was coming up.

I can hit 130 even when the passengers but even though this road is smooth---
No doubt. There can be no doubt right now.

Coming out of the last curve, the Driver floored the accelerator and the certified speedometer slowly rose from 120 to 125—

The Truck was still coming on.

"How can a truck go that fast?" Abigail's voice was shaky. "Fuck...I fucked up, Jesus. This is your way of showing me I have sinned and need to be punished—"

"Stop it!" the Driver yelled. "If you don't let me concentrate we will crash!" The speedometer edged past 130 but its progress stopped short of 135. She had never driven the Crown Victoria that fast, 120 was the old record. The Truck was right on their bumper, then dropping back a few car lengths, then right on their bumper.

How could they make a big truck go that fast? The thing is, it can clearly go even faster...

Maybe Abigail is right, maybe it is a vessel of God—

Stop. Just stop that shit, can't be thinking like that.

The road they needed to turn on was coming up. How fast could the Crown Vic make the turn safely? Even at sixty the rear end would come loose—and the Truck would probably ram them.

"Okay, guys," the Driver said quietly. "This is gonna be a little dicey—"

"Dicey?" Mary asked, eyes wide.

"You mean dic*ier*?" Rose asked.

The Driver hit the brakes, quickly dropping below 100, the Truck was right on them but the driver of the Crown Victoria jerked to the left, taking the car onto the shoulder of loose dirt and into a lightly banked culvert. The Truck didn't dare follow, the combination of loose dirt and its much higher center of gravity...the driver of the Crown Vic was counting on that. She slammed on the brakes right before the turn, driving on the loose dirt, off balance because she was partly in the culvert, it was worse than driving on ice. Jumping onto the crossroad, the Driver spun the wheel left and the tires bit on the pavement, the rear end coming loose as she expected. She dropped into third and the engine roared in protest as the revs climbed well into the red—

And she was back in control, moving up to fourth and getting up to seventy and shifting up to fifth.

"Where did it go?" Abigail was looking out the back window, her arm across the back of the seat.

The Truck was gone.

TEN

The passengers were rattled, not just by the chase, but by how the Truck had just *vanished*:

"How could it just disappear like that?"

"We're being punished, we're being punished…"

"I mean, *where did it go?!*"

"God sent it, I got lost, I just…"

Only Rose was silent, she was rattled as well but not as much as the others. *She would be the perfect plant, a Progressive…or so she is playing.*

The Driver felt stress but she also felt pride: She had handled the car like a pro and had even survived a run in with the Truck.

"Some call the Truck *the elephant*," the Trainer had told them after showing the grisly pictures.

"Because it's really big?" One of the Hatchers had asked. Jakob, he had been gunned down after being forced off the road by a couple of pickups a month after the Trainer's presentation.

"Partly," the Trainer had chuckled at that. "Back in the frontier days, people coming west had to cross a vast desert in Utah and Nevada. They called it *seeing the Elephant* when they got overwhelmed and had to turn back. We've lost five of you guys to the Truck, two quit after being chased by it, and three were killed as you see in these pictures."

"The Elephant," the Driver murmured to herself in the present.

"Pardon?" Mary asked, she had finally calmed down.

"If I want to back out," Abigail said. "What do I do?"

"When I get you to the hospital in Denver, you tell them you want to go home."

"Abigail," Rose looked over at her seatmate. "We just went through a traumatic experience…"

The other woman just held up a hand to silence her.

"What the heck am I doing?" Abigail asked thoughtfully. "I got in this situation because I was out, drunk, cheating on my guy…"

Her voice broke up and a line of tears popped out of her left eye. After a few seconds she composed herself.

"Mike…I am so lucky to have him. He stood by me even after I explained to him *how* I got pregnant, offered to marry me, the whole deal. But I didn't want that, a husband and a baby would just get in the way of me just…I don't know, living…I don't know how to say it."

She paused, looked out at the fields passing her window.

"And I was flirting with those guys at the truck stop," Abigail continued. "The Truck…I don't know, if you can't see you can't but I do."

Rose had no response to that.

"We need music," Mary nodded. "Driver?"

"Yeah, sure…as long as it isn't that newer crap they play on the radio."

Mary chucked at that, even Rose and Abigail smiled.

"Do you know what you're going to do, Mary?" Rose asked.

"Come on, Rose—" the Driver chided.

"No, no," Mary smiled. "That's fine. I am going to see about having an additional procedure when at the hospital."

The others in the car understood what she was inferring: *I am going to get my tubes tied.*

"Mary," Abigail said. "I know people who would love to take you in—"

"No," Mary said firmly. "My kids need me."

Abigail leaned forward, put a hand on the older woman's shoulder, and appeared on the verge of tears.

"The way you described your man and his people…they are going to give you a mean welcome home party."

"I know," Mary replied, almost too quiet to hear.

"Listen to me," Abigail said more firmly. "You ain't no use to your kids dead—"

"They won't kill me," Mary said, trying to be strong. "They're more creative than that, but things will settle after a while."

Abigail just sat back in her seat shaking her head.

ELEVEN

"Fuck! That is so, so *beautiful!*" Rose cried.

"Language, please," Mary replied, but she was smiling as they passed the Colorado Welcomes You sign.

"They still operate in Colorado," the Driver said, trying to keep the others grounded. "We could still be—"

"No," Abigail beamed. "We're going to be okay, I can feel it."

The Driver kept thinking of the Truck—the *Elephant*—as the miles passed.

"What is your car's name?" Rose asked out of the blue.

"Pardon?"

"Every car needs a name," the woman with piercings continued.

The Driver had to think about that for a few moments.

"Ruth?"

Rose seemed pleased by that and sat back in her seat with a smile. The Driver caught herself smiling at the rear view mirror but forced the smile off her face: *It could be her, she could have a tracker in that bag with the Siouxside and the Banshees badge on it.*

"Guys, I hate to do this but…"

"Yeah, yeah, the rules," Abigail smirked.

"That's right."

Rose put Abigail's blindfold on, the Driver helped Rose with hers and then put one on Mary.

Of course, taking the tracker into consideration…

They were still ten miles from the hospital. The Driver texted her handlers about the suspicion about the tracker. The handlers had a way of destroying trackers silently and electronically; they would pick the women up and deliver them the last ten miles. Due to the change of plan the blindfolds were taken off temporarily. While waiting, the Driver explained what was happening, studying the faces of the passengers, watching for any tells that they were guilty.

"Either I am off base or one of you should get a career in acting," she said.

"How could you suspect us?" Mary sounded offended. "After all we've been through together?"

The Driver wanted to embrace her, wanted to comfort her and let her know it wasn't *her* that Mara suspected—

And the Driver hated herself for that warmth, that weakness, and shook it off.

"You need to understand the people on the other side," she explained firmly. "We have had them access the inside, the very center of our operation…they are very intelligent and very resourceful."

"I get it," Abigail said with a nod. "You're just trying to keep us safe."

"Do you think I'm doing the Devil's work?" The Driver asked, the words out before she was aware they were being formed.

The younger woman studied her for a few seconds.

"I don't know, to be honest," Abigail replied. "I can see you are good at heart, beyond that…"

She trailed off and shrugged. A panel van was pulling into the turnout they had been waiting in.

A bald black woman around thirty wearing a dark blue, two piece jacket and skirt suit climbed out and approached the Driver.

"The water is deep and fast," Dark Blue suit said.

"But we know where to cross," The Driver finished.

"Ladies," Blue Suit smiled at the passengers. "Please, this van will take you the rest of the way."

Rose waved at the Driver and Abigail gave her a smile and a nod. Mary walked a couple of steps closer, Mara could tell by the older woman's arms that she wanted a hug—the Driver turned away, struggling to push everything she was feeling down. When the women who had been her passengers were safely in the van, Blue Suit turned to Mara with a concerned expression.

"I was worried about you last week."

"Yeah?"

"You never drink that much, it's not like you."

The Driver felt embarrassed.

"Please don't tell me I sent you some mawkish text."

Blue Suit smiled, took a step closer until she was only an arm's length away.

"Don't hate on yourself, you were stressed out and drank too much," Blue Suit looked over at the van. "I'd better get them to the safe place."

"Yeah, yeah—"

"We'll text you in a couple of hours about the next assignment."

"I'll be waiting."

Dark Suit climbed in the van and it drove off, towards Denver, a minute later.

The Driver climbed back into the Crown Victoria. She hadn't remembered a lot about that night aside from the pain the whiskey and cigarettes left behind the following morning. It was coming back, though.

TWELVE

The next assignment was in Missouri. The Driver filled Ruth up and started east. More and more details of the drunken night were coming back and they troubled her. She kept seeing Mary's face: *How could you suspect us?* That had been wrong—

The Driver recalled more and more about *why* she had been drinking, just being *done* with all the stress and, mostly, about always having to be *apart*, not able to get close to any passengers. It had worn on her by the twentieth delivery and she was well past that.

But I can't quit. How could I quit? Quit something so important—what kind of person would I be?

She thought of Abigail, Rose, and especially Mary, struggling to drive through her tears.

The Crown Victoria crossed into Kansas on highway 96 traveling at seventy miles per hour. She had dropped the women off shortly after noon and now it was nearly dusk. The road was surprisingly deserted so early in the evening, but there was a dot on the horizon. The Driver knew who it was, *what* it was; it had found her because she had enabled it to find her.

"Elephants can die," she whispered to herself. "Right? I'm pretty sure…"

She got Ruth up to eighty. The dot was becoming more distinct, a large truck with an oversized metal plate mounted on the front. The Driver, Mara one last time, braced herself, both hands on wheel. She saw Mary's worried face and smiled at that.

"You're going to be okay."

The Driver gripped the wheel, twisted it slightly to the left, and put herself into the path of the speeding truck.

Written 24-25 June, 2022.

THE CORRIDOR THE CORRIDOR THE CORRIDOR THE CORRIDOR
CORRIDOR THE CORRIDOR THE CORRIDOR THE CORRIDOR THE
CORRIDOR THE CORRIDOR THE CORRIDOR THE CORRIDOR THE
CORRIDOR THE CORRIDOR THE CORRIDOR THE CORRIDOR THE
CORRIDOR THE CORRIDOR THE CORRIDOR THE CORRIDOR THE
CORRIDOR THE CORRIDOR THE CORRIDOR THE CORRIDOR THE
CORRIDOR THE CORRIDOR THE CORRIDOR THE CORRIDOR THE
CORRIDOR THE CORRIDOR THE CORRIDOR THE CORRIDOR THE
CORRIDOR THE CORRIDOR THE CORRIDOR THE CORRIDOR THE
CORRIDOR THE CORRIDOR THE CORRIDOR THE CORRIDOR THE
CORRIDOR THE CORRIDOR THE CORRIDOR THE CORRIDOR THE
CORRIDOR THE CORRIDOR THE CORRIDOR THE CORRIDOR THE
CORRIDOR THE CORRIDOR THE CORRIDOR THE CORRIDOR THE
CORRIDOR THE CORRIDOR THE CORRIDOR THE CORRIDOR THE
CORRIDOR THE CORRIDOR THE CORRIDOR THE CORRIDOR THE
CORRIDOR THE CORRIDOR THE CORRIDOR THE CORRIDOR THE
CORRIDOR THE CORRIDOR THE CORRIDOR THE CORRIDOR THE

CORRIDOR THE CORRIDOR **THE CORRIDOR**

THE CORRIDOR THE CORRIDOR THE CORRIDOR THE CORRIDOR THE
CORRIDOR THE CORRIDOR THE CORRIDOR THE CORRIDOR THE
CORRIDOR THE CORRIDOR THE CORRIDOR THE CORRIDOR THE
CORRIDOR THE CORRIDOR THE CORRIDOR THE CORRIDOR THE
CORRIDOR THE CORRIDOR THE CORRIDOR THE CORRIDOR THE
CORRIDOR THE CORRIDOR THE CORRIDOR THE CORRIDOR THE
CORRIDOR THE CORRIDOR THE CORRIDOR THE CORRIDOR THE
CORRIDOR THE CORRIDOR THE CORRIDOR THE CORRIDOR THE
CORRIDOR THE CORRIDOR THE CORRIDOR THE CORRIDOR THE
CORRIDOR THE CORRIDOR THE CORRIDOR THE CORRIDOR THE
CORRIDOR THE CORRIDOR THE CORRIDOR THE CORRIDOR THE
CORRIDOR THE CORRIDOR THE CORRIDOR THE CORRIDOR THE
CORRIDOR THE CORRIDOR THE CORRIDOR THE CORRIDOR THE
CORRIDOR THE CORRIDOR THE CORRIDOR THE CORRIDOR THE
CORRIDOR THE CORRIDOR THE CORRIDOR THE CORRIDOR

THE CORRIDOR

He awoke in an orange, pleather chair; there was a moment of confusion
and then the understanding that he had drifted off in the waiting room—
It wasn't a waiting room anymore, though: The counter where the
receptionist handed over a clipboard with papers was gone. All that
remained were four orange, pleather chairs arranged with two chairs, a small
table with magazines, and two other chairs. The waiting area was along what
appeared to be a corridor leading off to his left and his right. Off to his left,
it was dim, slightly smoky. Off to his right, it was well lit and stretched off
as far as he could see. His phone was on the table with the magazines. They
were all beauty publications, attractive men and women with big, ghastly
smiles full of yellow teeth and titles including *Charmer* and *Trap*. They
distubed him enough that he quickly averted his eyes after grabbing his
phone. There was no signal. What was going on? What had happened to the
waiting area? He couldn't even remember whether he was there to see a
doctor or a dentist or something not health related. The corridor to his left
had grown smokier and there was the smell of sulfur. Laughter in the
distance, laughter without humor, the laughter of someone or something
that savors the pain of others. It made him uncomfortable enough to move
on; the man stood up and started walking down the corridor to his right.
Maybe he would get a signal if he walked a ways or would come across a
stranger who had signal.

The corridor was eight feet wide with white walls that appeared recently
painted. It made no sense, but the laughter and smell of sulfur told him he
needed to walk away from the orange, pleather chairs—the corridor had to
lead somewhere, right? He had been walking ten minutes and had yet to see
a door. The lights were recessed and set in the ceiling every ten feet.
Beneath his shoes was low pile, industrial carpet slate in color.
"Where the hell am I?" That question, out loud.
Maybe I died in that waiting room—
Just…no, not helping. I clearly wasn't in a waiting room, maybe I became faint and saw
the chairs and sat down to rest…

But why was he in the corridor? The lack of memory made him uncomfortable but not as uncomfortable as the dark end of the corridor at his back with the smell of sulfur and cruel sounding laughter.

The corridor opened into a room, a room large enough that he could not see the walls. On the floor was the same carpet with white foot prints continuing on in the direction he had been walking.
"Hello!" He called out, to his left and then his right. "Is anybody in here?!" No answer. He had been walking half an hour, had to have covered at least a mile—were there any buildings that large? And what was with a mile long corridor without any doors? Was that even to code, such a long hall without fire exits? That reminded him of the smoke and he shuddered. Looking over his shoulder, he saw the smoke maybe a hundred feet behind him, slowly drifting closer. Whatever was laughing was somewhere in the smoke, he could *feel* it. It was time to move on.

Maybe I had a serious medical condition and went into a coma and this is some kind of fucked up coma dream.
He pinched his skin hard enough to bleed; it hurt, whatever he was experiencing it was not a dream. After following the white footprints for what had to be ten minutes he came to the end of the room and the resumption of the corridor. Looking back, he didn't see smoke. Maybe he should have followed the walls and seen if there was a door in the vast room. That thought and then picking up on the smell of sulfur; the smoke and the laughter had to be close behind.

SUAVE 1 WITH THA SHORT EYES

The corridor widened from eight feet across to ten. There were four more orange, pleather chairs. A man in a suit was sitting in one, sipping something amber colored from a crystal tumbler as he started at the opposite wall where an old looking photograph in a simple, ash frame was hung. The picture was of a nude girl who couldn't have been more than thirteen.

"Thank, god," the man who had been walking said. "I've been walking for an hour—do you have phone signal?"

The man in the suit looked over with a smile; he looked debonair but debonair like an antique: Expensive suit. Pencil mustache and brylcreemed hair.

"Phone signal? No, there is not a telephone here." The man responded, he looked at the walker as if he were daft.

"Never mind—do you know where the exit is?"

The man in the suit looked back at the photo and took a sip of his drink. The other man looked at the photo, the girl seemed to be looking right at him, smiling lavisciously, he looked back at the man in the suit, unnerved, feeling as if he were in a spell.

"Sir, do you know what this place is?"

Suit man looked over with a smile and, surprisingly, a wink.

"Please, call me Errol. What about you?"

"I don't know, I woke up down the hall and started walking—"

"Your name, friend—you have one, right?"

"Dan."

Errol looked back at the picture and took another sip.

"Dan, a good name," he said pleasantly. "I have a brother named Dan, he lost his mind in the war but he's a good fellow."

"Please, do you know where the exit is?" Dan asked.

The man in the suit mumbled something that sounded like "Vancouver."

"Pardon?" Dan was getting desperate.

"What does it matter?" Errol smiled distractedly. "This is a lovely place."

"Errol, please, I need to know where I am."

"Dan, not to be rude, but if you can't keep quiet please move along."

Dan could tell he was getting nowhere with the stranger and walked on.

JUNCTION

This has to be a coma. What do we know about comas? Maybe in comas, unlike dreams, you can feel pain…and smell sulfur. This has to be a coma or an extremely lucid dream…
Or something else. Come on, you know what else this could be.
No, he wouldn't accept that.

The corridor came to a Y intersection. Both corridors looked identical—which one should he follow? There was something down the right on, a dot that was getting larger, moving like a person walking.
What if it's the laughing ghoul?
Should he quickly start down the left branch? Dan could faintly smell sulfur, the smoke had to have been approaching behind him. The figure down the right corridor was not walking, they were jogging. It was a young woman: Dyed black hair. Skinny. Afghan Whigs t-shirt. Early twenties. She looked scared.
"There's smoke," she was winded.
"Smell of sulfur? Laughter?"
"Yeah—"
"Then we need to go this way," Dan gestured towards the left branch.
The two of them started walking down the left branch.
"Does your phone have signal?" the woman asked.
"No, I was about to ask you the same thing."
"You don't know where we are, do you?"
"No. Did you wake up in a waiting area with orange chairs?"
She said nothing for several moments, finally muttering "What is this place?"
"I've been thinking I'm in a coma or something…"
She made a face, he continued.
"I mean, I've been walking well over an hour that has to be over a mile and a half. Are there any buildings that big?"
"I don't know. Did you see anyone else?"
"Some creepy guy named Errol."
"Creepy? Did he know where we are?"

"No."

The woman stopped, looking troubled by something.

"Errol…handsome? Thin mustache? Old fashioned clothes?"

"Yeah, he was drinking scotch and…."

"What?"

"It's really gross, I'd rather not—"

"I need to know."

"There was a picture of a girl on the opposite wall, naked," Dan said this reluctantly. "Young, twelve or thirteen. Errol was mesmerized by it, wouldn't talk to me."

He expected the young woman to wear a grossed out expression, maybe anger at the sexualization of a child. No, she looked scared, even more fearful than when she had mentioned the smoke.

"Errol…Errol Flynn," those words, barely audible as she stopped in her tracks.

"Who is he?" Dan had stopped, as well.

"An actor."

"Never heard of him."

"He was in movies back in the thirties—"

"Thirties, this guy was no more than forty years old, not a hundred plus." She just shook her head.

"I smell sulfur again," Dan said softly. "We'd better keep walking."

The woman just nodded and they walked on.

"It had to be another Errol," Dan said firmly. "Maybe someone obsessed with old actors who has emulated the way this Errol Flynn looked, his mannerisms.."

"Maybe," the woman sounded unsure.

"Look, I refuse to accept the alternative—"

"That we're dead and you saw an actor who died over sixty years ago?"

"Yeah."

"Oh fuck," she said, stopping in her tracks.

The smoke wasn't just behind them, it was *ahead* of them. Twenty feet ahead on the left was the first door Dan had seen. Could they reach it before the smoke did?

"Come on," the woman said, grabbing Dan's arm and pulling him into a run. Up ahead, they heard laughter, laughter and sexual moans that sounded an alchemy of pleasure and pain. The door was white but the knob was ornate, antique brass. The smoke was now on them, the smell of sulfur overpowering. The woman twisted the knob, fortunately it turned and the door opened.

DON'T COME ROUND HERE NO MO'

A man was sitting in a room full of musical instruments: A drum kit. Guitars and basses on stands. A couple of antique Fender Twin amps. He was sitting on a stool playing a twelve string Rickenbacker, simple blues leads coming out of one of the speakers. The smoke drifted into the room. "Y'all might wanna close the door," the guitarist said mildly, his accent southern, Georgia or Florida.

Dan did.

"What is this place?" The woman asked.

The guitarist looked around the room with a wry smile. He was wearing a suit jacket over a t- shirt and jeans, somewhere in his fifties with lank blond hair and a beard that was half gray.

"Last time I checked it was my practice space," he said.

"No, outside, the corridor."

"It's just a corridor," the musician shrugged, turning the knobs on his guitar and playing with the volume off.

"I've been following it for close to two miles, my friend here—" Dan offered.

"Mia."

"Yeah, Mia, she told me she had to have walked half a mile—how is a building this large?"

"Man," the guitarist smiled wryly and shook his head. "I've toured all over the world, seen some big ol' places."

Dan didn't have to look at Mia to feel that her fear had returned, it was coming off her in waves.

"Your name is Tom, isn't it?" She asked softly.

"Last time I checked," the musician said with a drawl.

Mia looked over at Dan and mouthed: *Tom Petty*.

First Errol Flynn and now Tom Petty. Were they in a version of Hell? What would Tom Petty be doing there? He always seemed like a nice enough guy.

"So," Dan said. "You've been out in the corridor, you must know where it leads."

"Ah, I don't go out there," Tom said. "In fact, that's the first time I've seen that door open."

He stopped playing and looked up at them in turn, it was clear he was struggling to be patient with them.

"Look, I've got people coming over and we've gotta practice so y'all need to leave. Not to be rude, but we have a lot to do."

"Is it George and Roy?" Mia mumbled.

Tom ignored the question.

"We don't mean to be an imposition," Dan said. "But there is heavy smoke out there."

"I bet it's passed by now," Tom said, getting up and putting his guitar on a stand. He opened the door and looked up and down the corridor.

"Well...off to my right I think I see smoke in the distance but off to the left it's clear as a bell."

He looked back at them with a knowing look.

"You're not worried about the smoke?" Dan asked.

Tom's smile became tighter, more secretive.

"Ah, things like that don't bother me anymore."

"So," Mia said a couple of minutes after leaving the practice room. "You see Errol Flynn and now we see Tom Petty and you still don't think we're in some sort of afterlife?"

Dan said nothing in response, how could he be dead. He was only....

How old was he? He looked down at his hands, they appeared to be the hands of a man in his thirties. And Mia was even younger, he'd guess she was 25 at most.

Twenty five years old can still die in accidents, workplace shootings, cancer—
Stop, just...stop. This isn't helping.

"I can't accept this," he said finally. "I mean, how can this be the afterlife? It's a *hallway*."

"What were you expecting? Clouds, people with harps? I mean, there is smoke and the smell of sulphur here, that fucked up sounding laughter—"

"Don't say it, please."

"Maybe we aren't dead," Mia sighed. "Because I am getting hungry."

The corridor opened up on the left where there was a small, Italian restaurant. No people were sitting at the four, square tables inside. A rotund man with a mustache and a happy smile came from the back with menus.

"Please, sit where you want. Can I get you something to drink?"

"Wine," Dan and Mia said in unison which made them smile despite their situation.

That pleased the man who laughed, nodded, and went back to presumably where the kitchen was.

"I don't even want to ask him if he knows where we are," Dan sighed after they sat down. "I can't help but feel he'll just blow us off like the others have."

The waiter came back with a bottle of wine and two plates full of some sort of pasta, red sauce, and meat.

They both thanked him and both were wondering the same thing:
Is he dead?

The food and the wine were delicious. After a couple of minutes, the waiter returned with a basket of bread and an apologetic expression.

"So sorry, forgot the garlic bread!"

"You guys been in business long?" Dan asked.

"Long time," the waiter smiled.

"Get a lot of customers?"

The waiter's smile thinned, the easy joviality replaced by something equally private and unreadable.

"Not too many."

"We're a little lost," Mia said. "Do you have a phone we could use?"

"Ah, no, sorry. No phone here—"

"In a restaurant," Dan sighed, taking a long drink of wine.

"How far is it to the parking lot?" Mia asked,

"Parking lot?" The waiter asked, his confusion clearly an act.

"You know, an exit, the outdoors?"

He just looked at her and then became jovial again.

"Hey, we have a big party, I've gotta go help in the kitchen!"

The waiter walked into the back.

"There has to be at least one cook," Mia said.

"Maybe a busboy, as well, let's check it out."

They got up and walked to the door the waiter had gone through. Instead of the usual swinging door one would find in a restaurant this was a heavy, steel door that was locked.

"I'm guessing we don't have to pay for our meal," Dan said.

"Your wallet, let's look at your ID!"

He reached in his back pocket; the wallet was there—why hadn't he thought of checking it earlier? The billfold was empty: No ID, no debit or credit cards, nothing.

Dan looked at Mia, she looked at him, there was nothing to say.

They sat at the table, Mia pouring them both another glass of wine. A couple of sips later there was a familiar smell, sulfur. She gulped down the rest of her wine and got up, it was time to move on.

"So, we've walked down this corridor for at least a couple of miles. We've seen Errol Flynn and Tom Petty, had some delicious Italian food…" Dan trailed off, none of it made sense. His empty wallet, for some reason, bothered him even more than the dead celebrities and the laughter in the smoke.

"We have to be dead—" Mia started, only to be cut off by her companion.

"But I tasted the food. My first mouthful was hot, I burned my tongue a little."

Mia did not respond for what felt like a minute.

"I don't want to consider it, either, but what else could it be?"

"I've read theories that our subconsciouses are joined—"

"Like we're both having the same dream—"

"Or both of us are in a coma—"

"Having the same dream," she was openly dubious. "We feel pain here, wherever this is."

"Feel pain, taste food…I could smell the wool of Errol's suit."

"I'm fucking tired of walking," he added, stopping and sliding against a wall to the floor.

Mia sat down next to him, staring at the white wall just like the white walls they'd been following for hours.

The faint smell of sulfur, laughter down the corridor they had walked down. Smoke, wisps at first and then puffs.

"What could happen?" Dan asked. "It's smoke…and some creepy laughter."

Before she could answer—

Dread. That animal instinct when something really bad is getting close, something that will hurt you in ways you've never been hurt.

Without a word, both of them got up and continued down the corridor.

After a few minutes, they came to a vast room with white footprints on the carpet not unlike the room Dan had crossed—

Hours ago? Days?

He had no idea and it bothered him as the empty wallet had. There was a shape off to the right, Mia started walking towards it. The object was a golf cart.

"Hey, you wanted a break from walking," she climbed behind the wheel and Dan got in beside her.

The key was in the ignition, after fumbling around for a few moments Mia figured out how to make it go forward and drove the cart along the white footprints. Smoke began filling the room, from behind them and coming from both sides; it was heavier than it had been before and the smell of sulfur was strong.

"Whatever is laughing is close," Dan said.

"Yeah," Mia agreed, pressing the accelerator to the floor.

"Wait, wait!" A woman's voice, off to the right. It belonged to a small, Asian woman somewhere in her thirties in an orange tank top, expensive looking jeans, and strappy sandals.

Mia slowed but did not stop, the woman leapt onto the bench seat that faced the back.

"Drive, fucking, drive!" She screeched.

The women behind the wheel pressed the pedal to the floorboards again, the cart felt slower, maybe it was the extra weight or—

Maybe the battery was draining.

The smoke was all they could see, all three of them coughed.

"My lungs are burning," the woman in the back moaned.

And then:

"Oh my God," those words, gasped.

"What? What?" Mia asked.

There was no response, all she could do was drive in the direction that footprints had been leading before they were obscured by smoke. Laughter, close now, it sounded only a few yards behind them. Footsteps, heavy footsteps, more than two by the sound of it.

"Hello, Satan, guess it's time for me to go," Dan sang.

"Not helping," Mia replied sharply.

A wall, a few feet in front of them. Mia jerked the wheel to the right but they still clipped the wall, bouncing off it. The woman nearly lost control but kept the cart from rolling. Now the left front wheel was wobbling and their speed diminished further. The footsteps were closer, the sound like a beast breathing, through the smoke she could smell foul breath. The woman they had picked up was leaning as far forward as possible. Looking over, Dan saw that her eyes were clamped shit and she was mouthing something, possibly prayers—

And then they were in another corridor and the smoke was clear. The sound of hooves and foul breath smell were gone, it was just the three of them.

Mia slowed the cart to walking speed.

"You can open your eyes now," Dan said.

"They are open, I was driving," Mia frowned.

"I'm talking to our new friend."

The woman opened her eyes.

"What did you see?" Dan asked.

The woman just shook her head, tears streaming down her face.

TH' WINDING SHEET MOTEL

The shuddering wheel made riding in the golf cart uncomfortable. Mia stopped and the three of them climbed out, the Asian woman looked dazed. "I'm Mia and that's Dan."

"Hazel," the woman finally said. "You guys wake up in the corridor?"

"Yeah, orange chairs. Was there a corridor coming into that room from the right."

"Yeah," Hazel said, nodding for good measure before looking up the corridor. "What is this place?"

"No idea," Dan said.

"Is it…" Hazel started but then trailed off and then closed her eyes again. "No, this is just a bad dream."

"How old are you?" Dan asked. "What do you know about your life?"

Hazel just looked at him, fearful again. She shook her head.

"We should walk," Hazel said, nodding her head, trying to look strong. "There has to be an exit."

Dan and Mia gave each other a knowing look and then fell into step alongside Hazel.

The three of them walked in silence. Dan and Mia refrained from speculating where they were. *If* it was indeed some variation of the afterlife; they could tell that wherever it was Hazel had seen had rattled here. With a sigh, the Asian woman stopped in her tracks, she appeared to be preparing herself for something unpleasant.

"It was a man but not a man. Very pale skin, smile, but a fucked up smile like he is looking forward to doing something bad to you. Short hair parted in the middle, slicked down. Old fashioned tuxedo."

"Old fashioned tuxedo," Mia repeated.

"Yeah, and he was floating," Hazel said hoarsely. "I knew he was about to smile bigger, I had a preview in my head…teeth, big sharp ugly teeth."

She closed her eyes and shuddered. Mia put a comforting arm on Hazel's shoulder but the older woman shook it off.

"We need to keep walking," she said roughly.

The corridor widened to fifteen feet. Off to the left was a desk, the front desk of a motel with a neon sign reading "No Vacancy."

"Ignore that sign," the man behind the counter said, his voice was low but musical. He was big, well over six feet tall with a soul patch and a name badge claiming "Mark."

"Like your shirt," he nodded to Mia.

"So, you have rooms?" Dan asked.

"Yeah," Mark replied. "But only one. It has three beds, though."

He rummaged behind the counter and pulled out a heavy looking skeleton key.

"So…how do you wanna pay for this?" the front desk man looked to his guests in turn.

"Just messing with ya," he smirked.

"Can you tell us where we are?" Hazel asked.

Mark looked at her, no expression on his face.

"A motel."

"A motel on an endless corridor, does that make sense to you?" Hazel pressed.

Mark shrugged.

"Look, lady, I'm just a front desk clerk—"

"Where do you go?" Dan asked, feeling he had come up with a good line of questioning. "Where do you go when you get off work?"

Mark stared at him, clearly starting to get annoyed.

"Off work? I don't know what you're talking about, man," Mark growled.

Mia grabbed the key and looked at her companions.

"Come on, I'm fucking tired."

A short hall next to the front desk ended at an ice machine. On the wall to a right was a door, one door. The one room in the motel. Mia opened the lock. The room smelled like cheap carpet cleaner and the freon from the air conditioner, *freon*, not the newer environmentally friendly stuff. There were three twin sized beds with floral throws.

"Bathroom is clean," Dan's voice echoed from the room with the toilet.

"Maybe Hazel is right," Mia said, sitting cross legged on the middle bed.

"Maybe this is just a bad dream."

"But we feel pain," Dan said, stepping out of the bathroom.

"Besides…whose dream would it be?"

"Maybe *dream* isn't right," Hazel said. "Maybe we're part of some government experiment, some type of virtual reality or something."

Dan lay on the bed and stared at the ceiling.

"All I know is it can't be real," he said. "Or at least not reality as I've known it."

"How do we know our names?" Hazel asked him. "We don't know why we were in the waiting room, we don't know our ages or anything about our lives and yet we know our names."

"Maybe they aren't our real names," Mia said softly.

Fifteen minutes later, all three of them were asleep.

Dan awoke in the corridor, startled—

Has it started over? Am I alone now?

No, Mia and Hazel were asleep in nearby and identical orange, pleather chairs.

"Wake up, guys," Dan said, trying to contain his own fear and anxiety.

Mia was instantly awake and appeared irritated.

"Are we back at the beginning? Does it just reboot every day?" She asked.

"I'm hungry," Hazel said, sounding groggy. "You guys had Italian food, I had nothing."

"I smell bacon," Mia nodded, down the corridor to their right.

"Me too, and it's better than what I smell off to the left," Dan said.

"The sulfur smoke?" Mia asked.

"Yep."

The three of them climbed out of their chairs and started walking down the corridor. A hundred feet along, the hall widened and there was a table with objects wrapped in wax paper. The bacon smell seemed to be coming from there. They looked at each other, what would they find in the wax paper? Food? A cruel joke? Something that would harm them. Mia walked over to the table and grabbed one of the packages. She unwrapped it, the object was a breakfast sandwich, egg and pepper jack cheese on wheat bread.

"It's my favorite breakfast sandwich," she said softly.

"This is weird," she added, looking at her companions.

"Fuck it, I'm hungry," Hazel said, grabbing her own parcel and unwrapping it.

"I don't usually eat bacon," she added. "But I love it."

"Is it your favorite type of breakfast sandwich like Mia's?" Dan asked.

"Yep," Hazel replied. "Bacon, egg, and American cheese on a bagel."

She took a big bite and chewed, nodding at the others.

The sandwich Dan picked was also his favorite. There were also three cups of hot coffee drinks to the exact specifications of each of them.

"This can't be a dream," Mia said as she finished her sandwich and grabbed her coffee.

"It doesn't feel like a dream," Hazel agreed, her mouth full of food.

"Maybe you were right about the government experiment," Dan gestured at Hazel with his sandwich.

"No," Hazel said matter of factly. "I think we're dead and this is the afterlife."

"I prefer the idea you had last night," Dan sighed, walking over to get his own coffee drink.

"So, they terrify us with the sulfur smoke and whatever was chasing us. But they provide us with food and a place to sleep," Mia said, it sounded as if she were talking to herself.

"And we meet up with Errol Flynn and Tom Petty," Dan added to her train of thought.

"Who?" Hazel asked.

"You know who Tom Petty is, right?" Dan asked her.

"I think, rock guy. What about the other one?"

"He was a movie star in the thirties," Dan said, running his hand along the wall. It was smooth and cool.

"Did you recognize the waiter in the Italian restaurant?" He asked Mia.

"No, but he could have been Oliver Hardy," she said.

"I know him!" Hazel beamed. "Laurel and Hardy, they were my father's favorite."

Both her companions looked at her sharply.

"You remember your father?" Mia asked.

"Just that," Hazel said quietly. "I have a picture in my head of me and an older man laughing as we watched Laurel and Hardy on television."

"I wonder," Dan said, stopping in his tracks. "I wonder if that memory could create a character in this place..."

"What do you mean?" Mia asked, pausing and looking at him.

"It's a strong memory," he struggled to explain himself. "What if she was thinking about Laurel and Hardy and it projected Hardy into that Italian restaurant?"

"This would mean we can control whatever this place is to some degree," Mia said.

"What if we could control the smoke?" Hazel said from a few feet further down the corridor.

As they had stopped walking, the smoke had begun to catch up with them.

"Let's try something," Dan said. "Get in a circle, let's join hands."

"What for?" Hazel looked suspicious.

"What if all three of us focus, picture the corridor free of smoke," Dan explained.

"It's worth a shot," Mia said, grabbing Dan's hand and one of Hazel's. The older woman shook her head but allowed her hands to be taken by her companions.

"Close your eyes," Dan instructed. "Just picture the corridor bright and with no smoke."

Each did, struggling with their own fears about closing their eyes in a strange place but glad not to be alone, squeezing each others' hands.

The smoke still bloomed around them along with the sulfur smell, the laughter.

The smoke grew thick, Hazel began coughing, all of them choking.

Dan opened his eyes first, the smoke was all around them, growing heavier, he could barely see the other two.

"We'd better keep moving," he said sharply.

"It was worth a try," Mia said a few minutes after nearly passing out from the smoke.

"What if this place put that memory in my head?" Hazel said. She appeared thoughtful at first but sad after a couple of moments; before she thought that she had a memory of a father she loved and loved her, now she had nothing.

"I don't know," Dan said. "This place can mess with us, that's for—"

"Shh," Mia said, holding up her right hand. "I hear something."

All three stopped and listened.

"Sounds like a city," Hazel said. "Up ahead."

"A city? In this place?" Dan mused warily.

"It's not like we can stop," Mia pointed out. "We may as well walk on and see what it is; the smoke will be along if we stay here."

The city sounds grew more distinct: Cars and their horns. Men hawking newspapers. Crowd noises.

And the smells also became clearer: Exhaust. Garbage.

The walls of the corridor became brick, dark from decades of soot and grime and weather.

Light, natural light.

"The exit!" Hazel said happily. "Maybe this is the exit!"

Mia and Dan looked at each other and recognized the doubt they felt on the other's face.

The corridor became a chain link fence that was ten feet high and with the sides wrapping up to meet over their heads. Above them was a blue sky, clouds, some haze from pollution.

"Wow, look," Hazel said, sticking her fingers through the fence.

All the cars were old, from before the Second World War as far as Mia could tell. This had to be a big city, a Chicago or even a New York—

If any of this is real, Mia thought. *This looks like the 1930s.*

"When is this?" Dan asked quietly, leaning against the fence.

"I was thinking the 1930s," Mia said.

"How do you know that?" Hazel asked her.

"What do you mean?"

"We know who Tom Petty is," Hazel explained. "You know how the 1930s look—"

"This place can get in our heads," Dan attempted.

"But you didn't know about Errol Flynn before I explained who he was—"

"What if they got that from you?"

"Guys," Hazel said. "What if these people can help us? Someone with wire cutters to get through the fence or something?"

Before her companions could respond she began shaking the fence forcefully.

"Hey!" She yelled at the people on the sidewalk, nearly close enough to brush her fingers. "Over here! Over here!"

"Hey!" Dan yelled, shaking his own section of fence. "Free money! Hot nudes!"

Mia laughed at that, she couldn't help herself.

Her laughter died when smoke began drifting in from both sides, darking the scene, getting between them and the blue sky.

"I hate this," Hazel whined, letting go of the fence.

The crowds on the sidewalk didn't seem to notice the smoke just as they hadn't seemed to notice the yelling and fence shaking.

The travelers again heard cruel sounding laughter from down the corridor they had come from and smelled sulfur. The smoke was heavy enough that they could barely make out the people on the sidewalk.

"Part of me just wants to be done with this," Mia appeared on the verge of tears. "Just wait for whatever is laughing back there."

"No," Hazel said firmly, grabbing one of the younger woman's hands. "I saw it, it's bad."

"And this smoke," Dan rasped. "I don't know about you, but when it gets strong I can't breathe—"

A little boy broke from the crowd and walked to the fence. He linked his fingers through the chain link and smiled.

"You see us?" Mia asked.

The child nodded and smiled shyly.

"What a cute little guy!" Hazel laughed. "What's your name, sweetie?"

"Jimmy," the boy said, his mouth opening wider, revealing misshapen yellowish green teeth. They looked chipped or maybe jagged. Dan recoiled and stepped back automatically.

"Come on," Mia looked over at her companion with a frown. "Poor little guy can't help it if his folks can't afford a dentist.

"We need help," she turned towards the child, coughing as she spoke.

Mia wondered how the child seemed unaffected by the smoke seeing as the three of them were rasping and hacking.

"Can you get your mommy or your daddy, a grown up?" she continued.

"We need wire cutters, can you find a grown up to bring them to us."

Jimmy just looked up at her, still smiling his wretched smile.

"There's no help for you," the child laughed. "You're dead."

Hazel stood up, backing away from the fence. She looked more than terrified, she looked as if she were going into shock.

"Come on," Mia said sharply, struggling to get words out as she choked. "Don't lose your shit, you know how this place has been fucking with us!"

"Yeah, yeah," Hazel sighed.

"We've got to move on," Dan coughed, grabbing an arm of each of his companions.

They walked on, through the smoke, Jimmy's childlike laugher growing fainter and fainter.

The three of them were back in the corridor, free of smoke. They could still feel it in their lungs, taste it in their mouths.

"I feel like I just smoked a pack of cigarettes," Mia made a This Milk's Gone Sour face.

"That boy," Hazel said. "He saw us."

"It's just this place messing with us," Dan countered. "It created Errol Flynn, Tom Petty, the waiter—"

"Mark Lanegan at the motel," Mia added.

"Who?" Dan asked.

"You see my shirt?" Mia asked. "The lead guy of the Afghan Whigs—"

"Your shirt doesn't say Afghan Whigs anymore," Dan sounded shaky.

Mia looked down, it was still a black tee but it was for the band the Gutter Twins. It didn't shock her, nothing would have shocked her in that place.

"It's because we were talking about Mark Lanegan," she explained. "He was in the Gutter Twins with the songwriter from the Afghan Whigs, the other band shirt I was wearing."

"At least you got a new shirt," Hazel griped. "We're gonna be stinky soon in the same clothes."

Before she could react, Mia came over and got her face close to the older woman's underarms, breathing deeply.

"Nope, you don't smell at all," the younger woman said before going to Dan. "You too, no smell."

"*No* smell?" Dan sounded uncomfortable with that."There should be something, a little sweat, deodorant, the laundry soap we use to wash our clothes."

"The food we ate," Mia added, looking troubled herself.

"This place isn't real," Hazel interjected. "It's like how you can't smell a movie."

"It's weird how we know some things and not others," Mia pointed out.

"You know that you can't smell a movie, I have my memories of bands and movies, history—"

"It's like we can't access our memories but this place can," Dan interrupted.

All three of them could pick up on the smell of sulfur smoke, it was time to move on.

THE BOAT

"Okay, this is a change," Mia said.

The corridor had opened into another vast room but instead of carpet with white footprints there was water. A dinghy with flaking, dark green paint bobbed in their path, moored by a line that ran to a steel o-ring driven into the wall where the corridor ended.

"I wonder how deep it is," Hazel frowned.

"I wonder what..." Dan started then cut himself off.

"What?" Hazel asked.

Her companion just shook his head, he looked scared. Both women understood not to ask further.

"We know that we have no choice," Mia undid the knot, keeping the line attached to the o-ring.

"Weird ass boat or choke on smoke," Hazel sighed, gingerly climbing into the ship.

Dan was next, and then Mia who dropped the rope into the bottom of the rowboat. She grabbed an oar and Dan the other. It took them a few moments to get into the rhythm of rowing in sync. Mia leaned over and shoved her oar into the water, it was at least four feet deep.

"This is actually kinda peaceful," Hazel smiled. "The gentle bob of the water."

The room was big enough that they could not see the walls in the distance. The ceiling, white as the walls of the corridor had been, appeared at least twenty feet above them with the same recessed lights as the hall.

None of them spoke, the only sounds were the dipping and splash of the oars and the boat gently smacking against the water as it moved—

And then the sound of bubbles, large bubbles rising and then bursting a few yards off to their left.

"Something is under the water," Hazel's voice was tense.

Why did you have to say that?" Mia thought, annoyed at the older woman and also fearful. *You make things more real here by acknowledging them.*

She laid into the oar. Dan picked up on the change and rowed harder himself.

"Think of the corridor, nothing else," he said firmly. "We must be close."

Mia wanted to point out that it had taken several minutes driving a golf cart at a good clip the last time they had crossed a room but understood pointing that out would make their situation worse.

She looked over and saw that Hazel had clamped her eyes shut and was wringing her hands.

"Hazel," Mia said as gently as possible, aware of the fear in her voice as much as she fought it. "Whatever you see, you need to put it out of your head."

Something bumped the bottom of the dingy enough to almost knock Dan out of the boat.

"Yeah, Hazel," he added. "*Please.*"

That's all he could manage, he was fighting against his own vision of what was beneath the water, something that was all tentacles and teeth and hunger.

A splash, something breaking the water off to their left followed by a distinct meaty smell not only when you open a cellophane package of a raw roast or ground beef.

It was a tentacle, to Dan it looked as thick as his forearm.

"Gross," Mia muttered.

"Not there, not there," Hazel sighed, her eyes still clamped shut.

Dan tried to look away from the tentacle but couldn't help himself; it was slithering across the water like a snake crossing a patch of earth—

Another sound, something breaking the water off to their right, a second tentacle, slithering slowly towards the boat.

And a third, off behind them.

And a forth, off to the left but ahead of them.

The first tentacle bumped the side of the boat, they could hear it rasping along the side.

"Gross," Mia muttered, a line of tears moving down her cheek as she rowed with renewed determination. "Gross, gross, *fucking gross.*"

The tentacle moved upwards, over the lip of the dinghy, towards where Hazel sat. Without thinking, Mia brought the oar out of the water and jabbed the slimy looking limb. The oar cut through the limb, severing it—there was a scream like a cat in agony and bubbles all around the boat. The end of the tentacle coming from under the water shot away in retreat, the severed end flopped in the bottom of the boat, spraying all three of them with dark blood.

"Gross," Mia muttered in a high pitched voice. "Gross, gross, so fucking *gross.*"

She got back to rowing. The tentacle still flopping in the bottom of the boat. It found Hazel's ankle and wrapped around it. Her eyes shot open and she looked down with surprise and then disgust. Dan started to pull his oar in to help her but she shook her head.

"Row, just row," Hazel said thickly. "Get us out of here."

She reached down and struggled to get the tentacle loose from her leg, it twisted in her hand once she got it from around her ankle and was difficult to toss free of the boat. The other tentacles were nearby but not coming any closer...for the moment.

Something bumped the bottom of the dinghy again...*hard*.

This time Mia was nearly pitched out.

"It's going to capsize us, throw us in the water," Dan said.

Another bump, but a moment later the dinghy was running aground in the corridor. The water was gone, the boat was sitting on the carpet. Mia dropped her oar and looked down at Hazel's ankle, the one tentacle had been wrapped around, clearly struggling to keep her shit together.

"Gross....that was just...gross," she rasped.

None of them were covered with blood anymore. Hazel looked back the way they had come, running her hands through her shoulder length, black hair.

"I hate this fucking place," she said

Every couple of minutes, Hazel would pause to scratch at the leg the tentacle had been wrapped around. Dan shuddered everytime she did, remembering the creature that had invaded the boat.

Not real. How could anything in this place be real?

The travelers came to a corridor branching off to the right but that passway had stone walls and ceilings, earth floors, and torches instead of recessed lights.

"I don't know," Hazel scowled. "It looks spooky to me."

"It's different," Mia countered. "Maybe if we try something different things will change."

"Yeah, but it might be a bad change," Hazel replied, lifting her leg to scratch where the tentacle had been; it did not appear she was consciously doing so. Both women looked at Dan who sighed.

"Great, looks like I'm the tie breaker."

He started down the stone corridor and the women followed.

The torches, like the recessed lights, were spaced every ten feet in iron holders. This corridor was cooler, probably due to the stones.

"I'm getting a bad feeling from this place," Hazel said loudly.

"Let's give it a bit further," Mia said.

Both women looked at Dan who rolled his eyes.

"Great, if this is a shit show I'm the deciding vote."

The corridor was widening: It had started off a couple of yards wide, then a few, and then the walls were a hundred feet away—

And then you couldn't see them nor the ceiling. Instead of white footprints there were orange stones every twenty feet. Trees, first one here or there and then the travelers were surrounded by them. They heard wind and birdsong, the croak of a raven.

"That would have to be a big ass raven," Mia observed.

"They peck your eyes out," Hazel said. "I saw it happen."

Both of her companions looked at her with disbelief.

"Okay, it was a movie," Hazel said awkwardly. "But those birds are too smart, they get up to no good."

The sound of horses in the distance.

"Over there!" A man's voice called. "Poachers!"

And then seven men on horseback were riding towards Mia and her companions.

"What did I tell you!" Hazel cried out.

They started running back to where the corridor had been, where they hoped it still was.

The sound of whistling, an arrow; it struck Mia in the shoulder and she cried out, stumbled, and kept running. More whistles, one his Dan in the lower back and he dropped to his knees, barely feeling his legs—

Must have hit my spinal cord...

He could feel it though, a burning sort of pressure and the sensation that something important inside him had been breached and was leaking. Hazel stopped to check on him and an arrow went through her skull. Her eyes closed and she started falling like a dead weight. Dan tried to catch her and the movement brought on the sort of pain he had never experienced—

HAVE IT YOUR WAY (BUT DON'T SHARE)

And then they were sitting in orange chairs, back in the regular corridor.
Waking up, Dan started feeling his back for an arrow—
"They're gone," Mia said softly from nearby.
Hazel was waking up.
"I told you that corridor was no good," she scolded Mia and then
something caught her attention.
"I smell bacon again," the older woman added.
"I guess it's morning again," Dan said.
Twenty feet down the corridor was a table with three cups of coffee and
nine breakfast sandwiches wrapped in wax paper.
"I'm curious," Mia said softly. "Yesterday they knew what we wanted on
them; I want to try something."
Dan looked over at her and she continued.
"Go ahead, Dan, pick one up."
He did. Mia went over and took the sandwich from him, making a disgusted
face a second later as a rotten smell came from the wax paper and a thick,
green liquid oozed out. Mia dropped the bundle and it splattered on the
floor.
"Maybe we shouldn't do that," Hazel observed.
They kept to their own sandwiches—which were perfect as the day
before—and there were no other issues.

The threesome walked on. After an hour they came upon an identical hall branching off to the left but after the experience in the woods elected not to take it. Not long after that, there was a familiar sound up ahead, wind, the sound of powerful wind coming through an open door.

"Awesome," Dan said flatly.

They came to a point where the walls and the ceiling vanished and there was just a bridge with the same low nap, industrial carpet. On the other end of the bridge the corridor continued, judging by the size of the aputure Mia guessed the bridge was about a hundred feet long. A yard from the opening on their side, the wind was strong enough that the travelers could barely stand up.

"You've got to be kidding me!" Hazel whined.

"Come sail away, come sail away with me," Dan sang softly.

On their right was a rope railing, it didn't not look sturdy enough to support even Mia's weight. Nevertheless, the youngest of the three started out. Only a foot outside of the corridor, the wind picked her up as if she were a paper plate and not a hundred-ten pound adult. The wind tried to jerk her off the bridge, she grabbed the rope with her free hand, burning both palms and being pulled nearly horizontal.

If I fall it's not permanent, I won't die, I'll just end up in those stupid chairs....

A hand on her ankle, Dan, he was lying part in and part out of the corridor they had come down.

"Can you get your legs up?" Hazel asked. "Monkey climb it."

"Monkey climb it?" Mia gasped, she was being pulled so hard her shoulders dislocating seemed eminent.

With what strength remained, the young woman moved her body, swinging her legs over and wrapping them around the rope.

"I'm facing the wrong way," she said.

"You are," Hazel admitted. "You need to turn around."

A wind gust, the rope creaked—it was a thin robe, it had to be on the verge of snapping.

"Pull yourself back," Dan suggested. "We'll pull you in and you can turn around."

"I'll try," Mia grunted.

How was she supposed to pull herself across the bridge? She felt winded and her arms ached.

Dan and Hazel struggled to pull their companion in, Mia lay gasping in the corridor.

And then, the smell of sulfur smoke drifting towards them

"You rest," Hazel said. "I'll try first."

Not waiting for a response, she backed onto the bridge, grabbing the rope with her hands and wrapping her legs around the railing. Expertly, she shimmied across—

At the halfway point, there was a gust that nearly sucked Dan and Mia into the void. The rope snapped, carrying Hazel off in a wild arc. The woman on the rope smacked against a wall (?) and grunted. Dan dropped to his knees and then his belly to crawl across, hoping to make it to the other end and pull Hazel up. Mia observed him, he was not a big guy, it would take both of them to pull up the woman swinging on the rope. She also dropped to her belly and crawled. The wind was fierce, they would nearly get pulled off one side of the bridge and have to quickly grab the other side before flying into the void. When both of them were on the other end of the bridge, Dan and Mia worked on pulling Hazel up, the latter wincing as her palms were severely rope burned. When Hazel was halfway up, the wind died and the older of the two women was able to shimmy up the line on her own. All three sat cross legged in the corridor, gasping.

"That genuinely sucked."

"It *literally* sucked."

"Maybe one of us was in the Taliban," Dan mused.

"What?" Hazel, looking confused.

"The Taliban outlawed kites," Mia explained. "Maybe their hell has a lot of wind, it would be sorta ironic."

"You guys are nuts," Hazel muttered, and then added. "None of us look like Taliban guys."

"Who knows if this is how we appear in real life," Mia shrugged.

"This place *does* fuck with you," Dan agreed.

They came upon a black door with a black antique door knob. Warmth was radiating through the door as if there was an oven on the other side.

"Not creepy at all," Dan sighed.

"Maybe somethings in this place look creepy but really aren't," Hazel suggested.

"Like the forest? Like the lake we crossed?" Mia countered.

Before her companions could react, Hazel opened the door. It was a large room with white walls and ceilings. There were small trees in planters and on the branches what had to be dozens of small parrots and macaws, the birds were chortling and making soft bird sounds.

"Ah, how cute!" Hazel smiled. "See? Just a bunch of birds."

"Hello," a green parrot with a yellow and red face called. "Hello."

Mia smiled at that, they *were* charming birds. They walked deeper into the room. The trees in the planters became thicker in trunk and taller, the ceiling appeared roughly thirty feet above them. The macaws and the parrots were laughing and bobbing their little heads as if enjoying the visitors.

"Welcome, welcome," a macaw rasped.

"Okay, this is pretty cool," Dan laughed.

"He's hungry," a good sized parrot cried from a higher branch. "So hungry."

"Okay, that is not so cool," Dan said, the pleasure dropping from his face.

"Who…is….hungry?" Hazel asked softly, the others could hear the fear in her voice.

"Mr. Mad," she added in a lower tone, screwing her eyes closed and wringing her hands; Dan expected her to start scratching her leg again.

"Who is Mr. Mad?" Mia asked, her voice shaking.

"Let's not stick around to find out guys," Dan said, both women could pick on the fact he was hiding something, Mia by the way he averted his eyes and Hazel by his tone of voice.

The three of them turned to head back to the door—

And the room went black.

"So hungry!" A bird called.

"Hungry, hungry!" Another agreed.

The three humans tried to run in the direction of the wall but only got a couple of feet before running into a tree, often startling the birds who bit at them with their powerful beaks.

And then there was a *presence*, all three of them agreed later there was something big in that room, a spirit, not unlike the thing that chased them when they were on the golf cart.

The sound of wind being moved…no, it was the sound of wings beating, massive wings.

"Drop to the floor!" Mia ordered.

They did. Something massive flew right over them, so close they could smell the dander on its wings.

A claw scraped Mia back, tearing open her shirt and gouging her skin.

"Fuck!" She cried out in pain.

"We gotta crawl!" Dan said.

They did. The sound of wings, closer, closer. Hazel cried out.

"It got me!"

Dan and Mia leapt up and managed to grab their companion's legs. Mia had a shoe and pulled it off, Dan compensated by becoming dead weight until the youngest of the group could grab an ankle. Amazingly, the giant bird or whatever it was had the strength to lift all three of them off the floor.

"Time to fly the unfriendly skies," Dan said, and then started laughing hysterically. "Fuck you, Mr. Mad! Fuck you fuck—"

And then he was curled in the corridor, Hazel and Mia crouched next to him, trying to reassure him.

"I'm okay, sorry—" He said.

Dan got those words out and then burst into tears.

"Sorry, sorry," he struggled to get under control and was failed. "It's just…this fucking place."

Hazel pulled him up and embraced him, Mia took one of his hands.

"We gotta go, Dan. You know?"

"Yeah," Dan said roughly, nodding and wiping tears away with the back of his hand. "I smell it, too."

"Who would you want to be?" Hazel asked a few minutes later.

"What?" Dan asked, still embarrassed about his crying fit.

"We talked about how we could be different outside of here," Hazel explained. "Maybe I'm a big black man, a basketball player."

"Hello, stereotypes," Mia muttered.

"No, no," Hazel frowned and then brightened. "I would like to be a big black man and I love to play basketball but I'm no good."

"I don't know," Mia said. "It still feels like stereotyping or something."

"Maybe you're a big black man and that's why this offends you," Dan offered with a smile.

"Come on, just play along," Hazel said. "I need something to distract me from *this*."

"I'd be a guitar tech," Mia said. "For a big rock band."

"A guitar tech?" Hazel asked.

"Rock bands need people to set up the instruments, keep them tuned and so on. I could be a guitar tech or a drum tech for that matter."

"Why not be a rockstar?" The other woman asked.

"Being famous always seems like an ordeal," Mia explained. "If you were a tech you could travel the world, stay in hotels, all the percs without the downsides."

"Maybe you were a rock star," Dan said softly.

Seeing the discomfort on Mia's face (*were*) he added: "Maybe you *are* a rock star."

"What about you, Daniel? We have a basketball star and a guitar tech, what about you?"

"I don't know, definitely not a macaw wrangler."

"Do you think that was what Mr. Mad was?"

Dan didn't speak for what felt like a minute.

"I know that's what he was," He said quietly, focusing on remaining composed.

Always gotta be the man, the tough guy—was I this macho in real life?

"A family friend had a macaw when I was a kid. Name wasn't Mr. Mad, it was Bubbles—"

"Seriously, Bubbles?" Mia arched her eyebrows.

"Yeah, I was attacked by a macaw named Bubbles," Dan said and then reflected before continuing. "I was being a stupid kid, poking it with a ruler. Well, Bubbles the macaw flew off his perch and went to town on my head, had to get eight stitches."

"Shit," Hazel nodded. "Bubbles was a badass."

"I had this recurring dream," Dan continued. "I was in a forest and this big macaw was chasing me, fucker was twice the size of an eagle…and I knew his name was Mr. Mad."

Mia stopped and burst into laughter, she couldn't help it. Dan was offended, but only for a moment before laughing himself. Hazel just stood nearby shaking her head.

"You two are lunatics."

Dan and Mia pulled it together and stopped laughing….until their eyes met and it started again.

"Mr. Mad!" Mia hiccuped laughter.

"Stop, I'm gonna piss myself!" Dan gasped, shaking with mirth.

The coming of the smoke broke the moment and they walked on.

"So…this is it?" Hazel said, frustration made clear by her tone of voice. "Walk and walk and walk this stupid corridor and if we stop we choke on bad smelling smoke."

Her companions had no response.

"Walk and walk and fucking walk some more," the older of the two women continued. "What is this place?"

She stopped, holding up her hands to get the others to stop.

"Are we being punished for something?" Hazel's expression had changed from anger to desperation, to Dan she appeared on the verge of tears. "Was I a terrible person? I can't remember!"

"I don't think so," Dan said thoughtfully. "I think this is the essense of who we are, three generally decent people…"

"With flaws like all normal people have," Mia added.

"What happens if we allow ourselves to choke on the smoke until we die?" Hazel asked.

"Death by smoke inhalation, not a good way to go," the other woman mused.

"We'd probably pass out and wake up in those orange chairs," Dan frowned, growing frustrated himself. "We'd wake up in the chairs, smell bacon, have delicious breakfast sandwiches and walk on and on…or stay after eating until we choke out and wake up in the chairs again and again and again."

"This place is doling out more and more memories," Mia said that softly, barely audible.

"What do you mean?" Hazel asked.

"You wanting to be a black basketball player," Mia rolled her eyes before continuing. "Dan being attacked by a bird. I think your memory of your father was real, for some reason."

"I think that, as well," Dan added. "I have the feeling this place has connected the three of us not just to wherever this is, but to each other."

"We're always connected," Hazel said to him. "Most people don't see it, they only feel it."

"Synchronicity," Mia agreed quietly.

71

"What's that?" The older of the two women asked with genuine curiosity.

"The Police's last album," Dan smiled.

"And a Jungian theory or philosophy," Mia explained. "That we are all connected on a subconscious level."

"Yeah," Hazel said quietly. "I've always felt that but didn't know what it was called.

"I only know about it because of Sting," Dan added.

Mia rolled her eyes at him and the three of them walked on.

THE MAW

Hazel was talking about food. That was one of the sounds they heard in the corridor, their voices and breathing, coughs and sniffles, and muted thump of their footsteps on the low pile carpet—

And, in that minute, another sound, a muted rumble: Something mechanical coming up behind them.

Hazel cut herself off in the midst of talking about steak and french fries—

"I don't like that sound," she frowned. "That is not a good sound."

Whatever was making the mechanical noise was getting closer, a dark shape. The corridor was three yards or meters wide at that point, wide enough for the travelers to walk abreast. Whatever was coming up behind them was closing the distance fast.

"It's as wide as the hallway," Hazel said, her voice tense.

They began jogging, the object was still closing the distance and the mechanical noise getting louder along with the smell of exhaust. None of the three were used to jogging and quickly felt winded.

"Oh, shit, blades!" Hazel gasped, looking over her shoulder.

"I believe that's a grain thresher," Dan managed, breathing heavily himself.

"I think I'm a smoker in the real world,"Mia wheezed. "This really sucks."

They had started off at a decent clip but quickly flagged. The thresher was a hundred feet behind them then fifty, the travelers could hear the whir of the blades. The maw of the machine took up the entire corridor, there was nowhere to go but inside it.

The thresher was fifty feet behind them, then twenty.

Will the pain be prolonged, something for this place to savor, or quick like the arrows?

Dan thought that, having no fuel left, ready to just…stop and let whatever was going to happen happen.

And then the corridor opened up with an alcove on the left a couple of yards or meters deep, they staggered into it, pressing themselves into the far wall, gasping, lungs aching, hearts pounding enough that Dan wondered if he was going to have a heart attack. A man around fifty was driving the machine, he was wearing overalls along with an expression of equal amounts disgust and contempt.

"Get the fuck out of my cornfield ya fucking crows!" He shook his fist at the travelers before driving on.

"Some people are so unfriendly," A woman's voice nearby.

"I don't see crows," she added. "No, the three of you don't look like birds at all."

The woman was roughly thirty with wavy reddish-brown hair. She was wearing a gold lame gown, her nipples visible through the fabric which was molded to her body. She was smiling as she cooked steaks on a grill.

"I do apologize," the cook continued. "All I have is steak, french fries, and a couple of bottles of red wine. I'm not sure what kind it is or if it's any good, the lady at the market suggested it and I was distracted, you know?"

Katherine Hepburn, Mia recognized the woman. *She looks like she did in Bringing Up Baby.*

There was a table near the grill, Katherine waved them over to it as she grabbed one of the bottles of wine. Four glasses were already on the table. The cook opened the bottle and then poured.

"You are so beautiful," Mia said softly. "I don't think there has ever been an actress as beautiful as you."

"Actress?" Katherine said in her New England accent, she looked confused but pleased and even blushed a little. "No, no, I'm just a cook."

She winked at Mia, stroked the side of the young woman's face. There was something between them, Hazel and Dan picked up on it and gave each other knowing looks.

"You are the gorgeous one," Katherine added, letting her hand drop from Mia's face and going back to her grill.

"Do you know where we are?" Hazel asked.

"Of course!" Katherine laughed and then looked at Hazel as if she were silly. "Isn't it obvious, you're in a corridor! Ah, well, it looks like these steaks are done. Pour me a glass, will you?"

She pulled the steaks from the grill and set them on a platter. And then pulled the french fries from the oven and set them on the table next to the platter.

"Oh, I'm not eating," Katherine smiled as the others dished up their food. "I will never get this dress off if I eat a big meal."

"And I intend to take this dress off at some point," she added with a wink in Mia's direction.

The cook sipped wine as they devoured their food, clearly enjoying their enjoyment.

"Ah, I really do like it when people enjoy my cooking," she said and then frowned a little. "Sometimes I make a mess of it, could burn water, you know?"

Mia stopped eating and looking at the woman in the gold lame dress.

"Who are you?" She asked softly. "I mean, you are clearly not Katherine Hepburn…though in this place I'm not so sure…why would Katherine Hepburn or her spirit or whatever be here?"

"I am just a cook," Katherine said, looking at the three of them in turn with such warmth and love that it left the three of them emotionally in knots. "But I am also everyone you have ever loved that you've lost."

The smell of the sulfur smoke, wisps already reading where the four of them were sitting.

"I don't want to leave you," Mia said shakily, a line of tears running down her face.

Katherine took the younger woman's hands in her own.

"Ah, this is the way it always is, the way it always has been," she said, clearly only focused on Mia. "We lose everyone we love in one way or another, you know?"

All Mia could do was nod, the other two were pulling her up as the smoke was already choking. When Mia was standing, Katherine walked over, gave her a long kiss, and then held her tight for a few moments. The three travelers were all coughing, Hazel and Dan led their companion away, further down the corridor. Mia kept up with them but was sobbing helplessly.

"That was fucking awful," she said a couple of minutes along. "This place is so cruel."

HER WORK

The guards hustled her away from the workstation, bruising her arm. It was for her safety, they said; what importance was her safety if her work was being left behind? Her work was everything, beyond her work there was just food she ate because she knew she had to and a room she slept in when sleep was insistent—

Her work was intricate, too intricate for rough people with guns. The people who would occupy the building would not know what to do with her work, they were just more rude men with guns. The woman was hustled down corridors into an elevator and eventually outside and into a dusty Chevy Suburban. A man in a dark blue polo shirt and jeans was sitting in the front passenger seat. He looked back at the woman as she climbed into the back seat.

"You've endangered all of us by delaying the exit," he said, anger in his voice, also anxiety.

"Drive," he said to the driver.

The driver did as she was told. There were five of them in the SUV, driving through the bombed out city.

"Prisha," the man in the polo shirt sighed. "I know how important this project was to you—"

"What did you think they'd do to me?" Prisha cut him off, feeling her own anger. "I'm a scientist, what would they have done?"

"I'm sorry," Polo Shirt almost looked apologetic. "It's just that you're the closest thing to a doctor we have, we need you."

"*They* needed me," Prisha sighed. "Now they're just going to be stuck in there forever."

"Not forever, they'll wink out when the power is disconnected," Blue Shirt said without thinking.

Had that been thoughtless? He knew how attached the scientist was to the three subjects.

Prisha did not seem to hear him, she had a dreamy expression as she looked out the window at a Rite Aid that had suffered a missle strike.

"Power doesn't matter, they're in the cloud, I thought you understood that."

"It's all part of the grid, and the grid is collapsing," Polo Shirt said flatly.
"Prisha, we need you to focus on real things—"
"What they are experiencing is real. You never really got it, Kyle, to you it's just," words failed her for a couple of moments. "Zeros and ones, an abstract…from what I can determine what they are experiencing is as real as what we experience out here."
"You don't give me enough credit," Kyle said defensively. "I totally understood the program: You have coma patients that you connected their brains to a supercomputer and somehow put them in this false place like virtual reality."
"An oversimplification—"
"Oh, sorry, I don't have an amazing IQ—"
"That's not what I meant," Prisha closed her eyes, distractedly traced her finger along the bottom of the window frame. "Honestly, I don't even know if I understand it."
She put her hands in her lap and looked defeated.
"What does it fucking matter," She added bitterly. "Before I could set it up to monitor them, so we could watch them like characters in a movie, the war came to the city. The human race is fucked because we're just violent moneys, this is why people like me can never finish our work."
"Who knows,"Kyle looked forward again. "I'm sure the other side has good doctors, maybe they'll come out of their comas."
"No, that is impossible now," Prisha replied.
He looked back, saw the guilt on her face, and was surprised at what she had done.
"Don't tell me you—"
And then an IUD exploded under the SUV and there was only bright light, a feeling like being pulled in a hundred different physical directions but no pain followed by darkness.

The sky. No sensation of her body, just an awareness of the sky and the brightness of the sun through the pollution. Was she dead? No, but the way she could not feel her body told Prisha the end was close. There was the crackle of flames, men shouting and running in the distance, a smell like a barbecue. It would have been a pleasant smell, a smell alluding to fun and easy times, summer, but Prisha knew the barbeque smell was her companions burning. She had delayed their exit and it had cost all of them their lives. But the three people in the machine were free, there would be no more ominous smoke or any other terrifying things, Prisha had made sure of that, it would be like heaven, a personalized heaven, if such a thing existed.

She would soon find out.

THE END OF THE CORRIDOR

"Do you sense something guys?" Mia asked, stopping in her tracks.
"Yeah," Dan replied.
Hazel almost asked what they were talking about but she felt it too.
"I feel good," she smiled. "I don't know why, but I feel good."
"Don't question it," Dan looked right at her. "Let's just enjoy it."
The corridor opened up but instead of another vast room they found themselves in a wooded area next to a river that was maybe twenty feet in width. There were a couple of tables with men and women of varying ages in clothing from different periods in history; they were people the three travelers recognized, a few waving over to Mia, Dan, or Hazel as they smiled. As with Katherine what the picnic tables were radiating was comforting and warm—love.
"This a good place," Mia said softly, the others looked over, the youngest of the three was crying but it appeared to be good crying.
"We're going to be okay," Mia added.

Written between 9 and 14 May, 2022

GREEN BOX TIME GREEN BOX TIME GREEN BOX TIME GREEN BOX TIME
GREEN BOX TIME GREEN BOX TIME GREEN BOX TIME GREEN BOX TIME
GREEN BOX TIME GREEN BOX TIME GREEN BOX TIME GREEN BOX TIME
GREEN BOX TIME GREEN BOX TIME GREEN BOX TIME GREEN BOX TIME
GREEN BOX TIME GREEN BOX TIME GREEN BOX TIME GREEN BOX TIME
GREEN BOX TIME GREEN BOX TIME GREEN BOX TIME GREEN BOX TIME
GREEN BOX TIME GREEN BOX TIME GREEN BOX TIME GREEN BOX TIME
GREEN BOX TIME GREEN BOX TIME GREEN BOX TIME GREEN BOX TIME
GREEN BOX TIME GREEN BOX TIME GREEN BOX TIME GREEN BOX TIME
GREEN BOX TIME GREEN BOX TIME GREEN BOX TIME GREEN BOX TIME
GREEN BOX TIME GREEN BOX TIME GREEN BOX TIME GREEN BOX TIME
GREEN BOX TIME GREEN BOX TIME GREEN BOX TIME GREEN BOX TIME
GREEN BOX TIME GREEN BOX TIME GREEN BOX TIME GREEN BOX TIME
GREEN BOX TIME GREEN BOX TIME GREEN BOX TIME GREEN BOX TIME
GREEN BOX TIME GREEN BOX TIME GREEN BOX TIME GREEN BOX TIME
GREEN BOX TIME GREEN BOX TIME GREEN BOX TIME GREEN BOX TIME
GREEN BOX TIME GREEN BOX TIME GREEN BOX TIME GREEN BOX TIME
GREEN BOX TIME GREEN BOX TIME GREEN BOX TIME GREEN BOX TIME
GREEN BOX TIME GREEN BOX TIME GREEN BOX TIME GREEN BOX TIME
GREEN BOX TIME GREEN BOX TIME GREEN BOX TIME GREEN BOX TIME

GREEN BOX TIME GREEN BOX TIME **GREEN BOX**

TIME GREEN BOX TIME GREEN BOX TIME GREEN BOX TIME

GREEN BOX TIME GREEN BOX TIME GREEN BOX TIME GREEN BOX TIME
GREEN BOX TIME GREEN BOX TIME

It all started with the lights—the lights weren't flickering, there was no evidence of burnt out bulbs or tubes, they were just *wrong*...subdued was the word that came to mind. Shadows were allowed to exist in areas they hadn't before; Marissa noticed this and wondered if others had, as well.

"Hello? Wow, Marissa is really zoned out!"

Laughter, genuine laughter filled with easy pleasure, Marissa mentally returned to the table.

"Sorry, what did you say?" She asked.

"Where were you?"

Thinking about the lights. Do any of you notice anything different about the lights?

"Sorry, guess I didn't sleep well last night."

Her friends looked at each other, curious, possibly suspicious. None of them—Marissa included—ever had sleep issues; when you wanted to sleep you just lay down and sleep came. They had no sleep issues, no health issues of any kind.

"I remember that can happen," one of the men said helpfully. "A glitch, but a minor one."

"I don't even want to think about minor glitches," the woman who had been talking to Marissa frowned. "If there are minor glitches there could be major ones."

"It only happened last night," Marissa forced a smile. "I don't think it's a glitch, I think it's my memory; in the past I had insomnia."

"Yeah, I remember that can happen," One of the men said, his face registering a returning memory. "It's like phantom limb syndrome or whatever they call it, people who lose legs but feel the missing foot itch."

The mood at the table lightened again. A plate of loaded nachos appeared along with drinks. The five of them dug in, laughing and talking about light and easy things like places they had traveled to or shows they were binge watching. Marissa smiled and nodded, laughed at the right times, and made a point not to zone out again. Inside, though, she was thinking of the lights. Even in that easy going place with light hits of the 1980s playing in the background the lights seemed different, subdued. At eleven, Marissa finished her drink and said goodnight to everyone. The others, like her, appeared to be around thirty with stylish but not flashy clothes. Pleasant looking, but none of them were notably beautiful or handsome; they were just normal people with straight teeth that were white but not bright white. Marissa walked out of the restaurant and looked up at the facade. There was no name, no advertisement of what the building offered. just a large plate glass window revealing tables of groups of people, all seemingly around 30, enjoying themselves as light hits of the 1980s played in the background.

It was a three block walk from the bar back to her row house. At eleven it was sixty degrees just as it was sixty degrees every night at eleven. No one else was out but there was the smell of jasmine in the air and a light breeze to keep the village fresh. Marissa found herself fixating on the streetlights; like the other sources of illumination they were different.
"Subdued," she said out loud.
Her row house was narrow but two stories in height, beige like all the other row hours with a tiny backyard with a tidy lawn that never required mowing or watering. Marissa did not fumble with keys because she didn't have any keys to fumble with, no one locked their doors. She had a car— a white sedan parked in the garage under her beige house—but it was accessed using her phone and not a key,. She walked in and closed the door without locking it, the lights had come on when the front door opened. The woman walked up to her bedroom and lay on the bed—
And then her phone was beeping; another morning had begun.

TWO

Streets of row houses surrounded the downtown area of the village where a couple hundred people lived. There were no schools because there were no children. On the edge of the village was a large rectangular building, beige like the houses, which contained the office nearly everyone in the village worked. Marissa's job, like those of her office mates, was to click on a green box on her computer monitor each hour on the hour. No one knew what happened if you didn't click on the green boxes, but they were all aware how other crimes were punished. When it wasn't Green Box Time, they leaned into cubicles or met in the break room to talk about the latest sports event or the shows people were binge watching or to share a cute animal video they had come across. After fifty-seven minutes, a voice would come over the PA:

"Three minutes to Green Box Time, three minutes."

No one would disrupt their speculations about the team's future performance or cease oohing and awwing over the antics of puppies and kittens; no one was more than two minutes from their cubicle.

"Two minutes to Green Box Time, two minutes."

Only then would people break away to walk to their cubicles with a comment thrown over their shoulder about the adorable animals or that they disagreed about the speculation of the sports team's future performance.

"One minute to Green Box Time, one minute."

Marissa dropped in her chair just as she did every hour at work. That morning, though, things were different.

What happens if we don't click on the green box?

They were all aware of the punishment if you hurt another person or stole from them—what about not clicking on the green box? How could doing that be of any importance? That morning she was curious, part of her needed to know what would happen if she just sat there, hands in her lap, ignoring Green Box Time.

Marissa thought of how the lights had been changing and clicked on the green box with eleven seconds to spare.

THREE

"That was totally unrealistic—"

"What?!"

"The parachute—"

"He's a scientist! He could totally make a parachute!"

Brad and Josh were arguing about the latest episode of the show everyone was watching. Mary and Jane were talking about the past, finding similarities in the lives they had led before coming to the village. Marissa smiled and nodded at the right times, didn't zone out. There was a huge platter of jalapeno poppers in the middle of the table that everyone helped themselves to. No one worried if the others had washed their hands or if they had a cold; no one got colds or sick from e coli or whatever else was passed by unhygienic hands.

"I didn't know you worked for a district attorney," Mary said to Jane before turning to Marissa. "Weren't you a cop, Marissa?"

"Yeah, but not at the end."

"Why did you quit?" Jane asked, grabbing a jalapeno popper without looking at the ex-cop and dipping it in green goddess dressing. She didn't worry about calories because there was no risk of getting fat.

"PTSD," Marissa said softly, trying to keep a smile on her face while feeling the bite of the past. "I got shot, nearly died, and when I went back on duty it made me anxious so I quit."

"Nearly died," Mary leaned forward. "How close?"

Marissa understood the subtext.

"Not that close. They had to put me in a medically induced coma for a few days but I was never technically dead."

"Wow," Mary said as Jane cut in.

"I've read that comas are an unknown, where we go—"

"Maybe it's like a dream," Brad suggested. The guys had dropped their own conversation.

"And dreams are an unknown themselves," Josh added.

"I don't remember anything, to be honest," Marissa replied.

The others at the table seemed disappointed by that.

"Do you guys ever think about Green Box Time?" Marissa asked.

She regretted the question instantly; there was a tension coming off the others, a couple of suspicious faces.

"What is there to think about?" Mary asked.

"Forget it," Marissa mumbled, sorry she had brought it up.

"No, no," Mary tried to look agreeable. "What have you been thinking about it?"

"Just...what if we didn't click on the green box?"

"The Gentlemen might come," Josh said, pronouncing each word deliberately as if explaining something to a child.

"Would they come for something as minor as that?" Marissa asked. "I mean, it's not like robbery or rape—"

"But it is important," Jane said, glass of sauvignon blanc in her hand. "If it wasn't important why do they have us do it every hour?"

"Are we doing it now?" Marissa leaned into the table. She had asked the question and now the question was her master. "If it's important, why don't we have to do it every hour we're awake?"

The others just looked at her or awkwardly moved their drinks from hand to hand or picked at a jalapeno popper, picking the batter off.

"Nevermind," Marissa said. "Forget I mentioned it, okay?"

She sighed, Mary reached across and took her hand.

"Cops don't see the world like the rest of us do, don't they?" She asked gently.

"No," Marissa sighed, accepting the hand and squeezing back. "To do the job right you have to recognize things out of the ordinary."

"I bet you were a good cop," Brad smiled.

That seemed to break the tension and Marissa was relieved: *And I will never mention Green Box Time again.*

"You know, I think I was," she allowed. "I got a lot out of that job, it was hard to leave."

"What did you do after that?" Mary asked.

Marissa didn't remember. It was one of the few things that troubled her...aside from the lights. But, she didn't want to create another awkward situation so she told a story about being a private investigator and how all her cases either seemed to be workers comp fraud or infidelity. Someone asked how many times Marissa had caught people "in the act" and that led to stories around the table about all the times they had walked in on people having sex—

Laughter, voices growing louder, more eating and drinking.

No one worried about the time because no one got tired if they lacked sleep, even if they walked to work directly from the bar.

No one worried about getting drunk because even after a dozen drinks the most you felt was slightly intoxicated, just enough to feel loose and happy and free of concerns.

The night went on.

FOUR

At one o' clock Marissa walked the three blocks back to her row house. At one o' clock it was 57 degrees just as it was 57 degrees every night at one o' clock. She did not lay on the bed because she was tired, feeling tired didn't happen; Marissa lay on the bed to sleep because she had done it all her life, it was a habit. When she lay on the bed and closed her eyes it was assumed sleep was what she desired and it came or some approximation: There were never any dreams and it only felt like a few seconds between closing her eyes and the phone beeping. The others were on the streetcar to the office and they waved and told Marissa to join them. The other four hadn't gone home, they had gotten into a conversation about a new show that was getting excellent reviews; Josh had started an argument that the premise was idiotic and Jane had countered that every show was, in fact, idiotic if you broke it down.

"It's entertainment, dude, what do you expect?"

And that had led to the four of them discussing what were considered great shows and films as they ate the poppers and then nachos and then fried chicken sliders and then it was eight—

"Oooh, time for work," Brad said, waving to the waitress and then ordering coffees for the group.

Mary explained all this to Marissa as the streetcar took them and a dozen other people to the large, rectangular building where they would spend the next eight and a half hours. Josh started making fun of Brad's shoes, how Brad was a "secret hipster" and the three women laughed but—

Something was in the air, Marissa picked up on it first—the feeling was worse than the lights or the tension she had created bringing up Green Box Time.

"The Gentlemen," Mary said quietly, fear in her voice.

Who were they coming for? And then one of the men—was his name Kyle?—was wearing a red polo shirt and everyone was moving away from him. Kyle was looking around, clearly terrified.

"Bro?" Josh asked. "What did you do?"

Kyle tried to grab onto people but was pushed away, everyone ran for the entrance to the office. It was a beautiful morning, only a few clouds in the sky, 64 degrees just as it was every morning at ten minutes to nine. Kyle tried to run into the office but a security guard pushed him back hard enough that the man in the red polo shirt fell on his ass. The security guard locked the doors, Kyle was on his own. Outside, four vaguely human shapes drifted down like leaves but there was no wind. The shapes were rail thin and impossibly tall, the ex cop guessed they were eight feet in height with a stovepipe hat adding to the effect. They wore old fashioned suits with billowing capes. Everyone crowded at the window including Marissa and her four friends.

"Bro," Josh said with quiet awe. "What did you do?"

The Gentlemen surrounded Kyle, the man in the red polo shirt tried to get away but the men in the capes were quicker and then Kyle was trapped inside the billowing capes. Screams, awful screams, and a spout of blood rose like smoke from a teepee. Then, the Gentlemen drifted off again and neither Kyle nor his blood were anywhere to be seen. The workers stared out the windows for a few moments before walking to their cubicles with out a word.

FIVE

Later in the break room, the five of them tried to remember how long it had been since the Gentleman had appeared. A month? A year? Longer? And what had Kyle done? When you came to the village and occupied your row house Mindy from Customer Service was there to go over the basics like how you weren't allowed to change the color of your row house, when the streetcar came, and that there were no locks on the doors or police.

"No police?" A new resident would usually ask with understandable trepidation.

"Crime is dealt with differently here," Mindy would smile, but it wouldn't be the easy, warm smile like when she was pointing out the neighborhood cats or how it was 72 degrees every day. "Don't be surprised when the Gentlemen appear to deal with a criminal."

Any further questions would be brushed off. When they made friends, it was expected the new arrivals would ask about the Gentlemen.

Some thought they were vampires but others would disagree: Wouldn't vampires drink the blood instead of just letting it spray everywhere? And, what crime warranted the Gentlemen showing up? Rape? Murder? Jaywalking? No one knew but anyone who had seen the Gentlemen in action warned newcomers to treat even tearing a mattress tag off with wariness.

"Three minutes to Green Box Time, three minutes," the voice came over the PA.

"We should get pizza for lunch," Jane suggested.

"We did that two days ago," Josh countered.

Marissa watched their argument and wondered: *I've always thought they were like me but what if they aren't? What if they're a simulation like the village?*

No, she needed to believe they *were* like her, that she wasn't alone there.

"One minute to Green Box Time, one minute," the voice over the PA announced.

Marissa just stared at the screen. If she didn't click on the green box would the Gentlemen come for her? Would she find herself wearing a red polo shirt with everyone, even her four friends, backing away from her?

It'd kind of be a relief.

Where had that thought come from? Why had it waited so long to make itself heard?

The village was an easy place, it was safe and the weather was always good and you could eat and drink all you wanted and never get fat or sick. There wasn't the dread of going to the dentist because teeth didn't develop cavities or wear down or crack on bones in food.

"It's fucking boring," Marissa said, moving her hand from the mouse.

Twenty seconds to Green Box Time, not an announcement, a timer on the monitor near the lower right corner of the green box which grew brighter the closer to Green Box Time.

Ten seconds.

What if I don't click on the Green Box?

And then she remembered Kyle's screams and the fountain of blood. With two seconds to spare, Marissa clicked on the green box.

The others had gathered around Jane's cube where she and Josh were still trying to reach a consensus about lunch. The other three just looked on, willing to wave the flag of the victor while giving comfort to the loser. None of them had fucked the others. No one ever had sexual desire or sexual interest of any variety for either gender.

"Are you going to the desert again?" Mary asked Marissa.

"Yeah, I found this amazing canyon I want to camp at again," the ex-cop replied.

Like any office, you sent an email to the Manager and asked to have time off. If you drove in one direction for fifteen minutes you ended up in the desert. In another direction there was a forest. In a third, was the sea. In the final direction there were lush meadows with rivers. The roads ended after an hour in any direction. You could walk on and on and the scenery would never change but occasionally you would find a small canyon or a creek you hadn't noticed before. There was no hunger or thirst or weariness but after a while the solitude would take on weight and even introverts like Marissa would walk back to their car and drive back to the village. You stayed in the desert or the seaside as long as you wanted and when you returned to the village it was exactly how you had left it.

Jane and Josh agreed on Chinese food. Marissa wasn't feeling it but said nothing, Josh and Jane were a team now, Team Chinese Food, and any opponents would be quickly worn down.

The lights were the first thing Marissa noticed. The second was a foul smell the day Kyle was taken away by the Gentlemen, the smell of a sewage leak which made no sense because there were no toilets because there was no bodily waste to deposit in them. She wanted to ask if the others smelled it but dreaded the same tension as when she had brought up Green Box Time.

"What is that stink?" Jane asked as they ate their Chinese food.

"I was wondering that, too," Mary said softly, chewing on an egg roll.

"It smells like shit," Brad said as he set down the bottle of Tsing Tao in his left hand.

"That makes no sense," Josh looked at Brad as if he were slow. "How can we be smelling shit seeing as we *don't* shit?"

"I've been noticing something else," Marissa said. "Lights, they seem to be getting softer.

"Yeah," Jane looked troubled. "I've been noticing them too."

Marissa felt a deep sense of relief that someone else had noticed the lights.

"I wonder if it's a glitch," Brad mused before taking a long drink of his beer.

"A glitch?" Josh pressed.

"In the Cloud," Brad replied.

"Don't say that," Mary looked scared and took an unsteady drink off the Sapporo she had poured into a paper cup.

"It could happen," Brad replied. The Cloud is run by computers, computers break down."

"Come on, guys," Jane said firmly. "Let's not go there."

Normally Brad would back down from an order from either Jane or Josh but that time he didn't.

"Something is going on, the lights, the smell of sewage—"

"And what good does it do to dwell?" Jane focused on Brad, leaning into the table. "Maybe there is a glitch in the Cloud in which case we are fucked and there is nothing we can do but enjoy our food."

But no one wanted to eat anymore, first Kyle and now the possibility of a glitch in the cloud. The day was uncomfortable and getting worse.

"Three minutes to Green Box Time, three minutes."
The five friends returned to their cubicles and sat in their respective chairs staring at the respective computer monitors. All hand their hands hovering over their mouses…except Marissa.
I'm gonna do it, this may be a bad bad decision, but I'm doing it…or not doing it.
Twenty seconds to Green Box Time.
Ten seconds to Green Box Time.
Marissa thought of the Gentlemen drifting in like leaves, the fountain of Kyle's blood…
Five seconds to Green Box Time.
It took all her willpower not to click on the Green Button.
Cut to Black.

SIX

Marissa was standing on a sidewalk. There was garbage all around, soda cans and paper and fast food containers. From nearby was the smell of human shit, someone had probably crapped next to the dumpster in the alley off to her right. After a few seconds she recognized where she was—*Stockton, California, the industrial part. East Taylor Avenue.*

The only car on the street was a bronze 1975 Chevy Biscayne, clearly an undercover car. No one was inside.

So…not clicking the green button sent me to Stockton, California in the mid seventies?

Looking down, Marissa saw that she was wearing the uniform of a beat cop down to a .357 strapped to her hip.

A rising unease, not unlike right before the Gentleman arrived—

She searched the sky, growing fearful…

"Hey!" A man's voice, he sounded a combination of angry and confused. The stranger was handsome, Arab in appearance, and wearing an expensive looking two piece suit with a pressed white, button down shirt.

"What is this?" He asked Marissa, gesturing around at the garbage and warehouses and vacant lots full of the crude shelters where the homeless probably slept.

And a woman was across the street, white, somewhere in her thirties like the man in the suit. She looked confused but was looking around in silence while walking towards Marissa.

"I'm guessing you guys didn't click on the green box," Marissa said quietly. Both strangers seemed to understand what she was getting at, but the ex (?) cop was confused.

This is clearly my personal punishment, returning to a place that caused me a lot of anxiety, but what about them?

The man in the suit stopped in his tracks and looked up at the sky. "Customer service!" He called. "Mindy, I need customer service!" Marissa had no idea what he was doing—

And a new sensation, her instincts: Something dangerous was in the crude shelters made of cardboard. Looking over, the cop saw that the keys were in the Biscayne's ignition. Marissa understood that it was her car which was odd because it was an undercover car and she was dressed as a beat cop;

maybe the Cloud didn't understand the nuances of being a beat cop which didn't—

A man emerged from a shelter. He was big, easily seven feet tall and built like a football player. His penis was nearly the size of her forearm and, like the rest of him, filthy looking with green gunk dripping from it.

"We need to get in the car," Marissa said firmly to the other two.

"Fuck that," the man in the suit said without looking at the cop. "I didn't pay ten million to have my life interrupted."

The large, naked man was striding towards them, a grim smile on his face. Marissa drew her service revolver but kept it pointed at the ground.

"Sir!" She said firmly. "I need you to stand where you are and lace your fingers behind your head."

There was stirring in the other shelters and the dumpster in the alley. The naked man smiled more broadly, his teeth crooked and dark. He began stroking his penis and it became erect. Something moved, a dark spot crawling out of the tip and flying away, probably a fly. He was still walking towards them but slower, taking his time as he masturbated. The woman cried out in disgust and slapped at her arm.

"I hate flies," she moaned. "And where this one landed, it itches!"

"Customer service!" The man in the suit yelled at the sky. "Mindy, get your ass down here!"

"Please get in the car," Marissa said to the woman who complied.

The cop looked over at the naked man, now he was only about twenty feet away. Marissa leveled her Smith and Wesson at him and cocked it.

And when he comes, it's going to be a swarm of flies.

"Last warning, sir!"

Still stoking and smiling an awful smile, the naked man kept coming. Marissa fired a round into his leg. Thick, black liquid oozed from the wound that smelled fetid. The sound of the report and the stink of the fluid snapped Suit Man out of his anger.

"Best get in the car," Marissa shrugged towards the Biscayne, watching the naked man closely. The injured man had stopped and was looking down at his leg with concern.

"Well," he said calmly. "Looks like my day is ruined."

A half dozen naked men and women emerged from the shelters, they converged on the man who had been shot, tearing at the wound to get to the black liquid and then tearing the man apart. Not taking his eyes off them, Suit Man climbed in the back seat of the Biscyane and Marissa got behind the wheel, quickly driving off.

SEVEN

"Was I correct about not clicking on the green box?" Marissa asked, a few blocks from where the naked man had been ripped apart.

"Yeah," the woman said quietly. "Do you know where we are?"

"Yes. Stockton, Calfornia. Judging by this car I am guessing it is the mid seventies."

"And they had zombies in Stockton back in the seventies?" Suit Man asked sarcastically.

"Drug zombies, maybe," Marissa mused before looking at the man in the rear view mirror.

"You didn't answer my question—"

"No, I didn't push the fucking button but, yes, I am going to chew Mindy a new asshole."

"It's odd the two of you are here," Marissa said, looking over at a taqueria she had eaten at many times. "This makes sense as my punishment, but—why are you guys here?"

"Maybe you're supposed to protect us," The woman attempted. "You're a Lower Tier, right? No offense, but I saw your confusion when the gentleman in the suit—"

"Tannen."

"---Tannen, thank you," the woman nodded at the man in the back seat. "I noticed your confusion when Tannen was calling for customer service."

"So," Marissa replied. "You guys have a high buy-in and you get percs like customer service?"

"Yes," the woman said. "Plus we get a custom package with add ons. What is Lower Tier like?"

And then Marissa stopped hearing the woman sitting next to her: An early seventies Cadillac had turned in behind them, a black Fleetwood. The feeling the cop got from the car was the same she had gotten in the homeless shelter.

"I'm Marissa, how about you?"

"Cindy."

"Well, Cindy, you'd better buckle up because we are being followed."

"This is absurd," Tannen scowled. "They never tell us the consequences of not clicking the green button; our being punished is unfair, some Lower Tier shit."

The cop ignored him, pressing the accelerator and getting them up to seventy miles per hour. There were no other cars on the street or on the road. The Fleetwood stayed roughly five car lengths behind, the windshield dark enough that Marissa couldn't see the driver or—

What the fuck?

The ends of the grill were tilting up as if the Fleetwood was trying to smile. Marissa floored it, the 350 V8 getting them to eighty, ninety, and then a hundred. The grill of the Fleetwood popped out and the hood opened wide. Where the grill had been was red but not paint red, red like a wound…or a mouth.

The Fleetwood closed the distance some; four car lengths away then three. The Biscayne had gotten up to 105 but seemed to be running out of steam. The front of the black car was changing into a red maw with white things that reminded Marissa of the teeth of a shark. The hood came down some then rose again, once, twice, three times—*chomp chomp chomp.*

Marissa swerved, stomped the brakes, and attempted to turn left onto a cross street. The Biscayne came loose and both Cindy and Tannen screamed.

"I wet my fucking pants," the man in the suit said through clenched teeth.

He wet his pants, does this mean this is real? That we will feel pain?

The cop got the Biscayne under control and back up to speed. The Fleetwood swept around the corner as if it were nothing. The mouth that made up the entire front of the car opened and closed lazily one, twice, and a third time—*chomp, chomp, chomp.*

The large, black car closed the distance: Four car lengths. Three. Two. One. The people in the Biscayne could see the yellowness of the fangs, smell the meatiness of its "breath." The mouth lunged and tore the rear bumper of the Biscyane off, the trunk lid popping up and creaking as it swayed up and down. The Fleetwood chewed, seeming to digest the metal that screamed in protest. The Cadillac mouth closed on the rear tires—

Once it gets them, we're fucked, game over.

There was the sensation of the back end being lifted followed by a large pop as the rear tires were punctured and burst.

Grinding, a sound that reminded Marissa of when a spoon gets caught in a garbage disposal but much louder.

The rear window bursting, Tannen scrambling forward, trying to climb into the front seat—

The first thing Marissa noticed were the lights: Fluorescents, the tubes humming. The smell of cleaners. A tile floor, white walls…a hospital. Cindy looked troubled, no Cindy looked distraught, on the verge of tears.

"Now we're in *my* hell," she said shakily.

Marissa knew she should put an arm around the other woman but couldn't bring herself to do, she had never been a touchy-feely sort of person.

Tannen was looking down at his suit pants. He appeared relieved, probably because they were urine free.

"This is where my children died," Cindy said quietly, struggling not to lose her composure.

"Jesus," Tannen flinched, he put a hand on Cindy's shoulder. "I'm sorry. You said *children*, as in more than one."

Cindy just nodded, walked over to one of the doors and put a hand on it.

"One died of leukemia, one was hit by a drunk driver, and Billy," she had to stop, clenching her eyes closed and struggling with her emotions for a few seconds before continuing. "They thought Billy had snitched or something and shot him. He was twelve."

Cindy had changed, her sadness turning to anger.

"I should have known I would be punished and this is perfect."

"What do you mean?" Marissa asked.

"It was good while it lasted," Cindy ignored the cop. "Having them all back home with me."

She removed her hand from the door.

"We need to get out of here," she continued.

Cindy began walking down the corridor and the others followed her.

"What was with the black car?" Tannen asked.

"What?" Marissa replied, though a moment later she understood.

"I was a cop," she continued. "When I got shot, before I lost consciousness I was staring across the street and there was a black, 1972 Cadillac Fleetwood parked there."

"So," Tannen continued. "We've been through your nightmare and now we're in Cindy's; I'm curious what they have for me."

"Whatever you do, don't think about it," the cop replied. "That area where we ran into each other, that was where I was ambushed. As I recognized the street I remembered the day I was shot."

"What about the zombies or whatever they were?" Cindy asked.

"No idea," Marissa said truthfully. "Just a bonus, I guess."

"Good to not have you yelling for customer service," she added with a shrug in Tannen's direction.

"I was in the middle of," he started and caught himself. "Something very enjoyable."

"So, that's your Upper Tier thing?" Marissa asked. "Hooking up with whomever you want to?"

"Part of it, getting to be attractive."

That caught Cindy's attention.

"So you were ugly in the past?"

"I guess," Tannen frowned. "It wasn't about then, it wasn't about the forty years I worked and didn't do anything for fun, it was about *now and forever*, which is why being torn out of my situation pissed me off so much."

"You must have been bored not to click on the green box," Marissa said.

"Bored?" Tannen said incredulously. "You have no idea who I was with or what I was doing to them."

"Maybe bored subconsciously," Marissa replied. "I know I was, no challenges, no change, no risk."

"What about me?" Cindy asked, Marissa had to look away from the older woman's earnest expression.

"What was your 'now' again?" She asked.

"Having my children back again living with me."

"Maybe you got tired of them," Tannen suggested.

"What? Are you…no!" Cindy protested.

"Let's just leave it as an unknown," Marissa cut in.

They approached a cross corridor. A form was on the floor twenty feet to the right, a child who appeared to be sleeping. Cindy was the first to walk towards the form.

"It could be a werewolf or something," Tannen said.

"It's a *child*," Cindy looked back at him with a frown before kneeling next to the child.

There were no more words, just muttering, little cries. the muttering getting louder. She shook the child, it was not stirring. Tannen and Marissa hurried over. It was a boy, not quite a teenager, tan foam around his nostrils.

"Fentynal," Marissa mumbled.

"Why the fuck is a little kid doing Fentynal?" Tannen sounded offended by the idea.

"It's Billy," Cindy's voice was barely audible.

"It's not real," Marissa attempted. "This is just—"

"It is fucking real!" Cindy screamed at her. "I bought these clothes for him, it's Billy's smell!"

"Is he dead?" Tannen asked warily.

"No," Cindy said softly. "But he's barely alive, his pulse is extremely weak." She struggled to pick him up, Tannen helped Cindy get the boy into her arms.

"It's a hospital," Marissa said firmly. "There has to be a doctor."

"You know there's no doctor," Cindy said bitterly. "The whole point of this is that I have to watch him die again."

They came to a bench and Cindy sat on it with Billy in her lap. She stroked his hair but didn't look at him.

"There was no way the old me could come up with ten million dollars," the mother said quietly. "But after Billy died, he was the last to go, something changed in me…"

"You dealt fentanyl to come up with the money?"

"Distributed but, yes," Cindy sighed.

"Wow," Marissa said flatly.

"You must have never been a mother," Cindy looked at the other woman sharply. "If you had been, you'd understand."

"This is how it was," she continued, stroking the boy's hair again. "When he was shot, the bullet destroyed a major blood vessel, there was nothing the doctors could do. They shot him as he walked up to our house. The hospital was only five minutes away but…he bled so much, my blouse was drenched, it was dripping off him and I understood that with each drop, the odds of him surviving were going down."

She stopped stroking her child's hair and stared at the opposite wall.

"So…yeah…I distributed a drug that probably killed at least a few people."

Cindy looked down at the child in her lap.

"I don't think he has much longer; would you guys mind waiting in the other corridor for me?"

Tannen and Marissa walked off, turning down the corridor they had originally been on. There was silence for nearly a minute, and then the sound of helpless sobbing.

NINE

There was the sound of sobbing then the sound of laughter, footsteps on tile, a mother reprimanding her child for being a pest, power ballads from the 1990s coming over PA speakers. The three of them were in a mall. Cindy and Marissa were confused, Tannen looked scared.

"This is your hell, I guess," Cindy said, her eyes still red from crying. "Tell us what horrible stuff is going to happen?"

"This goes back to how I made my money," Tannen was struggling to keep his composure.

He is scared, really fucking scared…in a stupid mall. Marissa saw nothing out of the ordinary.

"I programmed games," Tannen continued. "The biggest one was called Boomvest."

"Boomvest?"

"It takes place in a mall," now the man in the suit was struggling to get words out. "The player is a suicide bomber, the object is blow up as many people as possible."

"Lovely," Cindy said.

"This is easy," Marissa replied. "We just leave the mall."

They walked from one end of the mall to the other, no sign of an exit. When they got to a store, the gate was down. They'd walk away and the gate would be up with shoppers going in and out, but when the three of them tried the gate was down.

"Look," Marissa said firmly. "This is just a lesson, I think, reminding us about the problems in our old lives—"

"But this wasn't a problem to me," Tannen interjected. "I made a lot of money and people loved the game but…"

Marissa watched him trail off and waited a few seconds before pressing him.

"But what?"

"It's stupid," Tannen said, clearly hiding something.

"I can tell by your face it is not stupid, whatever you are hiding," the cop replied.

"We programmed forty levels," Tannen was chewing on each word, he wanted them out of his mouth but once they were out they were *free,* the words, the truth they represented. "And then people started reaching the 41st level and the 42nd."

"Was the game programmed with artificial intelligence?" Marissa asked. Tannen just shook his head, he looked deeply spooked, the olive tone of his skin paling.

"There is no logical explanation in this world."

A man was walking towards them with a tight smile. He was around sixty, hair slicked back, a well crafted two piece gray suit not concealing the fact the stranger was powerfully built. Marissa and the others were shocked that he acknowledged them, no one else in the mall had.

"In the world," the man said, looking at the three people in turn. "But you aren't in the world anymore, are you? You all volunteered—and paid—to have your conscious minds uploaded into the Cloud."

"Who are you?" Cindy asked.

The Devil, Marissa thought and the man focused on her.

"A cheap name," the man said, his smile disappearing. "If you need a name Max will do."

"So, we're here to get blown up?" Marissa asked.

"You are here to watch others be blown up, and watch your child die, and be eaten by black cars and relive your ambush over and over again."

Max looked around at the shoppers who were blissfully unaware.

"The green box is there to protect you," he continued. "By not clicking it you open a door and when the door is open…"

The older man stopped and looked at the three of them meaningfully.

"Now you are mine, to amuse me, for eternity."

Max swept his arm and they were in a small, open boat in a rough seat. A tentacle skittered across the water, entered the boat, and wrapped around Tannen who struggled and made mewling sounds.

Max swept his arm and they were in the middle of an ancient battle, men with lances screaming as they ran at Marissa, Cindy, and Tannen. Each was run through and the pain was amazing, they could feel organs bursting as they were skewered.

Max swept his arm, they were in a white space, just whiteness.

"I should have just clicked the fucking box," Marissa sighed,
The older man looked at her, smiled, and swept his arm.

TEN

Marissa was sitting up in bed, her phone beeping. It was another morning.
What if this is a trick? What if I walk into the kitchen and that man is there waiting to sweep me to some other awful place?
No, Marissa's instincts were telling her the experience had ended and she was back in the Village.
Until she decided not to click on the green box again.

The woman dressed and went to meet the streetcar. Her four friends were already on board and motioned for her to join them.
A cheap name.
Marissa smiled and nodded at the right time but she kept thinking of Max and his ability to sweep them from one reality to another.
Why do I get the feeling he wasn't part of the Cloud?
Josh and Jane were arguing about the old movie *Requiem for a Dream* but Marissa didn't really hear them. It was 68, another perfect day. That night they would meet at the bar and eat and drink until it no longer interested them. Jane had pivoted the discussion to *Top Gun*, and Josh jumped on her comparing the first movie to the second and—
Is that...body odor?
The smell of sweat made Marissa uneasy, people didn't have body odor in the Village. You could go without bathing a month and not smell like the bacteria that breeds in sweat.
She thought of Max sweeping his arm, sweeping them into another reality.
No, you're back. Even before you didn't push the green button you could smell sewage. It's a glitch in the Cloud, that's all.
Marissa labored to calm herself but her instincts were insistent:
Something is off; come on, you can't deny it.
And then she noticed crows feet around Josh's eyes, she was certain those hadn't been there—
"Earth to Marissa," a woman's voice, Mary was saying something.
"Sorry, what did you say?"

Mary smiled at that, her teeth were yellowing and a little crooked. It wasn't terrible, but Marissa picked up on it…picked up on it and worked to bury her reaction.

"We need to be a united front against Jane and Josh," Mary continued. "They really want Mexican for lunch but the bar has started making these amazing roast beef sandwiches."

"That does sound good," Marissa managed a smile.

"Is she trying to recruit you?" Josh broke from his conversation with Jane. "Come on, Mary, those roast beef sandwiches may be good, but they do not compare to Pedrobertos."

Mary meekly countered that and Marissa fell out of the conversation. They were approaching the office building where, most likely, the five of them would eat take out from Pedrobertos and click on a green box every hour. *Wait…*

There was something in the normally empty parking lot, a familiar shape; it was familiar but it didn't belong there. It took Marissa a moment to recognize it and a few moments more to accept what seeing it meant. Parked on the edge of the lot was a 1975 Chevy Biscayne.

Written 19-20 August, 2022

TWELVE MILES TWELVE MILES TWELVE MILES TWELVE MILES TWELVE
MILES TWELVE MILES TWELVE MILES TWELVE MILES TWELVE MILES
TWELVE MILES TWELVE MILES TWELVE MILES TWELVE MILES TWELVE
MILES TWELVE MILES TWELVE MILES TWELVE MILES TWELVE MILES
TWELVE MILES TWELVE MILES TWELVE MILES TWELVE MILES TWELVE
MILES TWELVE MILES TWELVE MILES TWELVE MILES TWELVE MILES
TWELVE MILES TWELVE MILES TWELVE MILES TWELVE MILES TWELVE
MILES TWELVE MILES TWELVE MILES TWELVE MILES TWELVE MILES
TWELVE MILES TWELVE MILES TWELVE MILES TWELVE MILES TWELVE
MILES TWELVE MILES TWELVE MILES TWELVE MILES TWELVE MILES
TWELVE MILES TWELVE MILES TWELVE MILES TWELVE MILES TWELVE
MILES TWELVE MILES TWELVE MILES TWELVE MILES TWELVE MILES
TWELVE MILES TWELVE MILES TWELVE MILES TWELVE MILES TWELVE
MILES TWELVE MILES TWELVE MILES TWELVE MILES TWELVE MILES
TWELVE MILES TWELVE MILES TWELVE MILES TWELVE MILES TWELVE
MILES TWELVE MILES TWELVE MILES TWELVE MILES TWELVE MILES
TWELVE MILES TWELVE MILES TWELVE MILES TWELVE MILES TWELVE
MILES TWELVE MILES TWELVE MILES TWELVE MILES TWELVE MILES
TWELVE MILES TWELVE MILES TWELVE MILES TWELVE MILES TWELVE
MILES TWELVE MILES TWELVE MILES TWELVE MILES TWELVE MILES
TWELVE MILES TWELVE MILES TWELVE MILES TWELVE MILES TWELVE
MILES TWELVE MILES TWELVE MILES TWELVE MILES TWELVE MILES

TWELVE MILES TWELVE MILES TWELVE MILES

TWELVE MILES TWELVE MILES TWELVE MILES TWELVE MILES TWELVE
MILES TWELVE MILES TWELVE MILES TWELVE MILES TWELVE MILES
TWELVE MILES TWELVE MILES TWELVE MILES TWELVE MILES TWELVE
MILES TWELVE MILES TWELVE MILES TWELVE MILES TWELVE MILES
TWELVE MILES TWELVE MILES TWELVE MILES TWELVE MILES TWELVE
MILES TWELVE MILES TWELVE MILES TWELVE MILES TWELVE MILES
TWELVE MILES TWELVE MILES TWELVE MILES TWELVE MILES TWELVE
MILES TWELVE MILES TWELVE MILES TWELVE MILES TWELVE MILES
TWELVE MILES

ONE

"This is not good."

Those words, softly, as the woman knelt next to the severed foot. The flashlight in her hand shook minutely as she struggled to ignore the coppery smell of blood. The ship lurched and the inspector nearly fell into the pool of dark liquid; it was the size of her torso and reminded her of the shape of Portugal. The woman stood upright and shined the flashlight on the surrounding deck: No drops of blood, the foot had been in a container and dropped where Mike had found it. Why? Why hadn't whomever had severed it just tossed it over the side? Was the victim dead—was there even a victim or had someone just sawed off their own foot?

Really? Why would someone do that? This is a murder...or a maiming.

Logically, the victim was dead and killed quickly—the screams from someone having a foot sawed off would echo through the ship. The woman took pictures of the crime scene from different angles and then walked back in the direction she had come in, away from the smell of blood and the pale foot with the jagged cut marks.

"What do you think?"

Mike's voice as her eyes adjusted to the sunlight. Six others were standing nearby; out of habit the woman with the flashlight studied their faces for guilt.

"Unless someone sawed their own foot off, we have a murderer or mutilator loose on the boat," she said.

"Do you know whose foot it is, Max?" A woman asked from nearby.

"I will soon," Max replied. "We need to do a head count and see who is missing...or at least missing a foot."

"No one is missing?" A man in a dress shirt was smiling in disbelief as Max delivered her report.

"No, but Kyle B is missing a foot."

Dress Shirt just stared at her, clearly not sure what his next question should be.

"So...does Kyle know what happened to his foot?" He asked.

"No, and he does not seem to have been given anything to render him unconscious or keep him in that state."

"It makes no sense," Dress Shirt looked troubled as he sat behind his desk. "Mr. Pearly—"

"Apso," Mr. Pearly said distractedly. "No misters on the seastead…..do you have any ideas, Max?"

"None aside from the obvious: A psychopath. But it'd have to be a psychopath with medical training; jagged as the cut was, they made it so Kyle didn't bleed out."

"How?"

"He or she cauterized the stump."

Apso cringed at that.

"Do we need to go on lockdown?" He asked.

"I don't see a reason for that," Max replied. "We're thirty people on a hundred-fifty foot boat, we're already kinda in lockdown."

"Seastead," Apso corrected her. "Not a boat—"

"Whichever it is, there is a psycho on board," Max said and then paused. "Which makes no sense, considering all the tests you ran on applicants."

Mr. Pearly was clearly bewildered and scared but was struggling to contain it and be the boss again.

"You're the closest thing we have to a cop, Max; I'm counting on you."

Apso looked at a framed photograph of Oppenheimer he kept on his desk; the woman understood it meant she was dismissed. Max shrugged and walked out of her boss's cabin.

The foot was not a surprise. Max had been feeling uneasy since boarding the seastead a month earlier. The boat had a story or many stories, she could sense that. It had been a cargo ship, originally licensed in Portugal in the early 1960s, moving from reputable shipping concerns to ones with less integrity and more guile—this determination was equally from research and instinct. Bad things had happened on the boat and now she was seeing shadows where shadows had no business being. So, the foot was not a surprise…..*no.*

TWO

Mari the nurse was, to Max's knowledge, the only individual with medical training on the ship. She didn't have the right vibe though; Max had been around genuine, clinically diagnosed psychopaths and Mari was not on the same wavelength. That left twenty-eight others, twenty-seven if you excluded Kyle, who could have had some secret medical knowledge.

But he had no signs of coming off anesthesia. I asked to draw blood so Mari could check for such things but Kyle refused and Mr. Pearly backed him up.

And Kyle's cabin was spotless during the black light check, for blood, at least. The stump had been immaculately bandaged so—

No signs of anesthesia. Stump is cauterized properly...so why the jagged cuts? Why was the foot carried off in a container and left down by the engine?

"Mr. Pearly is calling everyone onto the deck," a small woman with dreads said. "Sorry to sneak up on you, Max."

She hadn't. Max had smelled the oil in Jojee's dreads when the woman was beyond striking distance. Without a word, the inspector followed the woman up to the deck where a woman in a stylish bikini was lashed to a pole. Apso was standing nearby in his dress shirt, khakis, and Birkenstock sandals. No socks, mercifully. Stylish Bikini was alternating between sobbing and pleading with Mr. Pearly for mercy. Max understood what was going on and motioned for her boss to join her out of earshot of the others.

"Mr. Pearly—"

"Please, *Apso*, I am not comfortable with all that formal stuff," he smiled, bashful.

"Apso, is this really a good time for a flogging? We're all stressed out that there may be a Jack the Ripper on board—"

"Jack the Ripper killed," Mr. Pearly pointed out. "Besides, what if it was *Jaqueline* the Ripper, why couldn't it have been a woman? That's how Lizzie Borden got off—"

"Please, Apso, I'm just saying—"

"This is my seastead," her boss said firmly. "Look...there is never a good time for a flogging, totally fucks with moral, but Charity broke one of the biggest rules; she brought the outside world onboard. When I brought you on you agreed to the terms I placed on living and working here."

"Yes, sir, I did—"

"And don't call me, sir," Apso shook his head. "No mister, no sir, we should have left that crap in the twentieth century with all the other mistakes."

And capital punishment wasn't one of those mistakes?

"Come on," the boss sighed. "Let's get this shitshow over with."

"Apso, Apso," Charity brightened when Mr. Pearly walked back into view. "Please...I wasn't thinking, it won't happen again."

Mari had walked over to where Max stood, a small medical kit in hand...a medical kit for tending to Charity's wounds after the flogging. Apso ignored Charity's pleas and looked around at the people gathered on the deck, even Kyle had been asked to crutch up to witness the flogging.

"I hate this shit," Mr. Pearly shook his head, appearing remorseful. "But...the rules on the seastead are for a reason. We left the United States because it was stressing us out...all eleven of us and all the wonderful people who look after us. One of the biggest rules is not to bring that garbage onto the seastead, news of the dumpster fire our old country has become. Charity used the wi-fi to read the news and, well, if she wants to poison herself..."

He paused, seeming to be on the verge of emotions.

"But she shared the news with others," he looked over at Jojee. "How did what Charity shared make you feel Jojee?"

Jojee looked from Charity who was begging her with her eyes to Mr. Pearly. "Really, it's okay," Jojee stammered. "I mean—"

"Honesty, Jojee," Apso smiled. "It's okay, you're in a safe place—"

"When I mentioned it, I didn't want Charity to be punished!"

"Barbara told me you were stressed out," the boss said gently. "She said that, whatever Charity had shared with you, it had stressed you out."

Defeated, Jojee bowed her head. Seeing that, Charity struggled against her bonds and began screaming. Apso nodded to Max who gagged the woman in the stylish bikini, a bikini soon to be ruined with blood. Fitz, a strong looking woman with a flattop who was taller than most men, broke from the crowd, a cat of nine tails in one hand.

"As this is a first violation," Apso said, clearly uncomfortable. "The punishment is ten lashes."

He walked over to Charity and looked her in the eye.

"I hate this," Mr. Pearly was being honest, Max could see it. "But...the rules on the seastead exist for a reason."

Apso walked off and Fitz walked over with the whip. She was wearing a sleeveless, gray shirt that was already dark under the arms with sweat. One blow, a second, and then the blood began to flow from thin lines breaking the skin. The gag turned Charity's shrieks into odd, animal noises. After five blows she fainted. After the tenth, Mari rushed over to treat the wounds and then Mike helped her get Charity down into medical.

THREE

"I didn't think he would actually have us whipped," Charity said weakly as Mari checked the dressings on her back.

The whipped woman then looked up at Max accusingly.

"Why didn't you stop it? How could you let that happen?"

"You entitled people," Max started and then cut herself off. "Look...I can tell the flogging hurt—"

"I'm going to have scars, Max, *scars!*"

"Then why did you break the rules?" Max asked and then held up a hand when she saw the scarred woman starting to reply. "I don't have time for this, I have to figure out what happened to Kyle's foot."

"Maybe he cut it off," Charity frowned.

"No," Max replied. "In theory, you could give yourself a local but the logistics...and Kyle wasn't acting as if he was coming out of any sort of anesthesia—"

"How can you tell?"

"I just can."

"There are signs," Mari agreed, dressing the last wound.

"If you know all this medical shit," Charity looked over at Max. "Maybe you cut the foot off."

"I wouldn't have left it down by engines," Max frowned. "I would have just tossed it over the side, as close to Kyle's cabin as possible. What the amputator did was a big risk...of course, maybe that's part of the thrill."

"I don't remember anything," Kyle said impatiently. "How many times are you going to ask?"

"I'm sorry," Max struggled to be patient. "So...you went to sleep and you still had two feet, when you woke up one was gone."

Her eyes went to a poster on the wall, an old looking city with *Lisboa* in large letters on the bottom. Max got the weird feeling the poster hadn't been there before.

"Yep," Kyle said, his expression saying *now get the fuck out of my room and leave me alone.*

"It's just weird. If they had given you a general you'd feel it, a grogginess—"

"Come on," the footless man sighed. "Can't you just leave me in peace?" The investigator nodded and left the cabin.

Max was restless the remainder of the day. Thirty people, twenty-nine suspects. The internet had all sorts of information, *anyone* could learn how to cut a foot off without killing the victim; but, of those thirty people, how many could do something so violent, so pointlessly violent and yet skilled? *I could do the act, but I couldn't emotionally carry it out—how could you?* Everytime she crossed paths with someone, Max tried to *read* them but there was too much emotional cross talk; people were scared about what happened to Kyle and disgusted with the flogging.

"Look, I know everyone is upset about Charity," Apso smiled at everyone gathered in the crew lounge. "Believe me, I hated it—"

"Then why did you do it?" Jojee asked, a little timid but still angry. "This is your deal, you could have stopped it!"

Mr. Pearly didn't like that, Max could tell: *Maybe it was him, maybe the seastead is a sort of zoo for him...*

"Did you enjoy the way the United States was becoming, Jojee?" Apso crouched down in front of the woman with the dreads. "I remember your application, how you wrote about being sick of all the bad news and how it stressed you out."

"Yeah, but—"

"The purpose of the seastead is to remove us from all that," Mr. Pearly continued. "If I just punished Charity with a verbal dressing down, what stops her from doing it again? Now, she understands the consequences...right, Charity?"

The scarred woman just looked at him, fearful, hateful.

"Charity is not in a good place right now," Apso looked around the room with a smile. "That will change in time—"

"You flogged her, bro," Mike said harshly.

Mr. Pearly ignored him: Mike was one of the help like Max or Mari. Charity had bought in...and now she would have scars across her back.

"You make this big deal out of sharing news from the outside," Mike continued. "But Kyle losing a foot is no big deal?"

Mr. Pearly looked over at Max and nodded towards Mike. Reluctantly, the closest thing to a cop on the seastead walked over to the man speaking out. "Really?" He said to Apso. "You're kicking me out of the meeting because I dared speak out?"

"Mike…" Mr. Pearly was searching for the right way to express his thoughts, Max could see that. "Charity broke one of the biggest rules, a rule that is there for everyone's mental health. As for Kyle's foot, Max is on it and she is highly qualified to do so and I'm sure will get to the bottom of it."

He walked over to the staff member that had questioned him.

"Look, I respect the fact you are upset, what happened to Charity was *ugly*," Mr. Pearly continued. "If the way things are run upsets you, maybe you should reconsider your employment on the seastead."

The boss trailed off meaningfully. Max could tell by looking at Mike's face that the crew member had gotten the message and would keep his opinions to himself in the future.

FOUR

Max was the only one on deck at midnight. The sea was gentle but there were gusts. Daring herself, she looked over the railing at where the modest waves were; there was no moon so she had to imagine what they looked like. How far down was it? Twenty feet? Thirty? If you jumped would you be knocked unconscious or would you be aware of slipping below the surface? How far down would you go if you just *surrendered?* Max was both fascinated and terrified by deep water. It had to be a couple hundred feet deep where they were, they weren't over the Continental Shelf but it still had to be frighteningly deep. The rail was steel cables suspended by metal poles, she squeezed the cables, and could feel flecks of rust that went with the smell of salt and sea water. The foot was not a surprise; no, in a way it was anticlimactic.

This is not a good place.

Max had sensed that within an hour of boarding with her large duffel and new name. It may not have been a good place, but she had been short on options. A shape somewhere off to her right, she could have sworn she saw a man in a dark sweater and watch cap.

Don't be stupid, you're the only one out here?

Then why did she smell cigarette smoke?

In her cabin, Max undressed and lay on top of the covers naked. One by one she touched the red spots on her torso, ran a finger along the scars. Touching where she had been shot and the resulting scars was *real,* not apparitions or the smell of cigarettes.

FIVE

Mike again, clearly upset, and she hadn't even had her coffee.

"It's a skin rug, brah," he said weakly before lurching to the rail and vomiting over it.

Max waited until he was done coughing and spitting before asking for an elaboration.

"Same place?"

The crew member just nodded. Max grabbed her flashlight and proceeded below decks. She had to force herself into the guts of the ship just as she had when Mike told her about the foot; the intuitions got stronger down below, the sensation of being watched by something powerful—whatever it was made the woman's skin crawl and she got the feeling that whatever was watching her enjoyed that.

In the same place the foot had been discovered was a perfectly square strip of flesh Max guessed was a foot in length on each side..

Has to be the back, it's the only spot on the body you could get a piece this big.

She knelt down and examined the skin closely, there was hair so she assumed the flesh was from a man. Max took pictures and then walked up to the deck where Mike had his hands on the rail and was looking out into the distance.

"Gonna be a storm tonight," he said weakly. "We're gonna have to batten down…we're gonna be trapped inside with whomever cut off the foot and did…*that*—how do you skin someone like that, anyway?"

Max didn't know. Before she could speculate, screams were heard from down below.

The yelling came from Kyle's cabin.

"Again? Fucking *really*?" Kyle yelled, looking over his shoulder and then accusingly at the four people who had responded to his screams.

He was trying to tear at the bandages on his back but Fitz was stopping him, her body odor overwhelming in the small cabin.

"Dear lord, I won't fight if you back off, Fitz," Kyle gasped. "Just…please, you stink, Fitz."

The big woman didn't appear offended and backed away from the bed. The man lay back on the bed and looked over at Max who got closer.

"Okay, whomever the culprit is, they are targeting you, Kyle," Max managed a smile even though she didn't care for the man on the bed. "Who on the ship—" She continued.

"Seastead," Apso corrected from the doorway.

"*Seastead*," Max sighed. "Who are you at odds with? If it's a private matter I can clear the room."

"I don't know,"Kyle looked up at her, confused, frightened. "Jesus, what are they going to take next?"

Getting that much skin—*it's a skin rug, brah*—would have taken a lot of work, would have been painful—

And once again Kyle was lucid, not groggy. The culprit could have used a local, but Kyle was not showing any symptoms of even a local anesthesia. And, most importantly, if a local had been used Kyle would have been able to identify whomever was mutilating him. Apso saw someone approaching the cabin and stepped aside to let her in. Mari.

"I got the skin on ice, Kyle," she said apprehensively. "I can attempt to attach it but...honestly, I've never attempted anything like this before."

"Why don't we have a real doctor?!" Kyle yelled at Apso. "Ten million fucking dollars and what? What walk-in clinic did you kidnap her from??"

Max waited for Kyle to catch himself and apologize but the wounded man just glared at the boss.

"We'll find the culprit," Mr. Pearly said softly. "Feel better, Kyle."

"Where are we, Max?" Apso cornered Max in a passway, anger on his face and in his voice. "This is a clusterfuck...you're supposed to be a pro and now...what *is* next? Do you find his dick down by the engine?"

"Permission to speak freely, Apso—"

"No! You're not doing your fucking job. I'm sorry to raise my voice, please let me know if I am crossing boundaries but...what the fuck is going on? There are twenty-seven people besides us and Kyle, how hard can it be for you?"

He was just staring at her, mouth slightly open, face red.

I could just quit, get the fuck out of here...

Yeah, and you know what will happen if you show up back on the mainland.

"This is good, Mr. Pearly. Whomever has it in for Kyle, that narrows things down—

"Everyone hates Kyle," Apso muttered, looking over at a fire extinguisher in a glass case. "Guy was a manager of a rental car company until he made some wise investments."

"But not everyone could do *that*," Max pointed out. "Even if our culprit has the medical skill, one thing makes no sense."

"That there is no sign of anesthesia?"

"Yeah, having a foot cut off, especially. This is impossible, boss."

"Well…you need to do the impossible because the situation on this seastead is going fucking sideways."

Without waiting for a response, the boss walked off.

SIX

"Whatever did this to Kyle, it enjoyed the flogging."

Jojee was standing next to Max who was, again, looking out at the sea. The wind was bringing in waves—how big of a wave could the ship weather? *Whatever*, that description had caught Max's attention.

"What do you mean?" She asked.

Jojee grabbed the cable, pulled at it a little, looked down at the waves toying with the hull and then up at the sky which was growing darker.

"I don't know how to describe it," the woman with the dreads frowned before brightening and looking at Max. "You sense it, too!"

"Whatever I feel is immaterial because I can't define it," Max mumbled.

"No, no, this is good, it's really good."

"All I have is a sense of dread," the investigator protested, growing irritated with Jojee's *hippy dippy* shit, as Kyle would put it.

"But you feel the flogging is feeding whatever is on board?" She asked, too curious not to.

"Yeah," Jojee looked troubled again. "Maybe I should have kept on the festival circuit, at least you could get high…get laid, all that mainland stuff."

"Maybe we're supposed to be here," Words just came out of Max's mouth she wasn't aware of thinking.

"Maybe," the other woman said from some deep place. "This boat probably saved my life, I was getting into some heavy stuff on the circuit."

Max wasn't in the mood for Jojee's stories of music festivals and sleeping off drugs in dirty tents so she mumbled an excuse and walked away from the rail.

"This isn't an office," Apso said to Max after asking her to close the door to his cabin. "I have to think like a sea captain, keep in mind the importance of discipline."

It seemed he was saying that to shore up his own doubts and not to remind Max of something.

"Where did you get this boat?" She asked. "Before it was a seastead, what was it?"

The shrewdness that crossed his face for a moment—*he knows. He got an amazing deal on this boat because something fucked up happened on it.* Mr. Pearly quickly made his face an amiable blank again.

"My people found it," he said dismissively. "Just as they found you, Max." Apso winked at her, the wink said: *You should understand the consequences of asking about the past.*

"Why is only Kyle being targeted?" Max asked thoughtfully, as much to the ghosts she felt as to her boss.

"Honestly, if one of them is to be targeted I'm glad it's him," Mr. Pearly shrugged. "Don't like the guy."

"Then why did you bring him on board? Weren't you—"

Apso raised a hand to silence her.

"You have a finite amount of time and energy, Max; spend it on figuring out what the heck is going on."

He looked over at the framed picture on his desk: Tesla. Something about that seemed *wrong*; she could have sworn the picture was of Oppenheimer before.

"This is going to be the biggest storm we've weathered," Barbara said, making minute adjustments to the wheel as she watched the sky for clues.

"Can the seastead handle it?" Max asked.

"Guess we'll find out," the helmswoman smiled. "We've been mostly at anchor, now we're bringing the motor up so we don't get broadsided by the waves."

You could feel it through the ship, the rumble of ancient diesel engines now fueled by some sort of algae based biofuel Apso Pearly had a hand in producing.

"I"m asking people for ideas," Max pivoted. "You've heard about the mutilations?"

"Who hasn't? Thirty people on a relatively small cargo ship."

"Are you also aware that neither Mari nor I believe Kyle was given a general—"

"You mean anesthesia? Like when they knock you out for an operation?"

"Yeah."

"How do they do it without Kyle being able to identify them?"

"That's the big question. You couldn't just do either mutilation while a person was asleep, they'd wake up."

"And scream…"

"Yeah…"

"And on this boat everyone would hear it…."

"Exactly. If you were me, what would you be thinking?"

"That I had a shitty job."

SEVEN

"Whoo hoo, party party!" Apso had slapped on a big happy smile that didn't come within a million miles of his eyes.

This was his response to the people in the lounge drinking. The storm had found the ship which was rolling in the heavy weather. Occasionally, a big wave would strike the side and the boat shuddered. Max had broken down and was having a whiskey sour in the hope that it would calm her nerves.

Storms are a lot worse now than when this ship was designed and built—can she withstand modern weather? Have the bolts holding her together began to rust—

Stop, just…stop. This is not helping.

"You partyin' as well?" Apso asked, he was still smiling but his voice wasn't.

"Just one drink to calm my nerves."

Mr. Pearly nodded at that and looked around the room.

"We're all counting on you," he looked at her earnestly; oddly it didn't seem fake. "Max…I apologize for using my outside voice earlier. I *do* believe in you. I *know* you can figure this out."

She just nodded. Her drink was nearly gone and there was the desire for another one, a desire that she couldn't allow to be satisfied. The ship lurched to the side, beginning a roll. Someone cried out but the boat righted itself.

"You know," Apso said thoughtfully. "When a ship is battened down like this it is nearly impossible to sink due to imprisoned air."

"Seastead," Max mumbled, moving her empty glass from hand to hand.

The boss smiled at that and walked away.

The ten people who had paid millions were in the lounge getting drunk. As more alcohol entered their blood they moved to a different wavelength than Max who was largely sober; they began to annoy her but she didn't want to leave, didn't even want to be in the corridor alone.

Whatever did this to Kyle, it enjoyed the flogging.

The man himself looked grim, sitting by himself drinking tropical rum drinks with brightly colored paper umbrellas. The happiness of the umbrellas seemed weird in contrast to the misery on Kyle's face.

It has to be supernatural, whatever is happening to him—

Do you hear yourself? You're just feeding into this, soon you'll be spouting hippy dippy nonsense like Jojee…

But there was no logical explanation; she was trapped on an old boat in a storm twelve miles from the mainland with no explanation aside from something supernatural targeting one of the passengers. Max thought of her empty glass, she still hadn't set it down and the urge to refill it was almost too much to resist.

"You have to go down there," Barbara yelled at someone as Max approached the bridge. "I can't leave the wheel for a minute, I'm wearing a fucking diaper!"

Mike was the person the helmswoman was yelling at.

"Look at this shit," Barbara continued, gesturing with a free hand at the windows. "You need to stay on top of the engines or we're fucked!"

It was three in the morning. The drunks had passed out in the lounge or staggered off to their cabins leaving Max alone…alone with respect to the living. Ill at ease, she had walked to the bridge.

"I'll go with you, Mike," the investigator offered.

The engineer didn't like that, clearly he was still hoping to win the argument.

"Thanks, Max." He muttered.

Once they were out of the bridge he grabbed the investigator's arm to stop her. Something on Max's face let him know that was a bad idea and the engineer quickly let go and backed away.

"Sorry," Mike said. "I'm just…I don't know."

"This thing is like a cat leaving presents outside the door," Max said without thinking.

The engineer was openly terrified by that metaphor.

"How am I supposed to go down there after you saying that?" Mike asked, his voice higher pitched than usual.

"I'm with you."

The engineer chucked ruefully and shook his head.

"Come on, Max. No disrespect, but whatever this is…I don't know….it's like the boogeyman."

That caused ice water to run through the investigator's veins but she forced her fears down—mostly.

"There's no such thing as the boogeyman," she said.

Mike could tell she didn't believe that and smiled triumphantly.

"You say that, but—"

"It's fucking irrelevant!" Max snapped. "You need to stay on top of the engines, if you refuse to go with me I'll have no choice but to report this to Mr. Pearly."

"You'd rat me out to the boss?" Mike appeared surprised.

"I wouldn't need to," Max gestured up and down the corridor. "There are dozens of cameras and microphones all over this seastead."

The engineer looked defeated and started walking towards a stair leading belowdecks.

"Let's get this over with," he said.

EIGHT

"I don't even know what that is," Mike sighed.

"You're going into shock," Max said firmly. "Focus on the engines, focus on whatever it is you check, break the engine down into components, put this out of your head—"

"Come on," the engineer pleaded softly. "Just tell me what it is."

Max knelt down and shined the light on what they had found.

"A kidney, I believe," she said, struggling to remain strong—she *had* to be seeing as Mike was losing his shit.

"A kidney," the engineer said with wonder before something in him changed; it was as if he finally understood the consequences of losing his shit and found an inner strength he hadn't been aware of.

"I need to deal with the engines," Mike said in a firm voice, nodding. "Just one thing…"

"Yeah?"

"Stay down here with me while I do what I need to do."

"Sure."

"We're posting Fitz at your door," Apso smiled at the man in the bed.

"When Fitz is off duty, Max will be guarding."

"Why didn't you do that before I lost my fucking kidney?" Kyle asked.

It was odd, he didn't seem weak or adjusting to having lost an organ, he was just *Kyle*. Did the kidney even belong to him? Mari had examined his back and, sure enough, there were signs—in the subcutaneous flesh that remained—of an incision that would match where you removed a kidney.

"So, you *do* have some medical knowledge," Kyle observed sarcastically when the nurse shared her findings.

"Hey, Kyle, a little respect," Mr. Pearly smiled. "She's just trying to do her job—"

"Ten fucking million dollars," Kyle chuckled bitterly. "I want my money back, asshole, and I'm suing you for this. You need to have a helicopter here to pick me up *this afternoon*."

"Kyle," Apso said, uncomfortable with the passenger's anger but trying to work with it. "The storm hasn't let up, there's no way—"

"Then take this broken down shit heap as close to land as we can get and put me on an emergency boat!"

"I'll see what I can do, Kyle."

"I'll see what I can do, Kyle," the man on the bed mocked and then began sobbing.

Mr. Pearly led Max and Mari into the hallway.

"Yeah, he's a dick," Apso sighed. "But he has been through a lot."

"It's weird," Mari frowned. "In modern procedures, kidneys are removed through the navel so there is little scarring. They haven't removed them through the back for ages."

"Clearly the ghoul doing this isn't up on the most current way of removing a kidney," Mr. Pearly rubbed the side of his face with the palm of his hand.

"Guys…this discourse is lotsa fun, but I haven't slept the past two nights—"

Max got what he meant and led Mari away from their boss.

Max spent a lot of time on the deck in a parka, trying to find a logical explanation but having no luck. There was no sign of land and that surprised her; hadn't Kyle asked to be dropped off? It didn't make sense but after a few moments it did: If they returned Kyle to the mainland, cops would board the ship and conduct investigations. During those investigations they would discover that there had been a flogging. Even if it had occurred in International Waters, Charity was still, technically, a U.S. citizen.

"I don't think tonight will be as rough as last night," Apso was at the railing beside her.

"You're not dropping Kyle off, are you?" Max asked carefully.

The boss didn't respond for what seemed a long time.

"The investigations," Mr. Pearly said, looking over at his employee. "They won't stop with Kyle B," he continued with a meaningful expression. "They won't stop with the flogging, they will look into the background of everyone on this ship."

"True. But what about Kyle?"

"What about him?" Apso replied with a coy smile.

Max started out at the waves, clearly the boss wasn't going to bring her into whatever he was planning or knew—not that she wanted any part of it.

The investigator ran into few people on board that day and assumed that they were probably recovering in their cabins from the previous evening's debauchery. Seeing no one at the helm, Max hurried down to Apso's cabin and knocked on the door. When she explained what was amiss, the boss was clearly unconcerned.

"Oh…it was just easier to automate it and run it from here," Mr Pearly explained.

Did he even know how to pilot a boat? Max didn't want to get into that. After a cheap goodbye, she walked the corridors where the cabins were. The only person she saw was Fitz who was sitting on a chair outside Kyle's cabin. The large woman was just staring at the wall in front of her.

"You okay, Fitz?" Max asked.

"Yep, just keeping a lookout," her tone of voice was thick, almost slurred.

"Just checking," the investigator replied.

Fitz had never been the most animated person on the seastead, but now she seemed—

Like a zombie, like an animated dead person—

Not helping, not helping at all.

There were two people down the hall talking in an odd language—

Aren't Mike and Barbara trying to learn German together?

But it wasn't German, it was some sort of Latin language and—

It wasn't Mike and Barbara, it was two dark complexioned men in watch caps and sweaters. Seeing Max, they ducked around a corner—

She hurried around the corner but the men were nowhere to be found.

NINE

"Charity," Max couldn't contain her relief to find someone who didn't look like—(a zombie)—they were sleepwalking. "Does the ship seem deserted to you?"

"No, not at all," the other woman was smiling, but there was something to it that Max couldn't place but it made her uncomfortable.

"Is your back healing alright?"

"What?" Charity frowned.

"You said the scars were itching yesterday."

"Scars?" The other woman took a step back, looked confused. "If this is a joke, Max, I don't see the humor."

The investigator just walked away—what the fuck was going on?

Max stayed in her small cabin that night with the door locked, trying to make sense of how Fitz looked like a zombie and the dark men speaking the Latin language and Charity claiming she was unscarred—

Stress. This has happened before, for some reason the stress of the mutilations is messing with my head.

Portuguese, those guys were speaking Portuguese, I think, it was a Latin language but it wasn't Spanish, French, or Italian.

And the boat had originally been owned by a Portuguese company…in the 1960s.

Do you hear yourself? You're just diving deeper and deeper into this craziness.

The investigator didn't think she'd sleep but she did. Max had feared nightmares but didn't dream at all. On waking, the dred returned—what would Mike find next? But Mike wasn't leaning against a deck rail either appearing on the verge of nausea or actually throwing up. Apso walked up eating a mango.

"Everything good, Max?"

"Normally I run into Mike right here at the same time every morning. He hasn't missed a day since we came on board."

The boss just stared at her, took another bite of mango.

"Mike?"

"The lead engineer," Max explained, uncomfortable that she had to explain. "The guy who oversees the engines."

"They've been automated for a long time," Apso shrugged.

"But…I went with Mike to check on them yesterday, that's when we found the kidney."

Mr. Pearly frowned at that.

"Don't know what to tell you, Max," he clapped her on the shoulder and walked off.

She didn't want to go into the belly of the ship but nor could she fight her own curiosity: Something was waiting down there for her to discover it, another piece of Kyle. Max forced herself down the steep stairs. There was a sound below decks, not the engine…music. Old sounding pop music with people singing in—

"Portuguese," Max stopped in her tracks.

You've let control slip away and now you need to get it back. Come on, sergeant, you were trained for this—

"Trained? For *this*?" She laughed at that and removed her knife from her belt and cut her hand.

The pain helped clear her head as did the coppery taste of blood when she licked the wound.

"It's just stress," Max said to herself. "I may have been trained for this but this is still a weird, fucked up situation."

The investigator no longer heard the music; that was good, one hallucination out of the way. After a few seconds, Max arrived at where the other body parts had been discovered. Seeing an object, she knelt down next to the chunk of meat and studied it with the flashlight.

"I guess they got bored with you," Max said thoughtfully.

TEN

"Well, I have good news and bad news," Max said after Apso had granted her admittance into his cabin. "The good news is, Kyle B will no longer be complaining about what has been happening to him."

"I have no idea how they got past, Fitz," She added, again fighting off the idea that the big woman was a zombie.

"Old news," Mr. Pearly said, seeming bored.

"Old news? I just discovered the brain down by the engine. Did someone find Kyle dead?"

"Dead?" Apso looked troubled by that."Kyle isn't dead."

That shocked Max and she dropped into one of the chairs.

"The ghoul has picked a new victim," she said numbly.

"No, Kyle's brain *is* missing."

"Wait…this makes no sense: You say Kyle is still alive but his brain is missing…we don't have the machines to run the body without a brain."

Apso reached towards a bowl full of mangos on his desk.

"Want one? They're really juicy."

"Did Mari check him out? Does Kyle have any scars or bandages on his head?"

With his free hand, Kyle held up a black box the size of a man's billfold.

"I checked on Kyle this morning; no brainwaves."

"No brainwaves, no machine, still alive?"

"Yep," Mr. Pearly seemed pleased by that.

"None of this makes any sense," Max cradled her head in her hands.

"You worry too much, Max," Apso took a big bite of mango, juice dripping onto his desk. The framed picture was now of Ferdinand Magellan. "We're free of the old world, with all its noise and waste and craziness. There's nothing out here but nature…the storm brought so many things to life it's like a new world, do you understand what I mean?"

"No, Apso…I don't."

Mr. Pearly stopped eating and smiled at her, the juice on his chin looked red.

"You will."

Written between 28 and 29 June, 2022
Music listened to White Chalk by PJ Harvey

ALL THAT WAS BECOMES AGAIN ALL THAT WAS BECOMES AGAIN ALL THAT
WAS BECOMES AGAIN ALL THAT WAS BECOMES AGAIN ALL THAT WAS
BECOMES AGAIN ALL THAT WAS BECOMES AGAIN ALL THAT WAS BECOMES

AGAIN **ALL** THAT WAS BECOMES AGAIN ALL THAT WAS BECOMES

AGAIN ALL THAT WAS BECOMES AGAIN ALL THAT WAS BECOMES AGAIN

ALL **THAT** WAS BECOMES AGAIN ALL THAT WAS BECOMES

AGAIN ALL THAT WAS BECOMES AGAIN ALL THAT WAS BECOMES AGAIN

ALL THAT **WAS** BECOMES AGAIN ALL THAT WAS BECOMES AGAIN

ALL THAT WAS BECOMES AGAIN ALL THAT WAS

BECOMES AGAIN ALL THAT WAS BECOMES AGAIN ALL

THAT WAS BECOMES AGAIN ALL THAT WAS BECOMES AGAIN ALL THAT WAS

BECOMES **AGAIN** ALL THAT WAS BECOMES AGAIN ALL THAT

WAS BECOMES AGAIN ALL THAT WAS BECOMES AGAIN ALL THAT WAS
BECOMES AGAIN ALL THAT WAS BECOMES AGAIN ALL THAT WAS BECOMES
AGAIN ALL THAT WAS BECOMES AGAIN ALL THAT WAS BECOMES AGAIN
ALL THAT WAS BECOMES AGAIN ALL THAT WAS BECOMES AGAIN ALL THAT
WAS BECOMES AGAIN ALL THAT WAS BECOMES AGAIN ALL THAT WAS
BECOMES AGAIN ALL THAT WAS BECOMES AGAIN ALL THAT WAS BECOMES
AGAIN ALL THAT WAS BECOMES AGAIN ALL THAT WAS BECOMES AGAIN
ALL THAT WAS BECOMES AGAIN ALL THAT WAS BECOMES AGAIN ALL THAT
WAS BECOMES AGAIN ALL THAT WAS BECOMES AGAIN ALL THAT WAS
BECOMES AGAIN ALL THAT WAS BECOMES AGAIN ALL THAT WAS BECOMES
AGAIN ALL THAT WAS BECOMES AGAIN ALL THAT WAS BECOMES AGAIN
ALL THAT WAS BECOMES AGAIN ALL THAT WAS BECOMES AGAIN ALL THAT
WAS BECOMES AGAIN ALL THAT WAS BECOMES AGAIN ALL THAT WAS
BECOMES AGAIN ALL THAT WAS BECOMES AGAIN ALL THAT WAS BECOMES
AGAIN ALL THAT WAS BECOMES AGAIN ALL THAT WAS BECOMES AGAIN
ALL THAT WAS BECOMES AGAIN ALL THAT WAS BECOMES AGAIN ALL THAT
WAS BECOMES AGAIN ALL THAT WAS BECOMES AGAIN ALL THAT WAS
BECOMES AGAIN ALL THAT WAS BECOMES AGAIN ALL THAT WAS BECOMES
AGAIN ALL THAT WAS BECOMES AGAIN ALL THAT WAS BECOMES AGAIN
ALL THAT WAS BECOMES AGAIN ALL THAT WAS BECOMES AGAIN ALL THAT
WAS BECOMES AGAIN ALL THAT WAS BECOMES AGAIN ALL THAT WAS

ONE

The happiness she felt on opening her eyes was profound. Normally her emotions were a steady line; neither up nor down, little laughter or tears. Nothing particularly good nor bad. Not that morning--it felt as she would have imagined euphoria feeling. Where had it come from? The woman understood that feeling such joy was a gift, something to savor and appreciate, but the joy was a package on the front step with no return address.

Keep the door locked, don't reveal what the wrapper conceals.

She went through her work morning routine. The intensity of the happiness had dissipated some but was still a tape running in the background. The pessimist inside said it was a sign, a sign of *something big*. The *something* was a problem, an unknown. A slash of red above the normal steady line of her thoughts and emotions.

The woman put her lunch in a sensible box that was tucked in her stylish yet simple bag. Water had spilled on the counter so she wiped it up with a paper towel. The trash was full so she tied up the bag with the intention of putting it in the dumpster on the way to her car. The smell of the garbage and the simple act of closing up the plastic bag was comforting--real, easily explained and understood. The happiness had settled far in the background; she was neither happy nor sad or really anything. Buzzing insects with wings were circling the dumpsters. At first the woman thought they were flies but when one alighted on her arm it became clear they were bees. The bag was heavy and it took effort to lob it into the bin. The motion caused her stylish yet simple bag to slip off her left shoulder and down her arm. She was young though like she'd always be young and caught it before it hit the soiled cement. Her gaze had followed the progression of her bag. There was something on the ground--a piece of shiny paper.

No, a photograph.

Normally, that would be where such an observation would end: There were always odds and ends scattered around the dumpster, dirty unwanted things best ignored. Something about that photograph wouldn't allow the woman to just walk away and forget she had seen it like the countless odds and ends she had seen around that very dumpster. Before she understood what her body was doing the woman was kneeling and picking the photograph up. It was a black and white snapshot of a woman from the shoulders up. The photo smelled like perfume even though it had been sitting among the stray food cans and frozen meal boxes. The subject was looking boldly at the person behind the lens and her expression--

She loved whomever was taking the snapshot, that was clear; there was a playful sort of love in her eyes and expression. The woman holding the photo had never been looked at like that, she felt slashes of color above and below her normal steady line.

A sensible person would have dropped the photo and walked on to the rest of her day.

A sensible person would not be feeling intense emotions about a snapshot found next to a dumpster among stray food cans and frozen meal boxes.

So...why was she pinching the corner of the photo even tighter?

Why was there the feeling that the woman was looking at *her* with that love and playfulness?

It made no sense just as dropping the photo in her bag but that was what happened.

The woman walked through the beige complex to her white car and followed dark gray roads to the large, anonymous box where she spent five days a week. There were reports to complete and meetings to attend and she handled all her duties steadily and with competence. Normally focusing came easily, but that day the feeling of old photographic paper pinched between her right index finger and thumb was always in the background--

And the look in that woman's eyes, her smile.

Each time she pulled the snapshot out the woman reminded herself that the sensible thing to do would have been to toss that photo in the trash. Why had she picked it up? Someone else's garbage, an old picture of a stranger--

But the smiling woman wasn't a stranger; she was certain of that and the certainty frightened her.

Normally the woman had her lunch in the breakroom. It was all calculated; being social with coworkers, the right smiles and easy patter about safe subjects. The pretenses of professional friendships. That afternoon, though, she ate in her small office and looked at the picture. She felt weak and feeling weak made her ashamed--what was wrong with her? First there had been the sense of giddiness upon waking and now she was mooning over some tossed out photograph. The woman set her shoulders, drew a sharp breath, and tossed the snapshot in the trash.
Nine seconds later she retrieved it.

Driving back to her sensible condo the woman passed beige apartment complexes and drab strip malls. She drove the same route every day because it was the most efficient way to get from work to home in the late afternoon. All the complexes and shops had become a blur after passing them not dozens but hundreds of times. That afternoon, though, she saw something she hadn't seen before and locked the brakes. The shriek of tires on pavement was a sound her car hadn't made for her before and the person behind her honked; she hadn't been honked at since learning to drive over a decade earlier. After a guilty glance in the rear view mirror, the woman pulled into the strip mall and parked in front of a shop that she had driven by countless times but had never noticed. *Antiques*, that's what the sign that had nearly caused her first accident read.
A sensible person would have backed out of that spot, and gotten back into the flow of other cars commuting home.
A sensible person would be mulling what she would make for dinner and what series she wanted to start or continue binge watching.
Those thoughts, ignored.

The woman didn't like antique stores, the smell of old things. All the pieces seemed foolish and awkward, made before people understood the concepts of streamlining and efficiency. Everything in her life had been bought at

Target or IKEA, new things without old smells or awkward shapes. There was a counter area with a man standing behind it. He may have been forty or he may have been fifty, not fat but soft looking with sizable man breasts making shapes under a ratty looking cardigan. His mustache was like a still pet that needed to be groomed, the smile that formed beneath it was equally yellow and kind. His request to know how he could help her seemed genuine and something about it brought even more strange, determined emotions too close to the surface for her liking.

"I found this picture. It looks old, can you..."

She trailed off, unsure what to ask--unsure what she even wanted to know. He gently took the photograph. Emotions she couldn't decipher flickered on his face.

"It's old for sure, probably from some point between the wars," he said.

"Wars? Which wars?"

He looked up at her--what other emotions was she seeing aside from kindness? Had the photograph touched him as well?

Maybe the picture was magic--

Don't be an idiot, don't even think such ridiculous things.

"The world wars." He caught on to her incomprehension. "Between 1920 and 1940."

The man looked back down at the photo. Was he going to give it back now? What if it really was magic and he was going to try and keep it? What would she do, then? There was a heavy looking brass thing with arms nearby--

And then he was sliding the photo across the counter towards her, his expression intense, overwhelmed.

"She loved whomever was taking this picture. I mean...yeah, to be looked at like that."

The woman just nodded. Why was her breath hitching? What were her eyes doing? She couldn't even form a *thank you*, all she could do was walk out of the shop with the photo pinched between her right index finger and thumb.

TWO

It was one of the first time she had remembered a dream in years--
The woman was in their condominium but a couple of things were
different: The couch was a vibrant blue, not the background beige of real
life. The kitchen was much larger. There was a painting of the woman from
the photograph on one wall. A black man in a suit was leaning against the
counter and smiling at her. She could smell his cologne--spicy, a hint of
honey. Surprise was followed by a fear colored more and more by
indignation--what gave this man the right to enter their home and act like
he belonged there?
"What are you doing here? How did you get in?"
The stranger laughed a little.
"We're friends, Pha; you let me in."
Even if his face was unfamiliar his voice was; they *were* friends and he meant
her no harm. She took a step closer to him but was still confused.
"What do you mean? I didn't let you in."
His name is Sammy Dade. Someone was standing next to her; the woman in
the painting. She smelled like cotton candy and whiskey, looking at Pha with
the same expression she had worn in the photograph. The woman put her
arm around Pha and leaned her head on her shoulder. Close up, more
smells revealed themselves: Cigarettes and a minute amount of sweat under
the cotton candy.
Normally, Pha would have moved away when a stranger got so close---
But she is no stranger.
Sammy Dade walked towards the dreamer until there was only six feet of
beige carpet between them. The living room was gone. They were standing
on a stage faced by dozens of old fashioned chairs.
"Pha...there is going to be a bright light and it's going to scare you like
nothing else in your life has but I will be there. I will be waiting for you and
I will help you."
"A bright light? What do you mean?"
He just smiled again and the dream ended.

And there Pha was lying in bed with light starting to come through the blinds. Chase was already awake and reading something on his phone. The dream was still vivid--when was the last time she could remember dreaming? There was something disturbing about it--the subconscious message of a stranger in their home, an invasion--

And then there was the dancer...her *girlfriend*. Realizing that felt natural, comforting. The guilt she felt was not over loving another woman, it was about the man lying in bed next to her---

Pha wanted to return to the dream, to the woman who had laid her head on her shoulder and smelled like whiskey and cigarettes, but--

This is stupid. What is wrong with me? I can't just lie here, I should already be getting in the shower.

Should she tell Chase?

What would the point be? He doesn't believe in things like that; he will just pretend to listen and then go back to what he's doing.

Pha understood engaging with the man in her bed was the right thing to do, the sort of thing sane people who were having bizarre dreams did.

"What are you reading?" She asked.

It took Chase a few seconds to respond; he didn't look up from his phone.

"Kurt Cobain has new album out, it's called *1994*"

She had the feeling that the dream was her real life and this was a screen role she was playing. The cameras were hidden in the walls, the microphones were stashed under the bed.

You are the pragmatic girlfriend and daughter. Your motivation in this scene is to act interested in your boyfriend. Your being together is logical.

"I thought you said he was boring," she pointed out.

Did Chase ever dream of other men leaning his head on his shoulder? If so, did it excite him?

Stop it. It was a stupid dream, this is reality.

"This interview is crazy," Her boyfriend smiled and frowned. "He's going on about how when David Bowie died three years ago the world started coming apart--I can't explain it, do you want me to send it to you?"

What she wanted was to close her eyes, look over, and see the dancer. Amelia--that was her name.

Why are you doing this? There is so much to do and you're allowing yourself to get distracted.

"No, that's okay. You having coffee?"

"A little."

She climbed out of bed and walked to the kitchen wrapped in a beige robe. Every morning she put on either the beige robe or the white one. Every morning she asked Chase if he wanted coffee and he either said "no" or "a little." There were cameras in the walls of the kitchen, she was *sure* of it for a second---eighteen cameras scattered around the condominium. Soon the director would walk out from behind a false wall and yell "Cut!" and then he would smile and compliment Pha on her work…

Placing her hands on the counter the woman closed her eyes--she had been working over fifty hours a week, maybe the stress was getting to her.

No, there was no time for that; she had to be dressed and out the door in forty minutes.

Opening her eyes Pha looked over at the open bedroom door and saw what she could have seen with her eyes still closed: Chase was lying in bed scrolling through something on his phone just as he did every morning. He was just another actor hired for the way his appearance complimented hers. No, he was just a ghost in her condominium.

A text from Pha's mother came in as she was getting ready for work:

Julie. Your grandmother tells me you visited her the day before yesterday. That is very nice of you. Hope work is going okay. Love you, Mom.

Julie. Her mother never called her *Pha* and that was whatever it was—neither of her parents cared about the past or their family histories in Vietnam.

Why do you care about it? It was a terrible place, the Communists overran it and chased us out. Things are a lot better now that we are Americans.

Grandmother didn't really speak English and Pha's mother either had forgotten Vietnamese or refused to speak it. Mother had been two when they had come to America and had been the translator for her parents along with her two brothers. All three were now fully Americanized with American names for their children. Pha was the only grandchild who spoke Vietnamese and had taken a Vietnamese name. Her parents were not pleased and it was a subject the three of them had learned to avoid.

"On my way to work now. Love you guys."

She sent the text and then said goodbye to Chase. A quick kiss, very chaste. Pha imagined Amelia kissing the side of her face, how warm her lips would be--

No. No time for this.

"I got the new Kurt Cobain album on iTunes," Chase said.

Had she ever kissed him with passion? When was the last time he had kissed her with real feeling? Had either ever happened?

Words, he was watching her---words were expected.

"I thought you said he was boring and that grunge was stupid."

"The songs sound interesting, I guess he has been obsessing about the year 1994 for awhile, has had all these dreams of people having vigils because he died or something."

Maybe Chase would dream of Kurt Cobain resting a head on his shoulder. Cobain's hair was probably dirty and smelled like grease.

"Sounds weird," Pha replied.

She was an actor--no, she was a *robot*--looking down at the stranger in her bed, not remembering what his penis looked like; not wanting to see it, just trying to remember what it looked like.

"Maybe...I don't know. I shared it to the house account if you want to listen to it."

"No, thanks."

Did that sound curt? Pha didn't care. Sometimes she wished that one of them would rip the band-aid off and then she'd have the condominium to herself again. Those thoughts had made her feel guilty in the past, now they were starting to make sense.

He's going on about how when David Bowie died three years ago the world started coming apart...

Something about that after having the dream about Sammy Dade and Amelia made Pha feel unsettled, like something big and possibly dangerous was waiting in the near future. She remembered the day David Bowie had died because one of the temps had been upset by it. That girl had cried and cried and had to be sent home. Pha could take or leave music. She knew a couple of Bowie songs, one about "modern love" and another about dancing, but they were just old pop songs to her. Taylor Swift was the only full album she had ever bought otherwise it was just whatever was on the radio.

Halfway to her car, Pha stopped and looked back at the condominium. It was one of nearly two hundred in the complex. She had owned it four years and had shared it with Chase for nearly two years--

And now there was the strange feeling that she would be leaving it in the near future--

A memory of the dream, Sammy Dade smiling at her from the kitchen:

Pha...there is going to be a bright light and it's going to scare you like nothing else in your life has but I will be there. I will be waiting for you and I will help you.

She gripped her keys tighter and walked on towards her Camry. It was her second Camry, the first had been her parents and passed down to her. They had always driven Camrys as had many members of her family---

He's going on about how when David Bowie died three years ago the world started coming apart...

Anxiety. Why? What was giving her strange dreams and the sensation that her world was about to change in ways she never imagined?

Pha forced the thoughts away, climbed into her sensible sedan, and drove out of the complex.

THREE

Pha got caught in traffic and chided herself for daydreaming between the condo and the car. Normally she walked fast, with purpose, but something was wrong---

This is stupid. Nothing is wrong. I just had a weird dream and maybe I am realizing that I have to just tell Chase to move out.

The situation with Chase was the only thing she considered a loose end in her life. Aside from that Pha believed that she was on a good track: Job with a future. Condo in her name. Grown-up car. Regular dentist and doctor.

That is all this is--Chase. I will need to talk to him tonight and then all this anxiety will go away.

That was what Pha told herself; she almost believed it.

Traffic was a wash of lit tail lights and horns. Five minutes---Pha timed how long it took to go a single block and then understood doing that only made things worse. A song came on the radio, a bluesy folk song with a raspy singer that sounded familiar. Realizing it was Kurt Cobain, Pha turned off the radio and stared at the back of a GMC Yukon. There was a sticker suggesting "Make Portland Normal" and another one with an eagle and the acronym MAGA. Had it been two or three days since she had driven to Vancouver to visit her grandmother? Her *bai ngoai's* complex was shabby with rotten wood cladding and battered cars. In contrast, her grandmother's apartment was immaculate and smelled like incense. Pha had a key but always knocked out of respect. Even as a child the older woman seemed small, doll or midget sized; old age was making her even more diminutive like a star collapsing in on itself. She smiled as she opened the door and began chattering in Vietnamese.

"Come on, *bai ngoai,* you know I can't speak that well."

"No, you good!" That in English before going back to her native language."We will work on it. Maybe you can help me with English."

Pha had nodded agreeably and followed her grandmother into the kitchen where they sat at a plain wooden table. Her grandfather had made it out of pallets at some point in the past and sanded it down after the family complained about splinters. His ashtray sat next to the wall even though he had been gone over ten years. Did her grandmother really accept that her husband was dead? The older woman still talked about her husband as if he were out getting a newspaper. The two women exchanged small talk for a few minutes: Pha's job. How Chase was doing--(Grandmother asked this while making a *face*, she didn't seem to approve of Chase even if he was also Vietnamese). Whether or not grandma was taking her medication. It was a good visit; more than a day before the dream and the beginning of Pha's anxiety. Looking back as she stared at the taillights of an SUV she understood that shadows had already been forming. As her grandmother chattered about how her medication was not doing her any good, Pha found herself looking over at the ashtray.

"He was a good man."

Past tense. That is different.

"I remember," Pha smiled. "He used to take me to McDonalds."

Grandmother looked over at the ashtray. Seeing the sadness on her face Pha assumed that it was because she was finally acknowledging that her husband was dead and not just off running some errand. Pha took her grandmother's hands but the old lady shook her head and pulled her hands back.

"Your grandfather was very unhappy," she frowned.

Pha looked down at the table and started counting rusty nails. Did she want to find out any problems her grandparents may have been having? Her grandfather had always seemed a good man, gruff at times but always decent---what if there was another side to him?

"Did he miss Vietnam?"

Grandmother had gotten up to tidy the towels that hung from the oven door.

"No...not that. You know My Lai?"

It sounded like a woman's name. Maybe that was a good time to change the subject---

"Was that a friend of yours and grandfather's?"

"No, it was a town. Many people died."

146

Many people died--what a relief, Pha had been afraid it had been a woman; a woman would have inferred that her grandfather had been unfaithful.

"During the War?"

"Yes. It was not far from our town, we knew people there."

Grandmother reached over and touched the ashtray. She had closed her eyes, put her hands back in her lap, and then looked back at her granddaughter.

"There was a lot of killing back then but what happened in My Lai bothered your grandfather very much. He thought about it the rest of his life, said it was the start of the end."

"Start of the end?"

Pha still struggled with her Vietnamese and wasn't sure if she was understanding her grandmother correctly.

"Start of the end of the world," the old lady said in English.

"Well, here we are many years later."

Pha smiled as she said that but inside she was all tremors and chill.

Start of the end of the world

Her grandmother had smiled and taken Pha's hands.

"Very true." Her eyes said something different: *Maybe the end of the world won't happen over a few hours, maybe it will take a few decades.*

Pha forced the memory to the background as she parked in her designated spot, it even had her last name stenciled into the asphalt. The letters were starting to fade but she still could remember the pride she had felt that day, taking pictures to share with her family. The security guard was leaning against a big pickup and seemed to be staring at some trees on the edge of the parking lot. He wore a mustache and an extra seventy-five to a hundred extra pounds. The fact he was overweight made Pha uneasy---how was he supposed to stop anything bad from happening? Why was he just staring at trees when he should be walking around making sure that everything was okay?

"Lots of crows in those trees."

His tone was solemn and his voice had a tone overweight people get like they're gargling fat.

"Yeah?"

"Smart birds; they've been watching people come and go."

There was a gun on his hip but how long would it take his fat arm to grab it if they had an active shooter?

"Really?" She asked out of obligation.

Pha was edging towards the entrance and pulling her passcard out.

"They seem to think something is up so I watch them."

What, do you think they will talk to you or something?

"Yeah? Awesome. I'd better go and clock in, see you later."

He looked from the trees to the front of her blouse.

"Have a nice day."

She ran her passcard through the lock and pushed the door open. Before walking in Pha looked at the trees and saw all the crows passing time on the branches. They *did* seem to be watching the building. One called out harshly as if to end her daydreaming. She walked in and the door closed behind her.

Pha's office was typical for junior management: Small window. Barely large enough for a desk and two chairs. It was still an accomplishment---moving up from a cubicle---and as when her name had been written in asphalt the young woman took pictures and shared them on MeMeMe. Every morning she got coffee from the break room and then checked her email. The only one that stood out was from something called the Foresight Foundation: *Saw your resume on Monster and would love to talk to you about an exciting opportunity with our company! Great benefits! A worldwide organization that still treats its employees like family!*

She deleted the email. Her finger was still on the trackpad when an internal phone call came in; the day picked up momentum and all thoughts of her dreams and the visit with her grandmother were pushed into the background.

FOUR

Someone was watching *Poltergeist* in their cubicle during their lunch break. Pha stopped and looked in. She didn't know the movie, just saw what looked like a scared family being talked to by an odd, tiny woman. After a moment she was looking at a white version of her grandmother.

Stay away from the light, Carol Ann, it's the start of the end of the world

The other employee jumped when they saw Pha; she was not a camera on the wall, no, she was important enough to have her name printed on asphalt.

That's right. I'm their boss. Normal reaction, got it.

"Hey, uh, I'm just watching this on my lunch break," the employee said with a clench of a smile, resentment flashing like the spark of a gun in their eyes.

"Yeah, no problem. What are you watching?"

The smile clenched less but there was still the spark of wariness in the air.

"*Poltergeist.* You ever watch it?"

"No. Why is she telling her to stay away from the light?"

The employee--(Jason?)--was relaxing more but clearly confused. Pha knew she was seen as a no-nonsense/boring boss, generally benign without any perceivable imagination.

"The light is death, I think," Jason explained. "The bright light we're supposed to see when we die."

Pha casually put her hand on the cubicle wall because she was pretty sure her legs were about to give out.

"Yeah, I think I heard about that sort of thing."

She lost her words. There was the smell of cologne or perfume in the air, spicy with a hint of honey. Jason was looking at her, staring; it was up to her to end the conversation.

"Enjoy your movie."

She formed a smile and made her head nod before walking out of the cubicle and the building to her sensible sedan. Pha closed her eyes and ran her thumb and forefinger over the key fob, focusing on the feel of the plastic and depressions where the buttons were. Amelia danced into what she had hoped was a safe blank space where Pha could direct the clearing of her mind. The other woman was smiling like she had the sweetest love in her heart but only for one person---

I am. Losing. My freaking mind. No, I can't...it's just stress.

She opened her eyes and focused on the Camry. Her first new car. Dad had spent hours with her at the dealership making sure she got a good deal. Pha focused on him as she dropped in behind the wheel. Everything was going to be okay--

The bright light we're supposed to see when we die.

--soon, after clearing the nonsense out of her mind.

"Why did I have that dream? Why do I keep thinking about that woman?"

Dreams are the subconscious talking, maybe my body is telling me I have cancer or something.

She gripped the wheel and struggled to gain control of what was feeling like a panic attack.

This is stupid, I'm 28, too young to just die from cancer. I am probably just suffering anxiety because of work and the situation with Chase. If it is about death maybe it's about our relationship dying and Sammy Dade is another part of myself being reassuring.

The thought made enough sense to calm her. Relaxing some, she switched on the ignition and rolled down the windows to let in some air. A crow had alighted on the hood of a Yukon parked diagonally from her. It seemed to be looking right at Pha, studying her.

FIVE

She had been lost in a darkening city only to turn a corner and see no buildings, just harsh bluffs and chalky plains--a desert. Pha looked over her shoulder and saw that the town had disappeared and with it the crowds. The silence was crisp and dark bordered, the edges running in like devious ink. A spark of fear found fuel and every shadow held a potential fiend biding its time before leaping out to devour her flesh. Pha walked on. There was a shape out on a plain. As she got closer the young woman could see it was a person sitting on the ground. Her instincts told her that the stranger could help her find her way home. The seated person was very still but maybe they were meditating or lost in thought.

"Hello?" Pha, hoping not to startle the stranger.

They did not respond, did not move at all. Getting closer Pha saw why: The stranger was dead and had probably been that way for a long time. The body was little more than a husk covered by leathery skin that reminded Pha of beef jerky. A couple of feet in front of the crossed legs was a collection of charred sticks and branches.

They aren't dead, they are just...not here. Traveling.

Pha wasn't scared of the dead body, wasn't concerned that it would spring to life and assault her or any sort of thing that happens in nightmares---the person by the stilled fire radiated peace. She sat down beside it and crossed her own legs. Someone was smoking a cigarette nearby.

"Knew I'd find you out here. You know we only got five minutes, right?"

Amelia was holding a hand out. Pha accepted help getting up--

And they were walking into a circus tent. The seats were beginning to fill up.

"You got dusty, we need to fix your makeup."

Sammy Dade was talking to a small man with dirty blonde hair who was cradling a guitar. The small man sat in a chair on the side of the stage as Sammy walked over to the dancers. Pha caught a glimpse of herself in the mirror but she looked more Chinese than Vietnamese.

"Hey, glad she found you--you ready for tonight?"

151

She looked in his eyes, there was a lot of kindness there but also some concern.

"Sammy...I never dream. Why am I having these dreams? I know you're just a part of me...can you explain this to me? I feel like I'm losing my mind." Amelia was rubbing her shoulders as Sammy took her hands in his. The love coming off both of them was so overwhelming that she felt herself tearing up.

It was her family, a family before she was with the family she knew.

"It's going to be okay, Pha, really. I know right now is kind of confusing, but you'll be okay, I promise."

The small man started singing a song as he smoked. The only thing Pha could make out was "1994." She realized who he was and then the sound of sirens shattered the dream.

Pha's mobile phone had woken her up. Chase had already left her bed—Had he left in the morning? Had he even been there that night? She equally couldn't remember and didn't care. Her lack of remorse over the death of their relationship made her sad but the phone was ringing and she felt the need to be upbeat---

It was her grandmother and Pha instantly worried that the old woman was having a heart attack or some other serious problem. Her grandmother was in such a state that she couldn't remember the English she knew and the Vietnamese words she was rattling off came at such a clip that Pha couldn't translate them in her head.

"Please, *bai ngoai,* I can't understand you if you go fast."

"Sorry. I had a very bad--"

Dream? Sleep? Night? Pha wasn't sure but guessed it was the first one.

"What happened?" She thought of her own dream.

The older woman rattled off a bunch of words; the gist seemed to be that she had gone to My Lai in the dream but as she recollected it her speaking grew faster and Pha was unable to follow at all.

"Please, *bai ngoai,* I am not understanding."

"I saw you." Her grandmother said that in English: *I saw you.* She said that in the same tone she had said *the start of the end of the world.*

"You saw me in My Lai?"

"Yes. You had been shot but you were alive. You were sitting and talking with American soldiers and smoking with them. You looked happy, but you were dead."

Pha had grabbed her laptop to access the translation app.

"Grandmother, it was just a dream."

"I wouldn't have called you if it was just a dream."

This conversation is not real. I am still dreaming.

She dug her thumbnail into a finger, she was awake.

"What do you mean?" Pha asked.

"I called you because after the dream I remembered something that happened back home years before we came to America. We went to My Lai after the shooting. They were in the middle of burying the bodies but we saw one young woman who had been shot many times---"

The old woman suddenly became very upset and spoke very fast. Pha struggled to type in what she thought her grandmother was saying but she must have misheard because what the translator came up with made no sense:

The dead woman looked exactly like you--I think she was you.

Ten minutes later Pha was still sitting in bed with her computer in her lap. The phone call had been over half that time and her mobile lay on the bed beside her--

The dead woman looked exactly like you--I think she was you.

No. She had misheard her grandmother and typed the wrong thing in. Pha thought about the dream with the mummy by the fire and felt scared and alone and confused and--

This is stupid. Grandmother is old, I've seen her getting more confused and mixed up. She had a bad dream about me being killed at My Lai and now she thinks it really happened. It makes no sense; I was born in 1991, how could I have been killed in 1968...in Vietnam?

Pha told herself that and it sounded logical and sane but--

But the things grandmother gets confused about are usually things happening now. Her short term memory is getting bad but her long term memory is very strong.

The anxiety wanted to run free but Pha was determined to put it in a cage and hopefully kill it. She forced herself out of bed and walked naked to the kitchen for the first time since she had bought her sensible condominium. The young woman was unaware that she had forgotten to put a robe on until she felt the chill of the freezer on her bare skin. Normally, she felt uncomfortable walking around naked even if she had the condo to herself---*normally*.

But things had stopped being normal; normal had been left in the past.

They were playing the new Kurt Cobain song on the radio. Stopped at a light Pha had a vision of the singer sprawled in a greenhouse with a rifle lying nearby---

Someone was honking, the light had turned green. Jabbing the gas pedal Pha pushed a preset on the radio. A talk show she recognized as *Hollah Hour* was on. A woman with a brassy voice was talking about when she had been caught up in a workplace shooting and the health problems she had been experiencing since.

"Wow," the host exclaimed." Hey, we have to go to break but we'll be back with more from our special guest Dakota Barnes here on *Hollah Hour*."

Pha turned off the radio as every station was only adding to her anxiety. Was she having some sort of breakdown?

Why would I? Don't people have breakdowns because of some trauma or stress in their life?

Chase--*that* had been causing stress, the awkwardness of them being together, the anxiety of facing the fact that she needed to suggest they break up. Somehow *that* made sense to her and she found the anxiety drifting away. Pha resolved to start coming up with a way to make the break as clean and painless as possible. Her family would be upset. Even if they hadn't cared much for Chase their marriage had seemed very logical and sensible to everyone. Also, Pha was closing on 30---if she broke up with Chase how long would it take to find another suitable partner? Everyone wanted her to have children. Did she? Pha was uncertain.

The trees surrounding the parking lot were black with crows. Traffic, sirens, all the normal city sounds, were colored by their harsh voices. The security guard was sitting in his Kia Rio listening to the new Kurt Cobain song as he watched the birds. As Pha fumbled in her purse for her keycard a shadow filled the glass door in front of her. She was in her bag, unaware of her surroundings, and the door opening startled her.

"Sorry to scare you," the shape said in a masculine voice.

The shape became Matt. Her boss's smile gave his beard a weird shape.

"No...thank you," Pha replied. "I should just keep my passcard in my wallet."

"Sorry to ambush you, but we have a consultant coming in this morning and I wanted to bring you in the loop."

"Consultant?"

Those were never good: The company only spent money on consultants when they felt like big changes needed to be made--changes that usually involved layoffs.

"We've had interpersonal challenges recently so HR is bringing someone in to help us."

Matt paused, clearly struggling to find a *corporate friendly* way to express what was on his mind.

"Get along better as a team?"

"Yes." Her boss was relieved, even his beard looked relieved.

"Who is this consultant?"

"Her name is Abby Newall."

The smile retreated back into his beard.

"What?" She asked.

Her boss looked around to make sure no one was listening.

"She is..."

He caught himself and forced his smile to burst from his facial hair again.

"Nothing. I need more coffee. Check your email; I cc'd you in what Abby will be doing, team expectations and all that."

"Will do."

Pha forced a smile of her own. The world was feeling stranger all the time.

Kelly was making a fresh pot when Pha walked in the break room. She knew very little about K aside from the fact that they could key very quickly and seemed to bounce from department to department and special project to special project.

And I have no idea if you are a boy or a girl.

Kelly was either slightly tall for a woman or slightly short for a man, maybe five-eight or five-nine. He/She always wore loose clothes so it was impossible to tell if there were breasts or testicles or anything else that would reveal gender--it was just Kelly. K was a good worker but kept to him or herself. When they spoke, his/her voice was neither masculine nor feminine and peppered with slang.

"Thanks for making more coffee."

Kelly just nodded and walked out of the breakroom. Not wanting to wait for the coffee to finish brewing, Pha walked back to her office. K's cubicle was halfway between the breakroom and her desk. He/she was training a temp, an edgy looking man somewhere in his mid-twenties. The temp looked anxious and was fidgeting as Kelly showed them how to use the company software. The two of them felt Pha staring at them and turned towards her. Kelly nodded and the temp smiled with nervous teeth and jumpy eyes.

"Yo, Pha, this is Scott. I'm just showing him how to key in the databases."

"Welcome aboard, Scott."

"Thank you!" His voice was as bright as his eyes were dead looking. A robot man with a bug in the system. Something about him was unsettling; Pha gave the two of them a smile and a nod and went to check on the coffee.

SIX

Amelia was sitting with her behind the curtain that separated the stage from their dressing area.

"You getting cold feet? Your face tells me you're getting cold feet?"

Her beau died in the War. I was her friend but after that we became more than that.

With every dream Pha was remembering more and more about her life with Amelia.

"Cold feet?"

The other dancer smiled and removed the top part of her costume. Her breasts looked like they had never seen the sun and her nipples were the ghost of the color pink.

Tonight we talked about dancing topless for the first time.

She definitely was *not* doing that. A moment later she was untying her top and letting it fall.

"Safe to come in?"

Sammy Dade. She did not mind him seeing her. After all, they were all---

Family? I would be disturbed by this if it didn't feel so natural.

"Yeah."

"Okay, the music is about to start. We got a full house, lots of restless kids, so I hope you're ready."

"Of course."

And then Sammy was back through the curtain.

"Good evening, everyone. Tonight we have a very special show for you, a dance we brought over from North Africa by way of Paris, France."

A drum started playing a tribal beat accompanied by an amplified acoustic guitar. After the groove built Kurt Cobain started singing the "1994" song. Pha thought of how uncomfortable she had been walking around her apartment without a robe in the past and now---

Pha went to another dream where she was standing outside. An old-fashioned wagon with two high wheels and one horse was rolling fast over the prairie in silhouette. The man driving it was frantically shaking the reins, making them roll like a wave. Four men on horseback---presumably Indians---caught up to the wagon. They aimed with their bows and the arrows they shot perforated the man driving the wagon. His arms shot up as if he'd finished a race and then he tumbled off the seat and into the long grass. The wagon, now driverless, sped on.

The man on the ground moved weakly for a few moments before being swallowed by an intense, white light.

Pha was wide awake from the moment she opened her eyes. Chase was still sleeping beside her. She looked at him and was surprised to feel a fondness, maybe even some remaining love. Was breaking up the right decision? Or, were those moments of softness just distractions keeping her from a task she needed to complete?

A task I need to complete--has it really come to this?

C was happy with their life together or at least it seemed that way. If that was true Pha understood that he would be hurt if they broke up. What if she was wrong? What if this was something that could be fixed? Pha looked at him lying there and felt nothing---she had love for him but was no longer *in* love with him. She cared for him but didn't care to be around him anymore. Did she wake him up right then?

I can't do this right now. Maybe when I get home from work, I need to figure out what to say and how to respond to the objections he will have.

She looked away from him and climbed out of bed.

Pha thought about the last dream as she drove to work and remembered more details. There were eighteen school desks out on the prairie and the children seated at them were watching the man on the wagon being hunted down. A rotund man in a white suit and red moon face was standing nearby. "See, children, that was the menace of the red man. The man driving that wagon was innocent, he just rode through the wrong place and was riddled with arrows."

"What about the light?"

Pha asked that, dutifully trying to sit at one of the desks only to find she didn't fit.

"You'll understand soon enough, child," the man in the white suit smiled grimly.

Was that all of the dream or all she could remember? Pha had the feeling she was forgetting something, probably something important.

His name is Cofab Teel.

The new Kurt Cobain song came on the radio. Pha heard one lyric and thought it was "the start of the end of the world." Focusing on the traffic to calm herself she realized that she was stuck behind the same GMC Yukon as the previous morning. There was the Carl's Jr. she went to sometimes to pick up lunch. There was the Fred Meyer she bought groceries from after work. Pha passed the doctor's office then that of her dentist; her entire life was on that road. She looked up at her windshield to see when the next oil change was due--all things to remind her that the world was safe and predictable and even boring---

And yet it wasn't.

Pha got a cup of coffee from the breakroom. Kelly was working at his/her desk but there was no sign of the weird temp. The smell of McDonalds was coming from a nearby cubicle and she realized that she was hungry---did she have anything to eat in her bag? Pha chided herself for not making lunch before leaving the condo. She would stop at Fred Meyer on the way home and buy things she could bring for lunch. Matt saw her out of the corner of his eye as she went into her office and he joined her in the small room. His shutting the door with a pained look on his face didn't help her anxiety.

The consultant---am I going to be one of the layoffs? How am I going to explain that to Mom and Dad?

"We need to talk about Kelly." The tightness of his mouth made his beard pucker.

"What about?"

"I know that Kelly's numbers have been good, a real asset to the projects, but during the weekly check we found that Kelly was called in by Homeland Security."

"How come?"

"We don't have access to that but obviously it's a red flag."

"Maybe it's something innocent, questions about a friend or neighbor or something."

"Maybe." Clearly Matt hadn't considered that. "I don't want to have to take action against Kelly, a hard worker like that is an asset to the team."

"Do you know where Scott is today?"

"Scott?"

"The temp Kelly has been training?"

"No."Matt looked concerned again. "I'll call Indenture-Temps and see what's up."

"Let me know, okay?"

"Yeah, no problem."

After her boss left Pha started checking her emails and returning calls and going down her list of tasks. And then it was eleven and she realized that she was hungry. What sounded good for lunch? Pha was pretty sure she didn't want fast food---

You get in the habit of eating that crap and the next thing you know you're obese with all sorts of health problems.

Subway? Subway was pretty light--were people yelling? Was a game on or something? It seemed too early in the day for a Trailblazers game--was it even basketball season? A pop, then a second and a third. Pha realized what they were but what they were didn't make sense. She was more confused than scared---what should she do? Hide under her desk? Run for an exit? Try and reason with whomever was shooting?

If I get under my desk I'll just be trapped If I lock the door they'll just shoot through the glass.

Pha thought of her grandmother's dream; she had to run. What was going to happen after the shooting? Would they all be called in the next day to work or would it take time for the police to process the scene or whatever they did? More pops. Screams. She could hear someone begging not to be shot and then another pop followed by a scream of pain. Matt, that was who the begging voice belonged to. His shrieks sounded like a woman. Another pop and the screaming stopped. Pha went to her doorway and looked up and down the hallway. She wasn't scared, she was excited and felt as if she could run a hundred miles an hour. No one seemed to be out there. If she went left the exit was maybe thirty feet away. How long would it take to run it? Ten seconds? If she zig-zagged would it make it less likely she would be shot? Pha was in the hall and preparing to run when the weird temp backed into the hallway. He wasn't looking at her, he was aiming at someone else.

Shit. Should I go back to my office? No, if I did and he comes down this way---
No, I have to run, run now.
The temp turned towards her and their eyes met.
Maybe if I look in his eyes it will remind him I am another person and he won't shoot me. . . .
No, his eyes were blanks; they looked black even from thirty feet away. Pha started running towards the exit and got roughly ten feet. There was a pop that was much louder than the other ones followed by a sensation like someone hitting her in the back with something heavy like a board and it made her stumble. Pha cried out, realized she had made the same sound she made when she came and felt embarrassed. She thought of Chase lying there, how cold she had been to him---
I am sorry, I am so sorry.
There wasn't much pain, just a spreading numbness with fire crackling on the edges. Her hand hurt for some weird reason; it felt like a dozen bees had stung it.
Lying there, thinking of how gross the carpet was that her face was on...
And then all the details of the room were swallowed by a white light.
She fought the light. Pha knew her injury was bad, maybe she would even be paralyzed, but surely---
No, it was over.
A shape was coming towards her. What if it was the temp coming to put another bullet in her?
It didn't matter, she couldn't move.
A man was kneeling beside her, a handsome black man with a thin mustache.
"Come on," he smiled.
The smile was so kind and---

She realized that he was her best friend. No...they were brother and sister--it didn't make sense and yet it did. Pha took his hand and was surprised that she could stand. The numbness was gone as was the pain in her hand. They were walking down the hall to the parking lot but instead of small offices on one side there were hospital rooms. In one of them an old Asian woman was comforting an old white woman lying in bed and struggling for breath. Pha knew who the two women were and, for the first time, understood that Sammy Dade had told the truth when he told her that everything would be okay.

He squeezed her hand, and they walked on.

Written between 27 July, 2016 and 18 February, 2019
Music listened to: The Fixx "Beautiful Friction," Al Stewart "Year of the Cat," Elvis Costello "So Like Candy," Wilco "Shot in the Arm," Duran Duran (various ballads)

RESET RESET RESET RESET RESET RESET RESET RESET RESET RESET RESET
RESET RESET RESET RESET RESET RESET RESET RESET RESET RESET RESET
RESET RESET RESET RESET RESET RESET RESET RESET RESET RESET RESET
RESET RESET RESET RESET RESET RESET RESET RESET RESET RESET RESET
RESET RESET RESET RESET RESET RESET RESET RESET RESET RESET RESET
RESET RESET RESET RESET RESET RESET RESET RESET RESET RESET RESET
RESET RESET RESET RESET RESET RESET RESET RESET RESET RESET RESET
RESET RESET RESET RESET RESET RESET RESET RESET RESET RESET RESET
RESET RESET RESET RESET RESET RESET RESET RESET RESET RESET RESET
RESET RESET RESET RESET RESET RESET RESET RESET RESET RESET RESET
RESET RESET RESET RESET RESET RESET RESET RESET RESET RESET RESET
RESET RESET RESET RESET RESET RESET RESET RESET RESET RESET RESET
RESET RESET RESET RESET RESET RESET RESET RESET RESET RESET RESET
RESET RESET RESET RESET RESET RESET RESET RESET RESET RESET RESET
RESET RESET RESET RESET RESET RESET RESET RESET RESET RESET RESET
RESET RESET RESET RESET RESET RESET RESET RESET RESET RESET RESET
RESET RESET RESET RESET RESET RESET RESET RESET RESET RESET RESET
RESET RESET RESET RESET RESET RESET RESET RESET RESET RESET RESET
RESET RESET RESET RESET RESET RESET RESET RESET RESET RESET RESET
RESET RESET RESET RESET RESET RESET RESET RESET RESET RESET RESET
RESET RESET RESET RESET RESET RESET RESET RESET RESET RESET RESET
RESET RESET RESET RESET RESET RESET RESET RESET RESET RESET RESET
RESET RESET RESET RESET RESET RESET RESET RESET RESET RESET RESET
RESET RESET RESET RESET RESET RESET RESET RESET RESET RESET RESET
RESET RESET RESET RESET RESET RESET RESET RESET RESET RESET RESET
RESET RESET RESET RESET RESET RESET RESET RESET RESET RESET

RESET

MARA

OPEN

You are not in control, you are only a guest here.

When I was a little kid, they said the world was going to end in 2012; something about the Mayan calendar not going past that year. People freaked out about that, it was all over the news shows my parents liked to watch. The beginning of 2013 was celebrated with fireworks and other loud shit and there was this sense of relief: *We made it! Guess the Mayans were wrong?* What if they weren't?

What if the end, instead of the end just being a flash, it was really long and drawn out?

I look the way the world has been getting crazier, all the conflicts in this country, the fucked up weather---lot of signs---and realize more and more that the Mayans weren't wrong, our interpretation was.

I've been thinking about that for nine years.

"Come on," my brother whined from outside my room. "If I have to do it, you do, too."

He knocked on the door again, rattled the knob. Why did he rattle the knob? He knows I always keep it locked and yet there he was shaking it—*rattle rattle rattle*. Maybe it's to keep my family out or maybe it's to keep those creepy ass Mayans out.

Game night would best be described as my parents pretending they gave a shit about us being a family. Once a week during basketball season we would watch a Las Vegas Gamblers game; all four of us appearing to sit in the living room as a family unit but in reality being in four different places. At first, Mom and Dad didn't allow us to have our phones or tablets or whatever with us but then my parents had to do work and we all just ended up sitting with our faces in our phones—it was a fucking joke.

Why are we doing this? We don't watch the game, we just do our own shit, may as well be in our own rooms.

"We need to have family time, Mara. Just...just do it, okay?"

On what ended up being the last game night, I unlocked my door and walked into the living room doing shit on my phone just like Noah, Mom, and Dad were. The game was already playing on the eighty-four inch TV, tall bros running back and forth, occasionally throwing a ball. There were whistles and horns but none of us were paying attention.

Family night: What a fucking joke.

I was irritated that night because I had been in a groove; I had been working on this painting for a couple of weeks and not having much luck until that night. I was painting an old sailing ship, and while the ship had turned out really good, getting the ocean right was throwing me---but then something clicked...

And ten minutes later Noah was knocking on the door and reminding me about Gamenight. That night, Mom and Dad were deep in their tablets doing work shit. One of them had made a huge bowl of popcorn; none of us liked popcorn but I guess they thought that we needed to have fucking popcorn for family gamenight. No one had ever eaten the popcorn, at the end of the game our folks would ask Noah or myself to dump it into the trash. I felt bad...I mean, I would think about the hungry people in this town, maybe they would like the popcorn...

Maybe the homeless people would feel grateful to spend a couple of hours in our fancy, warm living room eating popcorn.

There was nothing I could do about that.

That night I plopped down on the couch and brought up mememe on my phone. Someone had posted some crazy cat video; this cat was stalking its owner and attacking him; maybe the Mayans got to that cat---

And then there was some kind of excitement coming out of the screen: One of the tall bros was doing all sorts of basketball stuff and it bent all the announcers out of shape. *Tyrell Dube*, that was the name the announcers kept saying, Tyrell Dube was like a machine making basket after basket. I looked up, glancing around I saw that Mom, Dad, and Noah had all been sucked into the game; Dad had even started eating popcorn. What the fuck? Then Mom was reaching for it and then Noah, as well.

"It's going to go into overtime," Mom said.

"What do you mean?" Dad asked.

"Watch," Mom replied.

Tyrell Dube made a long ass shot and the announcers confirmed what Mom had predicted.

"He loves it when they fall," Dad mumbled. "He likes it even more when they bleed."

"What?" Noah asked.

Before Dad could reply the front door opened and the world as we knew it ended.

HOME INVASION

There was a woman walking through the door. She was beautiful but talk show beautiful with a fake face, fake boobs, and expensive hair. I knew her---everyone knows Chelsea Seen. You see her walking in your house, do a *what the fuck* for a couple of seconds, and then you understand why she has just walked in your living room---

And it is too late.

Behind her were a man and a woman, both were muscular looking, wearing ski masks, and carrying small cameras. Dad got up, I guess he felt the need to "Be the man" and confront the strangers that had just walked in his house.

"What are you doing in our house?" He asked, trying to sound firm but you can hear a tremor in his voice.

Mom was up too and she knew some martial art so her getting up had some relevance. She was not talking, just approaching Chelsea who was smiling as if she was showing us a new car she wanted to sell us.

"I know what you're thinking, Megan," Chelsea said. "*I have a red belt in Kuk Sool. The thing is, both of my assistants have the equivalent of a Sabum Nim in Kuk Sool so it might be best to sit down.*"

Mom didn't sit down, but she did not get closer to the tough looking people with the cameras.

"What is this?" Mom asked firmly, no tremor to her voice.

"Reset," I said quietly. Mom and Dad looked at me, Noah didn't; he knew about Reset. My brother looked scared, scared as I was feeling.

"Reset?" Dad asked. The confusion and fear on his face made me love him but also pity him but in a way that I didn't want anything to do with him.

"It's the Mayans," I said quietly, mostly to myself.

Chelsea asked us to sit back down and for one of us to switch off the game.

"The Gamblers win," she smiled. "124 to 120, amazing game."

"How can you know that?" Mom asked.

Chelsea just smiled at her. Her expression was like one of those people on those morning talk shows where everyone is obnoxiously happy and talking in circles about absolutely nothing.

"It doesn't matter, Megan," Chelsea smiled. "This is not about the NBA, this is about the four of you."

She had a bag over her shoulder, it was the same color as her jacket and skirt: Mustard, but dark mustard like the fancy kind Dad preferred. Chelsea took a small camera out of the bag, set it on top of the television, and aimed it at the couch where Noah and I were sitting. The hostess backed away and looked at the camera.

"Welcome to another chapter of Reset," Chelsea said in a voice I recognized, having watched every chapter of the show. "Where you never see us coming..."

She turned towards the four of us.

"Or *three* of you didn't see it coming, Shone family," Chelsea added. "One of you contacted us, gave us the keys to your house and the alarm codes. We know everything about you, know about the 9mm handgun and the shotgun...we have accessed your bank accounts, car loans, the mortgage on this house, your 401ks---"

"Holy shit," Dad said weakly but then firmed up. "Wait---you can't just get to our money like that; there are passwords, security measures."

"If having faith in that makes you happy," Chelsea shot him with a finger gun. "Then...go with that!"

"What happens in this Reset, Noah?" Mom asked.

Of course she asked *the golden child* even though I was the one who---

Whatever, I'm not even getting pissed about that.

"Our lives are over," my brother said quietly. "Our bank accounts have been cleaned out, 401ks, whatever. The SUVs will be dismantled and sold for parts, the boat taken to Mexico and sold. When this is over, the furniture will be removed from the house and sold."

"So, this is a scam," Dad growled, taking a step towards Chelsea. "You just steal our money and stuff---"

"The money goes to charity," Chelsea clarified.

"That money is so our kids can go to college!" Mom yelled.

"Relax, Megan," Dad nodded with a grim smile. "There is no way they can get away with this."

Chelsea just looked at them, her sunny morning television persona hadn't flagged at all: She was going to put us in that new car---*what do I need to do to put you in a Mayan prophecy today?*

A small woman wearing a ski mask walked in. She was carrying a duffel bag that she sat on the coffee table next to the *Money* magazines and a book on Monet that no one but me had ever looked at.

"What's in the box?" Mom asked.

"There will be the temptation to go against the program," Chelsea said. "Inside the box is assurance that we can all get along and be civil to one another."

"The Diapers of Distress," Noah said.

"We prefer to call them *the Garment*," Our guest nodded to him.

The hostess opened the box and pulled out what looked like a diaper. Dad looked confused and then looked over at Noah and I for help.

"It's like a shock collar for your junk," I said.

"Uhn uh," Dad grimaced. "I am not putting that thing on."

"Please, Kyle," Chelsea said soothingly. "I won't hurt you or your family if you play along."

"Get the fuck out of my house!" Dad yelled, taking a step towards Chelsea.

The hostess had something else in her bag, a taser: She gave Dad a blast; he screamed and fell back, luckily into a chair.

"It doesn't have to be like this," Chelsea said sadly. "Put on the Garment, play along, and no one gets hurt."

"You just clean us out," Mom smiled bitterly. I could see the wheels turning; Chelsea *knew* where the guns were but Mom knew the house---

My mother turned to run towards the master bedroom; a second muscular woman had come from the kitchen and blocked Mom. Mother tried some martial arts thing but that woman in a ski mask laid her out. Mom staggered, the woman who had smacked her helped Mom to a chair.

"I'm sorry, kids," Dad said, looking at Noah and I plaintively.

"It's okay; we know there's nothing you can do," I replied softly.

THE GARMENT

The woman who had taken down Mom followed me to my room. I was
holding the Garment out in front of me like it was a bomb that needed to
be dismantled. In my room I didn't lock the door; locks had become
meaningless.

"This is really good," the woman said, looking over at my painting; she had
a gentle voice, kind even.

"Thanks, I still have a lot of work to do."

"I really like the way you painted the ocean," she said.

The woman was reaching out towards the painting—was she going to touch
it, feel the texture of the paint? Would it be worth asking her not to? I
mean, the paint *should* have been dry at that point.

"How about you put the Garment on?" She added. " And in order to give
you some privacy I will keep checking out this painting."

"Okay."

I took off my pants long enough to slip on the Diaper of Death. It fit
perfectly---*of course* it did.

"It's on," I said.

She turned to me and nodded, smiling a little through the hole in her mask.
Green eyes, the woman had beautiful, green eyes.

After the four of us had put on our Garments we met back in the living room.

"Are you going to tell us your name?" Mom asked Chelsea.

"I'm sorry," the intruder laughed. "How rude of me! My name is Chelsea Seen. Your kids have seen the show but clearly you haven't."

"Must be a Generation Z thing," Dad mumbled before focusing on Chelsea.

"You say you cleaned us out," he continued. "Why are you still here?"

Chelsea smiled at him like she was flirting and took a step closer.

"What's wrong, Kyle? Don't you like me?"

Dad looked from Chelsea to Mom and then back at Chelsea, no words coming, my father just looking more and more uncomfortable. The hostess laughed and took a step back.

"This isn't just about money," Chelsea said. "One of you told us all about the situation around here. We dug deeper---"

She nodded at Mom before continuing.

"---the Shone family is kind of a fucked up mess, isn't it?"

"You have no right to judge us," Mom said quietly but harshly. "You broke into our home, you assaulted us---"

"And I may be able to save you," Chelsea smiled.

"Save us?" Dad laughed. "You took all our money. How the hell are we supposed to live? We were saving that for retirement, for the kids to go to college!"

"Noah and Mara will still be able to go to college," Chelsea said. "We would not deprive them of that. All the money we get goes in a pool, a chain of investments. You will not be homeless, your children will not be denied an education."

"I don't get this," Mom mumbled. "Can I get a drink?"

Dad, Noah, and I looked at her; Mom stared back.

"It's okay," she said. "This is kind of a special situation."

"You don't want us to call your sponsor?" Chelsea teased.

Mom looked at the hostess hatefully.

Dad kept a six pack of beer in the fridge. While Mom was recovering he kept it in a small fridge in his office but after a few months she was okay with it being in the fridge. Dad only had a beer or two a night, there were three left in the fridge.

"If you want anything else we can get it," Chelsea said.

"Great, turn my wife back into a drunk," Dad said ruefully.

"I was never a drunk," Mom turned on him. "I always took care of things, always brought money in."

"I'm not judging," Dad said though he clearly was.

"You don't have any place to judge," Mom snapped at him. "You can't even please your wife!"

Silence; a big awkward silence. Noah and I looked at each other and then at the strangers in our living room, wishing we were anywhere but *there*.

"I think I'll have a beer, too," Dad said quietly.

What Mom had accused him of had clearly shaken him.

You can't even please your wife!

Great: Cue mental imagine of your parents having sex. Fuck you, Mayans.

"I'm not talking about it on some fucking show," Mom said quietly, taking a long drink of beer.

Mom *hadn't* ever been a "drunk," she had handled her shit even if there had been a lot of bottles in the recycling--*a lot*. And her moods could be dark.

174

She went to AA and got the sponsor Chelsea mentioned; this had been explained to Noah and I during a family meeting.

"I want a bottle of scotch," Mom said. "Good scotch."

"Megan," Dad said gently, looking at her with a love that surprised me. "You don't want this, you really don't."

Mom looked at him then looked at the carpet.

"We're not getting into this, Kyle," she said firmly. "Eventually these people will leave our house and I will call Rick---"

"Wait, Rick is still your sponsor?" Dad looked confused, possibly angry. Mom looked really uncomfortable, the bottle of beer was nearly empty. The tension in the room---

"Can we have drinks, too?" I asked. "Maybe white wine or something."

"No," Dad said firmly, and then he looked at Mom again. "We talked about this, I thought you were getting another sponsor."

"We are not talking about this now," Mom said flatly, her tone of voice shutting Dad down.

THE COWBOY AND THE OCEAN

"You can't even please your wife!"

"Rick is still your sponsor?"

There was something there, some connection between those two outbursts.

Had Mom hooked up with Rick or something?

"Can I go back to my room and paint?" I asked.

"Sure," Chelsea winked at me. "If I can interview you as you do it."

"Uh...okay."

The hostess took a camera from one of the muscular people and we walked to my room. Once inside, she locked the door and winked again.

"You like it locked, right?"

"Usually just when I'm alone but...whatever."

I looked at the painting, not sure I could work on it with someone watching. Chelsea put the camera on the bookcase so both of us were in frame. She sat on the bed, pointedly not watching me paint.

"You're different from the rest of your family," she said. "It must make you feel lonely sometimes, like you have no one to talk to."

I didn't respond, totally seeing through her "interviewer tricks." I was thinking that I had to be someone else, someone worth watching on a show. Mara but not really Mara.

"Your parents are all about their jobs," Chelsea continued. "Your brother has all these plans for his education---"

"Noah isn't who you think he is," I said that without thinking.

I couldn't see her face but I could *feel* Chelsea smiling; it wasn't the happy morning television smile, this one was real, more cunning.

"Who do we think he is, Mara?"

"I don't know...forget it."

"You are struggling, aren't you, Mara?" Chelsea asked, her voice was so gentle I wanted to share whatever shit was in my head. Almost.

"I don't know...I just don't..."

No words were coming, it was just a feeling or feelings. Sometimes in the middle of painting everything gets clear, I could totally talk and explain things, but I wasn't in the middle of painting; a stranger was sitting on my bed and I couldn't put my thoughts into words.

"We patched into your mememe---"

"That doesn't mean anything," I snorted. "I just put up a bunch of memes and shit---"

"You're intelligent enough to understand the phrase *reading between the lines*. It's not just the memes, it's your search history...it's you being inspired to paint a ship in a storm and---"

She gestured at another painting of mine over the bed.

"A cowboy lost in a desert," Chelsea got up and studied the painting. "I love the detail work, the way you did the textures of the cowboy's shirt, the cactus, the ocean in the one you're working on."

The hostess walked over and put a hand on my shoulder---

Normally I hate being touched and will jerk away if anyone reaches for me; I didn't, then.

"I don't know," I sighed. "The three of them have shit figured out and I have no idea what I'm going to do. I like to paint...it's going to be okay, everything is gonna work out, I *know that*...I just don't know how."

Chelsea squeezed my shoulder, grabbed the camera from the bookshelf, and left my room.

WHAT IS THE DEAL WITH RICK?

I wasn't painting, just moving the brush towards the dab of oil and just...
Poke at it, stir it, tease the oil---

"Okay, what is the deal with Rick?" I asked Mom and Dad that after
walking back into the living room.
"Noah was telling us about these kittens he found at school," Dad frowned
at me.
"Fuck the kittens," I said.
"Mara," Mom said quietly, looking into the glass of neat scotch she was
sipping. How had she gotten it so fast? The show must have known she'd
ask for it.
"I know this is a weird situation," Mom continued. "But we need to be civil
to each other."
She looked up at Chelsea with open dislike.
"And we are not discussing private family business with strangers," Mom
added
"Maybe they already know," Noah said softly.
"Yeah," I agreed. "They've probably already interviewed Rick, if you guys
were texting or whatever---"
The look Mom gave me caused me to back up, it was definitely a *we're having
a serious conversation when these people leave* look.
Dad was chuckling, it was the sort of laugh you do when you understand
that everything is fucked up so badly you may as well laugh about it.
"I haven't texted him since our conversation," Mom said firmly, looking
over at Dad. "I have been totally straight with you---"
"No," Dad said, I could see him struggling with his anger. "Rick is still your
sponsor therefore you have *not* been straight with me."

"What do you care," Mom said so quietly I could barely hear her.

"It's going to be okay, guys," Dad said to the three of us, giving Mom the most cursory glance. "Your mother and I still have good jobs---"

"Actually," Chelsea said. "You don't."

"What?" Dad frowned.

Mom looked amused and took another drink.

"Megan resigned effective immediately," Chelsea explained. "On Monday you, Kyle, will be called into a video conference with HR. They are going to have to let you go."

"And why is that?" Dad asked with a caustic smile.

"They found a bunch of pornography on a work computer---"

"Of course they did!" Dad laughed. "You people thought of everything!" He scowled and shook his head before walking into the kitchen to get a beer.

"You've completely fucked us," Mom mumbled. "Lovely."

Chelsea had brought a chair over so she could face the three of us, focusing on Mom.

"Why do you look at it that way?" The hostess asked. "Neither you nor your husband enjoy your jobs."

"Enjoy?" Mom said with a cold smile. "Life is not about *enjoying* things. We have two kids to think about, we have a mortgage and car payments---"

"Not anymore," Chelsea clarified.

"Whatever," Mom replied. "When you leave we will just have to get new jobs and buy new cars and everything else."

She sat forward in the chair and hard stared the hostess.

"All you've done is make our lives more difficult, that's all; all so you have your stupid show."

"Maybe we need this," I said.

"Why do you have to be like this?" Mom turned on me. "I love you but...it would be easier---for *you*, Mara---if you could be more like your brother. He isn't into all this *dark shit*, he has friends and works hard in school, he befriends the mentally challenged kids, he even rescues kittens."

"Come on, Mom," Noah said. "Leave her alone."

"I love Mara," Mom continued, starting to slur a little. "But I just wish she was more like you, *for her sake.*"

"You don't know anything," Noah said softly.

NOAH IN THE CONFESSION BOOTH

Noah wanted to go to his room. As in my case, Chelsea went with him leaving the rest of us with the two camera people who knew martial arts.

"This is stupid," Dad said. "Why are you filming us when she isn't here?"

"Why don't you just pretend she's here," the male cameraperson said, like the woman he had a gentle voice.

"This is just *ridiculous*," Dad added, slumping in his chair. "I'm guessing we will get kicked out of the house."

"In a manner of speaking," the man with the camera said. "But there is a place for it if you want it. Chelsea will be able to explain it better."

"Why don't you talk about the text from Rick?" The woman camera operator asked, focusing on Dad and then Mom.

"I am not talking about that with strangers," Mom said firmly.

"It's safe to assume that the Show has access to your text messages," the male said. "What would stop us from cutting to the texts from this discussion?"

"Uh, because we could sue your asses!" Mom said loudly. "Because those are private conversations and there are laws protecting people."

"We entered your house and are holding you against your will," the female said. "Do you really think the Show is concerned about *laws*?"

"Ah, you got to a good part without me!" Chelsea laughed as she walked back into the room.

"Is Noah okay?" Dad asked.

"Yeah, he just got to talking about stuff and it got emotional," Chelsea smiled kindly. "He just needs a few to get it together."

She sat back down, looked from Mom to Dad and back to Mom again.

"You were about to talk about the texts, I can smell it!" She said.

"Rick and I were sexting," Mom said softly. "We never did anything, but it has been tempting."

"*Has* been tempting," Dad said bitterly. "Note how it is *present tense*."

"What do you care?" Mom turned to him with a frown. "If I *was* with someone else it would take you off the hook."

She took a sip off her drink, reading her lines off the bottom of the glass.

"You always close your eyes," she said softly. "I ask what you're thinking about and you always say you're just enjoying the moment--I know you're thinking about someone else. And then there's the history on your phone…"

She trailed off with a shake of her head.

Dad looked uncomfortable and equally ashamed and sad.

"What did you mean when you said we'd be taken care of?" Dad asked.

"Some of the money from our contestants goes to the Haven," Chelsea explained. "It's a rural place, a bunch of cabins, sustainable---contestants can stay out there as long as they want but if it's full time they have to do work around the farm."

"Sounds lovely," Dad frowned.

"It kind of does," Mom said softly. "Just...relax."

Chelsea seemed pleased by that.

"It's a good way to reset," the hostess nodded. "Clear your head, see what you really want in life."

Something about that triggered something in Mom who looked up at the hostess with venom.

"We had what we wanted: We had a home, we had been saving money for our retirement; we provided for our kids---"

"This place is depressing," I said.

"Then we will legally emancipate you and you can live in a fucking squalid art studio or whatever it is you want!" Mom shouted at me.

And then the words she had said snapped back in her face as if on rubber bands, I could see it. She looked sorry, she looked hurt; I could tell she wanted to suck the words back in, take them back in the deep, rotten place she keeps thoughts like that but it was too late. I turned away from her.

"Mara," her voice was shaky like she was on the verge of tears. "I don't...I don't know what to do with you. I love you so much but I don't know...we're so different."

That's all she got out; if she had tried to say anymore Mom would have cried and I know her well enough to understand she would never cry in front of Chelsea.

I still wasn't looking at her; the way I was feeling I never wanted to look at her again.

Noah walked back in with his phone in his hand, the female camera op took it from him.

"Sorry," Chelsea said. "No phones, no tablets, no laptops."

"Afraid we'll call the cops?" Dad smirked.

"No," Chelsea said with a tight smile. "So you can focus. This is important, the most important weekend of your lives."

"You're going to be here the whole weekend?" Mom sighed.

"That's usually how long it takes," Chelsea replied.

CAN'T SLEEP

A few minutes after midnight I was nodding off. We were allowed to go to sleep whenever, the catch was there would be a camera in our rooms. The only place without cameras were the bathrooms. Having seen every chapter of the show, I knew that anything that could be used as a weapon---or as a means of committing suicide---had already been removed. There was probably a mobile truck parked nearby, more strangers watching us as we lay on top of the covers unable to sleep. I kept turning over and over how Mom had laid into me and then how guilty she looked---what fucking ever, I already knew the truth. Why wasn't I more like Noah with his 3.6 grade point average and all his friends and good deeds and solid plans for when he graduated in two months. When they bought him a used car he didn't want a sports car or whatever, he wanted a used Prius. Of course he did; my brother was always going on about the environment. He went through a period of not flushing his piss to "save water," I quickly put a stop to that. But I always loved Noah. I may have been the younger sibling but it was me who worried about him because I saw a disguise taking over his life.

So...Mom wasn't getting laid enough and Dad probably all sorts of porn in his search history---
It was really gross to have that shit rattling around in my head but it was too late.
You know, as much as I stressed about having no fucking idea what I was going to do after graduating I understood that I was better off than my family; plans are not always good. Having a plan...it can be a prison. The plan comes, it involves being a responsible adult or whatever along with the understanding that you have to follow it: College. Solid Career. Investment shit. Big beige house.

I don't know...I'm probably projecting my own shit because I didn't like our house. We had the living room that we sat in once a week, the dining room we used twice a year. Mom and Dad never cooked, it was all delivery or picking something up. Noah complained to them about all the plastic bags once---*once*.

A knock on the door. I walked over and unlocked it. It was Noah, he closed the door behind him after walking into my room.

"I'm sorry Mom was shitty to you," he said, and then walked over to my work in progress. "This is turning out really good; I still like the cowboy the best."

"Everyone does."

He sat on the floor crossed legged, back against a wall, the same way my brother always sat in my room.

"Who do you think contacted the show?" He asked.

"Does it matter?"

Noah had to think about that one for a few moments.

"I guess not. Whoever did it, I think it's a good thing."

"You good with being broke and homeless?" I asked before smirking at him. "What am I saying, you work at the food bank, your customers there will probably show you the ropes."

I made sure to smile when I said that; my brother studied my face, tense at first but then relaxing.

"I know that you think I'm too earnest for my own good," he said.

No, I understand you more than you realize.

Should I have said that? I wasn't sure so I kept that thought to myself.

"I just miss us being weirdos," Was my eventual reply. "I remember when you were a punk, not that wearing black jeans and listening to Green Day

186

makes you a punk, but you were snarky, you could be really fun in a sick way."

"I changed," he said softly.

His words said one thing but his face was saying something else.

"Yeah?"

"It wasn't fun for me," Noah continued. "Something needed to change."

He got up, looked at my work in art before leaving.

"You need a guy on your boat," he said.

"A guy?"

"Yeah," he said with his hand on the doorknob. "A guy, just one."

ON A YACHT

"I really like this song!" Six year old me said that.

I had started dancing like a dorky little kid to the Hall and Oates song Mom had put on. She looked upset or at least suspicious, like she thought I was making fun of her corny music or whatever. It *is* corny music, but I love Hall and Oates and Michael McDonald and all that shit they call yacht rock. I remember that day very clearly; six year old me spazzing out and jumping around to "I Can't Go For That" or maybe it was "Private Eyes." Kids at school think I'm being ironic, that listening to yacht rock is part of my shtick or something and I let them think that because it works for me.

After Noah left I lay back down on bed and thought about when I was six and Noah was eight. We had just bought our stupid house. Mom and Dad had a smaller ranch house before that, it was pretty old but I loved it. There was this cool old oak tree in the backyard and the trunk was all gnarled. I knew all the kids on our street and we'd go to each others houses to watch stupid kid videos or play Xbox or other kid stuff. I didn't know any of our neighbors after we moved. The only time I saw other kids was when I went to school. At the new house, the backyard was a small square of juvenile grass and a sapling being held up by a stake. Dad bought an expensive barbeque and plopped it on the cement porch but I think we've used it like two or three times. It's pretty rusty now.

Why was I lying on bed thinking about being six and dancing around like a dork?

And then I remembered---

When Mom understood my joy was real she had laughed and danced with me...

And when we were done she had picked me up and held me and, ten years later, I could see feel how much she loved me---

And then I thought of how she had yelled at me in front of Chelsea and everyone else---

I turned towards the wall, not wanting the camera to capture me crying.

SATURDAY MORNING

"I remember Saturday morning when I was a kid," Dad was talking when I walked into the living room. He wasn't looking at anyone, maybe my father was talking to himself. "I used to watch cartoons. I'd take a bowl of cereal into the living room and watch cartoons. Scooby Doo was my favorite."
Chelsea had been drinking from a mug, coffee by the smell of it, and smiling a little as my father talked.
"I liked Scooby Doo as well," she replied with a nod. "Then they brought in a little dog---"
"Scrappy Doo---" Dad scowled.
"Yeah," Chelsea laughed a little. "*Scrappy Doo*, and it wasn't as good anymore."
"Scrappy Doo was the nadir of that cartoon," Dad sighed.
"Is there more coffee?" I asked.
"I don't know," Dad smiled over at me.
"A little," Chelsea nodded over at me. "Get it before it's gone."
I didn't ask where Mom was; I didn't care.

There was barely enough coffee to fill a mug. I used the dark green one, Mom's usual cup---
Fuck her, you know, *fuck her*.
I was trying to be angry but what I really felt was hurt.
Dad was still talking about when he was a kid, before the internet, when there were only four channels that came in at his house or some blah blah blah like that. I stood on the side of the living room, watching him regress to a simpler time; if we had milk and cereal he probably would have been eating it as he tried to find Scooby Doo on the television. Mom walked in. She looked over and had to see that I was using her cup; I could tell by

watching her face that Mom had noticed that I was using her precious cup but I could also see that my mother understood that she didn't dare say anything after all the shit she had said the night before. Megan looked sad, maybe hurt herself---good.

Mom walked into the kitchen then walked back out into the living room a minute later.

"Where are the filters?"

I rolled my eyes and walked into the kitchen. Megan followed me.

I got the filters, pulled the coffee out of the cupboard, and set up the coffee maker to brew another pot.

"You have every right to be pissed at me," my mother said.

She was looking for forgiveness but I wasn't sure I had it for her. That hadn't been the first time I had gotten the "weird daughter" treatment: Two years earlier I had been full on Goth down to the black lipstick; Mom had taken me to a mall to show me *how normal kids dressed*. We had been good up to that day...no, maybe we hadn't. If I look back there were signs before our mother and daughter trip to the mall. I had been getting more Goth over the course of a few months: First the black clothes and then the make up. With each step Mom was talking with me less and less; I was no longer her little girl, she could probably see that I wasn't going to grow up like her---she must have been disappointed and that trip to the mall was...I don't know, maybe it was her last attempt to get the old Mara back.

"You make it strong, don't you?" Mom, in the present, talking to my back.

"You used to like it stronger," I said, tense like a stretched rubber band. "I learned to make coffee when you'd be nursing a hangover."

Mom winced, I could feel it even though I wasn't looking at her. I turned the coffeemaker on but kept looking at it; if I moved Mom would see my face, see how she had hurt me---*again*---and I was determined not to give her that.

191

"You knew I was going to come in here, Mara," mother said softly. "You knew I was going to follow you in, part of you wants to talk to me."

The coffeemaker was burbling, I could smell the steam reinvigorating the old grinds that had fallen into the machine---

Part of me *did* want to talk to her but that part had no idea what to say.

"You were just telling the truth," I said softly but firmly. "It's what you feel...whatever."

Dad would have taken a step forward, awkwardly put a hand on my shoulder. Mom was tougher or maybe she feared rejection more deeply...I don't know.

"I'm not upset with you, Mara, I just worry---"

"I'm okay," I interrupted her. "Worry about Noah."

"I do," she replied. "But I worry about *you* because neither your father nor I understand you; you're all about art...you see the world in a way we don't---how are we supposed to guide you, help you make decisions?"

I forced myself to face her. Mom looked anguished; I don't think I had ever seen her look that vulnerable. I almost wanted to hug her but neither of us are huggers.

"Maybe you're not supposed to," I said. "Maybe all I need is for you to be there for me."

I couldn't deal with the pain on her face; there had been a lot of times I had wanted her to be human, to be gentle with me, but when she was actually being open and vulnerable it just weirded me out.

"Sorry I took your cup, coffee should be done in a minute."

I said that and walked out of the kitchen; Mom didn't try to stop me.

NOAH

THE BRIDGE

You are not in control, you are only a guest here.

I had a weird dream: I was crossing a bridge that was full of people. They weren't walking, everyone was just standing around talking and it made it difficult to get across. I was late for school and had no idea where I was but believed that if I got across the water there would be a landmark or something. The bridge was jammed, though; no one was moving, just standing around. I tried to edge through the crowd but there were too many people. I asked them to move; even though I was polite everyone ignored me. The wind picked up and the bridge began swaying. It felt unsafe, like there were too many people on the bridge and their weight would cause it to collapse and fall into the water. A small boy appeared to my right: Somewhere between six and eight. Blonde hair. Serious face. Gray school uniform with a yellow and blue striped tie. Looking right at me.
"You are not in control," he said. "You are only a guest here."

I turned that dream over and over in my head all day, even looked up what it meant when you dream about crossing a bridge; there were a lot of different answers and none seemed to fit my life.

The smell of popcorn--*game night*. Mom and Dad mean well, I get that they want us to retain some sort of connection to each other. Mara doesn't see that: Honestly, she is too cynical for her own good. Mom and Dad sit on the couch with the big bowl of popcorn on the coffee table that no one eats and there is a gap between Mom and Dad, a dead space large enough for a third person. No one ever sits there; who knows Mara's reason but I have the feeling the space is very cold, uneasy. Mara was still in her room and when I walked to her door I could hear old music coming through it, a pop song with someone singing "I can't go for that."

She always does this, tries to avoid game night. At least Mom and Dad are trying, a lot of parents don't. I knocked on my sister's door.

"Come on," I said firmly. "You need to be out here, too."

I rattled the knob in case she couldn't hear my voice; she always locks her door and I'm not sure why. I heard Mom musing about it to Dad, wondering if Mara had been taking drugs. Fortunately Dad stood up to Mom for once and firmly told her that, no, Mara was not doing drugs.

Once a week during basketball season we watch a Las Vegas Gamblers game together. It always seemed random for Mom to come up with the tradition seeing as none of us are sports fans. All four of us have different viewing tastes; Mara said once that Mom picked something we equally hate but, again, my sister is too cynical for her own good.

I heard the lock click and Mara walked out, face in phone, walking to the living room and dropping into one of the chairs. Mom and Dad were sort of watching the game while looking at their own phones and soon I was doing the same though....

You are not in control, you are only a guest here.

I kept thinking about that dream. The last time I dreamt about crossing a bridge had been years earlier, when I was a little kid.

No one ever eats the popcorn. Late in the game Mom or Dad ask Mara or myself to dump the popcorn in the trash. I feel bad: When Mom started game night and Dad began making the big bowls of popcorn that never got eaten I got the idea in my head that maybe the homeless people would want it. Certainly they would feel grateful to spend a couple of hours in our fancy, warm living room. I bagged it up one time, a plastic bag full of cold popcorn, and took it down to the homeless shelter to see if they wanted it. This old homeless man with soup in his beard looked at me as if I was insane.

The game was just like any other basketball game, tall men running back and forth, throwing a ball at a ring of metal with fabric hanging from it--- And then there was some kind of excitement coming out of the screen; one of the tall men was doing something out of the ordinary and all the announcers started shouting. *Tyrell Dube*, that was the name the announcers kept saying, Tyrell Dube took over the game, tossing the orange ball through the metal ring with fabric hanging from it over and over. All four of us looked up from our phones and got caught up in the action; Dad had even started eating popcorn. Then Mom was reaching for it and I did, as well.

"It's going to go into overtime," Mom said.

"What do you mean?" Dad asked.

"Watch," Mom replied.

Tyrell Dube made an astonishing shot and the announcers confirmed what Mom had predicted.

"He loves it when they fall," Dad mumbled. "He likes it even more when they bleed."

"What?" I asked.

Before Dad could reply the front door opened and the reality as we knew it changed forever.

There was a woman walking through the door. She was beautiful, the beauty of local beauty pageants and make-up counters in department stores. After the surprise dropped from flare to glow I recognized her as Chelsea Seen. I recognized her, remembered why she was famous and---

And it was too late.

Behind her were a man and a woman, both strong in appearance, wearing ski masks and carrying small cameras. Dad stood up, I'm not sure why.

"What are you doing?" He asked, his tone was firm but you could hear shakiness in his voice.

Mom stood up, too. She knows some martial art so her standing up could have been useful. Mom was not talking, just moving slowly towards Chelsea who was smiling as if a potential customer were approaching her make-up counter. Chelsea said something to mom, something about the people in the ski masks knowing the same martial art as my mother. Mom didn't sit down, but she did not get closer to the tough looking people with the cameras.

"What is this?" She asked levelly.

"Reset," Mara said quietly. Mom and Dad looked at her, I didn't, already knowing about Reset.

"Reset?" Dad asked. The confusion and fear on his face was pathetic; in my head I heard the click of the scissors Mom used to remove his testicles.

"It's the Mayans," Maya whispered; why she was thinking of Mayans I have no idea.

Chelsea asked us to sit back down and for one of us to switch off the game. Her expression was like one of those people on those morning talk shows where everyone is obnoxiously happy and talking circles about absolutely nothing.

"Don't worry, Gamblers won," Chelsea said.

Mom asked for clarification.

"It doesn't matter, Megan," Chelsea smiled. "This is not about the NBA, this is about the four of you."

Chelsea took a small camera out of a bag, set it on top of the television, and aimed it at the couch where Mara and I were sitting. The hostess backed away and looked at the camera.

"Welcome to another chapter of Reset," Chelsea said in a voice I recognized, having watched a few chapters of the show. "Where you never see us coming…"

She turned towards the four of us.

"Or *three* of you didn't see it coming, Shone family," Chelsea added. "One of you contacted us, gave us the keys to your house and the alarm codes. We know everything about you, know about the 9mm handgun and the shotgun…we have accessed your bank accounts, car loans, the mortgage on this house, your 401ks---"

"Shit," Dad said weakly but then firmed up. "Wait---you can't just get to our money like that; there are passwords, security measures."

"Of course there are, Kyle," Chelsea shot him with a finger gun.

"What happens in this Reset, Noah?" Mom turned to me.

"Our lives are over," I said, wondering why Mom hadn't asked Mara who we all knew was obsessed with Reset. "Our bank accounts have been cleaned out, 401ks, whatever. The SUVs will be dismantled and sold for parts, the boat taken to Mexico and sold. When this is over, the furniture will be removed from the house and sold."

"So, this is a scam," Dad growled, taking a step towards Chelsea. "You just steal our money and stuff---"

"The money goes to charity," Chelsea clarified.

"That money is so our kids can go to college!" Mom yelled.

"Relax, Megan," Dad nodded with a grim smile. "There is no way they can get away with this."

Chelsea just looked at them like they were dim and she was struggling to remain patient. A third person wearing a ski mask walked in carrying a duffel bag that she sat on the coffee table next to the *Forbes* magazines and a book on some painter that was dusty because no one had ever read it.

"What's in the box?" Mom asked.

"Insurance," Chelsea said. "Insurance that we can all get along and be civil to one another."

"The Diapers of Distress," I said.

"We prefer to call them *the Garment*," Chelsea smiled at me.

The hostess opened the box and pulled out what looked like a diaper. Dad looked confused and then looked over at me for help.

"It's like a shock collar for your junk," Mara said. I thought that was clever.

"Uhn uh," Dad grimaced. "I am not putting that thing on."

"Please, Kyle," Chelsea said soothingly. "No one is going to get hurt as long as you play by the rules."

"Get the fuck out of my house!" Dad yelled, taking a step towards Chelsea. The hostess had something else in her bag, a taser: She gave Dad a blast; he screamed and fell back into a chair only to slip off and land on the carpet.

"Don't make us do things we'll regret," Chelsea said, fake sad. "Put on the Garment and no one gets hurt."

Mom mumbled something, smiling a hard smile. I could see that she was thinking---

And then Mom turned to run towards the master bedroom; a second muscular woman had come from the kitchen and blocked Mom. Mother tried some martial arts thing but that woman in a ski mask laid her out. Mom staggered, the woman who had smacked her helped Mom to a chair.

"I'm sorry, kids," Dad said, looking at Mara and I plaintively.

"It's okay, there's nothing we can do," My sister replied softly.

IT CAN GO OVER YOUR UNDERWEAR

The woman who had taken down Mom followed Mara to her room. She was holding the Garment out in front of her like it was a spider she had caught on a paper towel and was going to drop it in the trash. The two of them were in Mara's room for a few minutes and then one of the men in ski masks followed me to my room. There was no polite turning away, the man just stared at me, waiting for me to put the Garment on. I wanted to ask for privacy but he was just doing his job. Turning my back to him, I undressed from the waist down.

"It can go over your underwear," the man said.

"Pardon?"

"It doesn't need to be against your skin. In fact, we prefer if you wear the garment *over* your underwear; they are very difficult to clean because of the electronics."

I nodded and pulled my boxer briefs back on.

As I wriggled the Garment into place I saw the bridge in my mind, the one in the dream. It was empty; there was something ominous about that.

MOM GETS TRIGGERED

Dad was the last one to put a Garment on. He was taken back to the master bedroom and returned a few minutes later with the zipper down on the front of his Dockers.

"Hey, Dad," I said, motioning at my own zipper.

He smiled and nodded to me and then the smile left his face when he turned to Chelsea.

"You say you cleaned us out," Dad said. "Why are you still here?"

Chelsea smiled at him and took a step to close the distance between them.

"What's wrong, Kyle? Aren't we friends?"

Dad looked from Chelsea to Mom and then back at Chelsea, no words coming, just looking more and more uncomfortable. The hostess laughed and took a step back.

"You're mistaken if you think that this is just about money," Chelsea said. "One of you told us all about the state of your family and we looked into it---"

She nodded at Mom before continuing.

"---the Shone family is kind of a mess, isn't it?"

"You are in no position to judge us," Mom said quietly but with a toughness. "You broke into our home, you threatened us---"

"And I may be able to save you," Chelsea smiled.

"Save us?" Dad laughed. "You took all our money. How the hell are we supposed to live? We were saving that for retirement, for the kids to go to college!"

"Noah and Mara will still be able to go to college," Chelsea said. "We would not deprive them of that. All the money we get goes in a pool, a chain of investments. You will not be homeless, your children will not be denied an education."

"I don't understand any of this," Mom mumbled.

She didn't look strong anymore, my mother looked anxious.

 "I want a drink,"

Dad, Mara, and I looked at her; Mom stared back.

"Don't worry," she said. "This is kind of a special situation."

"You don't want us to call your sponsor?" Chelsea teased.

Mom looked at the hostess with contempt.

Dad kept a six pack of beer in the fridge. He only had a beer or two a night, there were three left in the fridge.

"If you want anything else we can get it," Chelsea said.

"Great, turn my wife back into an alcoholic," Dad said, clicking his teeth in anger.

"I was never an alcoholic," Mom snapped at him. "I never missed work, there was always food in the kitchen and the bills were paid."

"I'm not judging," Dad said but clearly was.

"You don't have any place to judge," Mom said loudly. "You can't even please your wife!"

Silence; the living room had become the most uncomfortable place in the world. Mara and I looked at each other and then at the strangers in our living room, wishing we were anywhere but *there*.

"I think I'll have a beer, too," Dad said, a whisper really.

What Mom had accused him of had clearly shaken him.

You can't even please your wife!

I saw the bridge in my head again; both of my parents were naked.

"I'm not getting into things on some fucking show," Mom said, taking a long drink of beer.

Mom *hadn't* ever been a "drunk," she had always made sure things were taken care of, but there had been a lot of bottles in the recycling--*a lot*. And she was not always pleasant to be around. Mom went to AA and got the sponsor Chelsea mentioned; this had been explained to Mara and I during a family meeting.

"I want a bottle of scotch," Mom added. "Single malt, the kind where you can taste the peat."

"Megan," Dad said gently, looking at her lovingly. "You don't want this, you really don't."

Mom looked at him then looked at the carpet.

"I'm not talking about this now, Kyle," she said. "Eventually these people will leave our house and I will call Rick---"

"Wait, Rick is still your sponsor?" Dad looked confused and angry.

Mom looked uncomfortable, the bottle of beer was nearly empty. She tipped it back to suck out the foam.

"Can we have drinks, too?" Mara asked. "Maybe white wine or something." She wasn't speaking for me; I think drinking is gross. I drank one time, just to try it out, and all it did was make me sick. Lesson learned.

"No," Dad said in a tough tone that sounded foolish coming out of his mouth, a comedian playing in an action movie. He looked at Mom again, and spoke in a careful tone of voice. "I thought you were getting another sponsor."

"We are not talking about this now," Mom said, something in her tone of voice shut Dad down.

WHAT IS THE DEAL WITH RICK?

"Okay, what is the deal with Rick?" Mara asked Mom and Dad after walking back into the living room as I was telling a story.

"Noah was telling us about these kittens he found at school," Dad frowned at her.

"Fuck the kittens," Mara said, pursing her lips, clearly enjoying tossing her little bomb.

"Mara," Mom said quietly, looking into the glass of neat scotch she was sipping. They had brought the bottle in two minutes after she requested it; the producers were clearly a thousand steps ahead of us.

"I know this is an unusual situation," Mom continued. "But we need to be nice to each other."

My mother looked up at Chelsea with a hate she didn't bother to conceal.

"And we are not discussing private family business with strangers," Mom added

"Maybe they already know," I said even though I knew *maybe* didn't belong in my observation.

"Yeah," Mara agreed. "They've probably already talked to Rick and if you guys were texting or whatever---"

The look Mom gave Mara made my sister flinch; it was definitely a *we're having a serious conversation when these people leave* look.

Dad was chuckling, I had no idea how he could find anything that was going on funny.

"I haven't texted him since you and I discussed things," Mom said, looking over at Dad. "I have been totally straight with you---"

"No," Dad said, you could tell he was upset. "Rick is still your sponsor therefore you have *not* been straight with me."

Mom said something so softly I couldn't hear her.

"Things will work out, guys," Dad said to the three of us, giving Mom the most cursory glance. "Your mother and I still have good jobs---"

"Actually," Chelsea said. "You don't."

"What?" Dad frowned.

Mom seemed to think that was funny and took another drink.

"Megan resigned without notice," Chelsea explained. "On Monday you, Kyle, will be called into a video conference with HR. They are going to have to let you go."

"And why is that?" Dad said with a caustic smile.

"They found a bunch of pornography on a work computer---"

"Of course they did!" Dad laughed. "You people thought of everything!" He scowled and shook his head before walking into the kitchen to get a beer.

"You've completely fucked us over," Mom mumbled with a dazed expression. "Awesome."

Chelsea had brought a chair over so she could face the four of us, focusing on Mom.

"Why do you look at it that way?" The hostess asked. "Neither you nor your husband enjoy your jobs."

"Enjoy?" Mom said with a cold smile. "Life is not about *enjoying* things. We have two kids to think about, we have a mortgage and car payments---"

"Not anymore," Chelsea clarified.

"Whatever," Mom replied. "When you leave we will just have to get new jobs and buy new cars and everything else."

She sat forward in the chair and stared at the hostess.

"All you've done is make our lives more difficult, that's all; all so you have your stupid show."

"Maybe we need *this*," Mara said.

"Why do you have to be like this?" Mom turned on her. "I love you but...it would be easier---for *you*, Mara---if you could be more like your brother. He isn't into all this *dark shit*, he has friends and works hard in school, he befriends the mentally challenged kids, he even rescues kittens."

"Come on, Mom," I said. "Leave her alone."

"I love Mara," Mom continued, starting to slur a little. "But I just wish she was more like you, *for her sake*."

"You don't know anything," I replied. It was the truth, she didn't.

DEAD KITTEN

Chelsea had me take her into my room; I'm sure many people have had fantasies along those lines. I respected the fact that she was a strong, successful woman in a patriarchal world but she seemed fake: Clothes I am guessing were expensive. Elaborate hair style. Perfume. Bleached teeth. The only thing that seemed real were her eyes, they were hard, cunning. Alive. We went into my room and closed the door. She motioned for me to sit on my bed and then she sat next to me; close. I could feel her clothes against mine and the warmth beneath them. She was doing something, that was obvious, trying to get in my head or something like that. Chelsea was looking around my room as if she were seeing it for the first time; I knew the show enough to understand that the *Reset* people knew every piece of furniture and poster, probably knew every piece of clothing I owned.

"You rescued some kittens the other day," Chelsea said softly, it reminded me of the tone of voice my girlfriend used when feeling romantic.

Fake. I told myself that but still felt aroused. Chelsea looked down at the front of my pants; it was a quick look which was clearly a part of her whole performance.

"Yeah, it was no big deal," I replied. "Someone had dropped them off, wrapped them in a dirty sheet and left them in some bushes."

"How did you find them?"

The top couple of buttons of Chelsea's blouse were unbuttoned and you could see the top of her breasts, they looked tanned, like she had been out in the sun naked---

And here you are objectifying women like one of those bros in day glow shorts with date rape drugs in their wallets.

I pointedly looked away.

"I heard them making kitten sounds---"

"Mewing?"

"I guess. The sheet was filthy, I didn't want to touch it but I was worried---"

"That the kittens could be in trouble?"

"Yeah."

I was still fully aroused and it made me feel....

Weird? No, not just weird but weird was part of it.

I felt guilty for objectifying her, but also I felt weak because Chelsea was clearly playing a game and I was falling for it---

I also felt guilty because I wanted her to see my hard dick; it felt like my erection was part of everything....

I can't explain it, I'm sure that thought makes no sense at all.

"What did you do?"

"I grabbed a corner of the sheet. They started mewing even more...the sheet smelled like feces---"

"You can say shit, Noah---"

"Okay. Anyway, I grabbed a corner and tried to shake it out. I could feel them, little balls of weight; I was being gentle as I could but I really was grossed out by the sheet...the shit smell."

There were four kittens but one was dead. It tumbled out and didn't move like the other ones; just a tiny thing, dead long long before its time---

And my erection was gone. And I was crying. Chelsea was the last person I wanted to cry around but I couldn't help it: Tears ran down both cheeks. I opened my mouth and gasped; the grief was too strong for the prison of my body.

She patted my leg, it was terrible.

"We both know this isn't about a dead kitten, is it?"

I said nothing in response.

NO PHONES, NO TABLETS, NO LAPTOPS

I grabbed my phone on the way out of my room. When I got back to the living room the female camera op took it from me.

"Sorry," Chelsea said from behind me. "No phones, no tablets, no laptops."

"Afraid we'll call the cops?" Dad smirked.

"No," Chelsea said with a tight smile. "So you can focus. This is important, the most important weekend of your lives."

"You're going to be here the whole weekend?" Mom sighed.

"That's usually how long it takes," Chelsea replied.

A few minutes after midnight Mara was nodding off. Chelsea suggested that my sister go to bed. Knowing her she was probably just lying in bed thinking about things, about the things Mom had said to Dad, about Rick. I walked to her room and knocked on the door.

"It's unlocked," Mara said.

I opened the door, walked in, and closed the door behind me.

"I'm sorry Mom was mean to you like that," I said.

Her new painting was turning out really good, not as good as the cowboy but still something she had every right to be proud of. I told her the painting was good and she smiled at that. Art is my sister's whole identity and that makes me worry, like she's setting herself up for disappointment.

"But do you like it as much as the cowboy painting?" Mara asked.

"No... almost, but the cowboy is still my favorite."

"Everyone says that."

I sat on the floor crossed legged, back against a wall.

"Who do you think contacted the show?" I asked.

Honestly, I suspected it was Mara since she was the one obsessed with the stupid show.

"Is it relevant.?"

She had a point.

"I guess not," I replied. "Whoever did it, I think it could be a positive thing."

"Are you comfortable with being broke and homeless?" Mara asked.

Then she smirked in a way that irritates everyone who knows her before continuing.

"What am I saying? You work at the food bank, your customers there will probably show you the ropes."

I know what my sister thinks of me, that I'm too serious, and I said as much.

The smirk left her face; I could tell she was thinking about something, something big and possibly sad and asked what it was.

"I just miss us being weird kids together," Mara eventually replied. "I remember when you were a punk with your black jeans, listening to Green Day. You were snarky back then, you could be really fun."

"I changed," I said. It sounded lame out in the air but it was the best way to sum it up.

"Yeah?" My sister was clearly expecting more.

"It wasn't fun for me," I continued. "Something needed to change."

I stood up and looked at her painting again. The boat looked lonely, it seemed to need a lonely man standing on it; I said as much to my sister.

"A man?" She sounded unsure.

"Yeah," I said as I reached for the doorknob. "A man, one man with a lonely face.."

I wanted to stay in my bedroom but a few moments after my eyes opened a man in a ski mask walked in and told me I needed to dress and go to the living room. Dad had this wistful look and was turning over the remote control over and over in his hands, looking at it as if it had some precious memories. Mara walked in. She had forgotten to put on a bra and one of the guys in the ski masks was staring at her like a creeper. The front of his pants changed, I felt disgusted.

"I remember Saturday morning when I was a kid," Dad said. "I used to watch cartoons as I ate my cereal, Speed Racer was my favorite."

Chelsea had been drinking coffee from a mug and smiling a little as my father talked.

"I was more into Scooby Doo," she replied with a nod. "Then they brought in a little dog---"

"Scrappy Doo---" Dad scowled.

"Yeah," Chelsea laughed a little. "*Scrappy Doo*, and it wasn't as good anymore."

"Scrappy Doo was the death of that cartoon," Dad sighed.

"Is there more coffee?" Mara asked.

"I don't know," Dad smiled over at her.

"A little," Chelsea nodded over at my sister, she seemed to be looking right at her breasts. "Get it before it's gone."

Mara walked back in a few seconds later carrying Mom's favorite mug. I saw it for what it was, one of my sister's little *fuck yous*. Dad was still talking about when he was a child, growing up before the internet; I can't even imagine how people kept from going crazy back then. Mara stood on the side of the living room, it was clear she was disgusted with our father and it

213

made me kind of disgusted with her. Mom walked in. Mara was watching her face, probably waiting for a reaction related to her using our mother's favorite mug. I couldn't see one. Mom walked into the kitchen then walked back out into the living room a minute later.

"Where are the filters?" She looked from Mara to me.

My sister rolled her eyes and walked into the kitchen, Mom followed her.

I had to wonder if they were going to argue; honestly, I didn't want to know.

KYLE

THE VICTORY OF TYRELL DUBE

I have lost track of the number of times Megan has started a Serious Discussion when I was falling asleep. One moment she'll be doing something on her laptop, usually work stuff, and the next moment the laptop is on her nightstand and her arms are crossed as she stares across the room. It's my job to ask what's up, not to ask *If there's a problem why didn't you bring it up hours ago*. This is the way the game is played. As tired as I was of those eleven p.m. Serious Discussions I rode them out; I love my family and would do whatever it took to keep it together. This is why when Megan suggested having a family game night I smiled and acted agreeable even though it made no sense; none of us are sports fans though Megan was on the cross country team in high school. She was not a sprinter, sprinters are good only for a short distance. Being a cross country runner takes more thought, more planning—you have to be able to look into the future and plan how to get there. I wasn't on a team in high school, not baseball or football or cross country; this is why my wife can run circles around me.

I made popcorn on family game night. No one ever ate it but I still made it, wanting to contribute something seeing as Megan had come up with the idea of family game night. She was always using words like *contribute* and *participate* and *being proactive* as if I was doing none of those things. I always bit my tongue when she said things like that; when she was boozing it up it was me who made sure the kids were doing okay, tried to let them know they were still loved and cared for, that we were still a family and eventually their mother would get help.

We were all doing stuff on our phones or tablets when the game changed; it became the sort of game that even people who aren't into sports become engrossed in. A player for the Gamblers, Tyrell Dube, started making basket after basket; he was moving like a dancer, none of the players on the opposing team could stop him. All four of us watched, sucked into the game—

"It's going to go into overtime,"Megan said with a mouth full of popcorn. What do you mean?" I asked.

"Watch," My wife replied.

Tyrell Dube made a long ass shot and the announcers confirmed what Megan had predicted. It reminded me of a dream I had in the recent past, I was in the stands sitting next to a fat man in a white suit who said---

"He loves it when they fall," I mumbled the words a man in a white suit had said to me in a dream. "He likes it even more when they bleed."

"What?" Noah asked.

And then the front door was opening; the door wasn't kicked in, whomever opened it had the key to the locks. I was half watching Tyrell Dube shoot another basket and half looking over at the door—

Was a stranger really walking in our house? How did they have a key? It was a blonde woman, good looking, it seemed she had work done. Behind her were a man and a woman, buff looking, the woman was built like a man but you could tell she had breasts. Both were wearing ski masks and carrying small cameras. I got up to confront the strangers; I have no idea what I thought I could do, I just wanted to protect my family—it should have been Meagan, at least she knows Kuk Sool. The blonde woman just smiled at me like a game show host as I walked up to her, asking what she was doing in our house.

Meagan must have gotten up behind me because the blonde was looking over my shoulder; her face had become shrewder, her smile thinner. Blonde

Woman said something about martial arts, how the two people in ski masks knew them as well.

"What's going on?" My wife asked.

"Reset," Mara said.

I turned to look at her and saw Megan doing the same. Noah looked frightened and it made me angry...angry and helpless.

"Reset?" I asked my daughter.

She looked at me in a funny way; it almost looked as if she pitied me.

"It's the Mayans," My daughter clarified.

The blonde asked us to sit back down and had one of the people in ski masks switch off the television. When the screen was black our guest told us that the Gamblers would win the game

"The game isn't over," my wife pointed out.

The blonde just smiled at her; she looked like a game show host again.

"It doesn't matter, Megan," the intruder smiled. "This is not about the NBA, this is about your family."

She took a small camera out of the bag, set it on top of the television, and aimed it at the couch where Noah and Mara were sitting. The blonde woman backed away and looked at the camera.

"Welcome to another chapter of Reset," She said. "Where you never see us coming..."

She turned towards the four of us.

"Or *three* of you didn't know this was coming, Shone family," The blonde added. "One of you contacted us, gave us the keys and alarm codes. We know everything, where you keep guns...we have accessed your bank accounts, car loans, the mortgage on this house, your 401ks—"

Those words, that claim...I felt sick...and then I realized that the intruder had to be lying.

"Wait---you can't just get to our money like that," I pointed out. "There are passwords, security measures."

"If having faith in that makes you happy," The blonde laughed at me. "Then...go with that!"

"What happens in this Reset, Noah?" Mom asked.

"Our lives are over," my son said. "Our bank accounts have been cleaned out, 401ks, whatever. The SUVs will be dismantled and sold for parts, the boat taken to Mexico and sold. When this is over, the furniture will be removed from the house and sold."

"So, this is a scam," I said firmly. "You just steal our money and stuff---"

"The money goes to charity," The blonde clarified.

"That money is so our kids can go to college!" My wife yelled.

"Relax, Megan," I said. "There is no way they can get away with this."

The blonde intruder looked from Megan to myself, still a game show host: *Do you want to spin the wheel or pick one of the three doors?* A small woman wearing a ski mask walked in carrying a bag that she sat on the coffee table next to the *Money* magazines.

"What's in the box?" My wife asked.

"It will be tempting to cause trouble," the intruder said. "Inside the box is assurance that we can all get along and be civil to one another."

"The Diapers of Distress," Noah said.

"We prefer to call them *the Garment*," Our guest nodded to him.

The blonde opened the box and pulled out what looked like a diaper.

"It's like a shock collar for your junk," Mara said, registering my confusion.

There was no way I was putting the damn thing on and said as much.

"Please, Kyle," The blonde said. "I won't hurt you or your family if you play along."

That was my breaking point, I told the blonde to get the hell out of our house and stepped towards her. Again, I am not a tough guy; I was just reacting, trying to protect my family as a man is supposed to do. The blonde reached in her purse and pulled something out—a taser. It hurt like hell but I didn't fall down, was able to make it to a chair.

"It doesn't have to be like this," The blonde said, she almost looked as if she had regretted tasing me. "Put on the Garment, play along, and no one gets hurt."

"You just take everything," Megan said.

I didn't see what happened, the taser had kicked my ass; I heard running, a scuffle, my wife crying out in pain, and then the sound of her falling into a chair. I looked over at Megan, she looked at me—all the problems we had been having no longer mattered. We were helpless for the moment, but we would figure out how to protect the kids; the look we exchanged said that.

"I'm sorry, kids," I said, looking at Noah and Mara plaintively.

"It's okay, there's nothing we can do," My daughter replied.

ACCUSATIONS

Mara was the first taken into her room to put on *the Garment*. I was worried but at least it was a woman who had followed her in; if they had wanted to rape my wife and daughter it was clear they could have done that at the beginning. The children were taken to their rooms and then the man in the ski mask took me to the master bedroom. He set the Garment on the bed and stood there watching me.

"Come on, dude," I said. "Give me a little privacy."

"You don't have to take off your underwear,"he said flatly. "In fact, we prefer that you don't."

Seeing no choice, I removed my pants, put the "Garment"over my boxers, and then pulled my pants back on. There was a small bulge in the back the size of a box of matches; it touched the base of my spine when I was standing up—what were the long term effects? If they jolted us could it lead to permanent paralysis?

"You look worried,"Ski mask said, his voice was gentle for a big dude in a ski mask.

"I'm just wondering if this thing could cause permanent effects."

"No, sir,"I saw a smile through the mask, it looked genuine, kind. "You may lose control of your bowels, but that is the worst thing that has ever happened.

"Lovely," I replied.

Back in the living room, Megan was asking the blonde her name.

"I'm sorry," the blonde laughed. "My name is Chelsea Seen; your kids have seen the show but maybe that's a generational thing."

I was confused: Why were they still there? Why had they made us put on the Garments? If they had our money and everything else why were they sticking around? Was that part of the show? I asked Chelsea for clarification. She smiled at me, it looked like she was flirting—damn, she was good, not a game show host, someone who could sell a dozen cars a day.

"What's wrong, Kyle? Don't you like me?"

I just started back, Chelsea was the first to blink.

"This isn't just about money," She said. "One of you told us all about the situation around here. We dug deeper---"

She paused to nod at my wife.

"---the Shone family is kind of a mess, isn't it?"

"You have no right to judge us," Megan said, kind of bitchy, not that I blame her. "You broke into our home, you assaulted us---"

"And I may be able to save you," Chelsea smiled.

"Save us?" I had to laugh at that. "You took all our money. How the hell are we supposed to live? We were saving that for retirement, for the kids to go to college!"

"Noah and Mara will still be able to go to college," Chelsea said. "We would not deprive them of that. All the money we get goes in a pool, a chain of investments. You will not be homeless, your children will not be denied an education."

"I don't get this," My wife mumbled. "I need a drink."

Mara, Noah, and I looked at her—her worried and caring family---Megan stared back.

"It's okay," she said. "This is kind of a special situation."

"You don't want us to call your sponsor?" Chelsea teased.

My wife looked at the hostess hatefully, I didn't understand why until a few minutes later.

I kept a six pack of beer in the fridge. While my wife was recovering I kept it in a small fridge in his office; I told her I was going to stop drinking to support her and Megan got angry. *Angry.* Really? I was trying to be the good guy and that was what I got? So, I kept beer in my office. After having a beer I'd suck an Altoid before being around Megan again. After several months my wife told me that she was okay with the beer being in the fridge. I only drank one a night; when Chelsea showed up I want to say there was half a six pack in the fridge.

"If you want anything else we can get it," Chelsea said to my wife.

"You must know that my wife has been fighting a drinking problem," I said.

"I was never a drunk," My wife turned on me. "I always took care of things, always brought money in."

"I'm not judging." I wasn't, I was concerned.

"You don't have any place to judge," Megan shrieked. "You can't even please your wife!"

Why…why would she say such an awful thing, especially around our children? Stuff like that messes kids up---

"I think I'll have a beer, too," I said.

I was allowed to get my wife and I beers from the kitchen. Standing next to the fridge, I looked over at the knife rack—

Yeah, right; me with a knife against tasers and martial artists.

I really was tempted by those knives, though; I needed to do *something.* Maybe Megan was right, maybe I had been sleepwalking through my role as a husband and maybe even as a father, as well. I grabbed the beers but not a knife; what kind of man was I?

When I walked back into the living room my wife was yelling at Chelsea.

"I'm not talking about it on some fucking show!"

Megan roughly twisted the cap off the bottle and took a long drink. She had let the cap drop to the floor; my wife was always just leaving stuff around…dirty clothes in the bathroom that I would put in the hamper. I watched Megan's neck as she drank, worried she was jumping back into something much stronger than herself. As she said during many Serious Discussions, Meg had always met her responsibilities, had never missed a day of work…but we were just ghosts to her. Me…whatever…but I can tell it hurt the kids. They would never say anything, teenagers don't talk to their parents---we think they do but they really don't—but I can read Mara and Noah.

My wife killed the beer and set it on the coffee table; I set it on the art book so it didn't leave a ring. Megan burped a little and told Chelsea that she wanted a bottle of good whiskey.

"Megan," I said with a wary sort of love. "You don't want this, you really don't."

She looked at me….was she mad at me? Why *then*? A second later my wife looked down at her feet.

"We're not getting into this, Kyle," she said firmly. "Eventually these people will leave our house and I will call Rick---"

That hit me like the taser, but instead of shock it was like my stomach was being twisted.

"Wait, Rick is still your sponsor?"

The guilt I saw on my wife's face turned the twisting sensation in my guts to nausea.

"Can we have drinks, too?" Mara asked. "Maybe white wine or something."

"No," I said firmly before looking at my wife. "We talked about this, I thought you were getting another sponsor."

"We are not talking about this now," Megan said flatly, her tone of voice shutting me down.

RICK

Chelsea and Mara went into my daughter's room and closed the door. It may have looked as if I was watching them but I was averting my face from my wife's view. The conversation reminded me of the texts, *sexts* is the modern expression, I guess. Rick started the whole thing, openly flirtatious. Megan's replies were also flirtatious, but that wasn't the problem; the problem was that she didn't stop him.

You're my sponsor, I'm depending on you helping me through this without these heated texts.

Did she text that? No, she flirted back. Rick got more and more lurid, going from telling my wife how pretty she was and how beautiful her eyes were, to what he thought about her breasts, how he imagined her nipples were. By that point, Megan had stopped responding…that didn't stop Rick from sending a dick pic; either he had small hands or a large penis. I found the sexts because Megan had been acting weird, she seemed especially weird when checking her phone. So, the next time she left her mobile unsupervised I snooped. When I confronted her, my wife was defensive, *defensive*—how could she be defensive when she was in the wrong?

"We need to report him," I told her.

"No, no just…let me deal with it."

Megan later told me she texted Rick, told him his texts were inappropriate, and that if he sent any more she'd report him. That was what my wife told me, at least. During the next argument, Megan said that at least Rick was interested in her, that at least he desired her and wanted to fuck her. Even after nineteen years of marriage my wife still expected us to have sex basically every day; was that reasonable? If we didn't have sex for a week or two Megan grew moody and eventually angry. After the sexts, she would remind me that there were men out there who wanted to fuck her…

I think the worst part of the situation was that, thinking of Rick fucking my wife with his big cock, I got turned on a few times. Even jerked off once.

It was easy to see that something had been bothering Noah, that he had been preoccupied with something even before the home invasion. My son looked around at the invaders and the cameras and then told us about some kittens he had found at school---

And then Mara walked in from the hallway.

"What is the situation with Rick?" She interrupted, looking from Megan to me and then back to my wife.

"Noah was telling us about these kittens he found at school," I shook my head.

"Fuck the kittens," Mara said.

"Mara," My wife said quietly, looking into the glass of neat scotch she was gulping down.

"I know this is a weird situation," she added. "But we need to be nice to each other."

Megan looked up at Chelsea with open dislike.

"And we are not discussing private family business with strangers," My wife finished.

"Maybe they already know," Noah said softly.

"Yeah," My daughter agreed. "They've probably already interviewed Rick, if you guys were texting or whatever—"

I thought of Chelsea seeing the dick pic, wondered if it would turn her on, and then I imagined Rick fucking *her* and became aroused, crossing my legs before anyone could see. Megan gave our daughter a dirty look; it was definitely a *we're having a serious conversation when these people leave* look.

Everything was so fucked up and ridiculous I started laughing, chuckling at first, then really laughing—I couldn't help it. Megan gave *me* a dirty look and I pulled myself back together.

"I haven't texted him telling him to stop texting me," My wife said firmly. "I have been totally straight with you—"

"No," I replied, struggling with my anger. "Rick is still your sponsor therefore you have *not* been straight with me."

"What do you care," Megan said so quietly I could barely hear her.

The rest of my family was bummed out, *I* was bummed out but knew either my wife or myself had to rally the troops.

"It's going to be okay, guys," I said, looking to my wife to back me up.

"Your mother and I still have good jobs---"

"Actually," Chelsea said. "You don't."

"What?" I asked.

Megan looked amused and took another drink; why was she smirking?

"Megan resigned effective immediately," Chelsea explained. "On Monday you, Kyle, will be called into a video conference with HR. They are going to have to let you go."

"And why is that?" I asked..

"They found a bunch of pornography on a work computer---"

"Of course they did!" I laughed; the show's producers really *had* thought of everything.

I told everyone in the room that I was getting a beer and asked if the kids needed anything from the fridge. Neither responded. I walked in the kitchen and looked at the knives again. Maybe they would break a wrist or an arm if I ran in with a cleaver or the butcher knife, maybe the pain would have been a welcome distraction—I didn't want another man fucking my wife. The thing was, I had no interest in fucking her myself. I had no idea why and had no idea how to fix the situation. I had suggested marriage counseling but my wife had shot that down.

You're the one who needs therapy to work through your shit! I'm too busy to coddle you and hold your hand!

But I *had* gone to a therapist and she had told me that both my wife and I were to blame and that we should find a couple's counselor. Again, my wife shot the idea down.

In the present, I opened the fridge and grabbed a beer. I took one more look at the knives and then walked back into the living room.

My wife was yelling at Chelsea and then shaking her head as she smiled ruefully.

"Whatever," Megan said. "When you leave we will just have to get new jobs and buy new cars and everything else."

She sat forward in the chair and hard stared the hostess.

"All you've done is make our lives more difficult," my wife added. "Is this how your stupid show got so popular, ruining the lives of good people?"

"Maybe we need this," Mara said.

"Why do you have to be like this?" Megan turned on our daughter viciously. "It would be easier for you if you could be more like your brother. He isn't into all this *dark shit*, he has friends and works hard in school, he befriends the mentally challenged kids, he even rescues kittens."

"Come on, Mom," Noah said. "Leave her alone."

It should have been *me* defending our daughter, but I was in shock how brutal my wife was being.

Maybe I should divorce her and fight to get custody of the kids.

"I love Mara," Mom continued, she sounded sloppy drunk. "But I just wish she was more like you, *for her sake.*"

"You don't know anything," Noah said softly.

Noah wanted to go to his room. Chelsea went with him leaving the rest of us with the two intruders in ski masks.

"This is stupid," I pointed out. "Why are you filming us when she isn't here?"

"Why don't you just pretend she's here," the male cameraperson said, like the woman he had a gentle voice.

"This is just *ridiculous*," I added. "I'm guessing we will get kicked out of the house."

Even more of a reason to split up, get a fresh start for the kids and I.

"That's part of it," the man with the camera said. "But there is a place for you if you want it. Chelsea will be able to explain it better."

"Why don't you talk about the text from Rick?" The woman camera operator asked, focusing on me and then Megan.

"I am not talking about that with strangers," She said firmly.

"It's safe to assume that the Show has access to your text messages," the male said. "What would stop us from cutting to the texts from this discussion?"

"Uh, because we could sue your asses!" Megan slurred loudly, weaving like a snake in her chair. "Because those are private conversations and there are laws protecting people."

"We entered your house and are holding you against your will," the female said. "Do you really think the Show is concerned about *laws*?"

"Ah, you got to a good part without me!" Chelsea laughed as she walked back into the room.

"Is Noah okay?" Dad asked.

"Yeah, he just got to talking about stuff and it got emotional," Chelsea smiled kindly. "He just needs a few to get it together."

She sat back down, looked from Megan to me and back to Megan again.

"You were about to talk about the texts, I can smell it!" Chelsea said.

"Rick and I were sexting, he did most of it," my wife said softly. "We never did anything, but it has been tempting."

"*Has* been tempting," I replied. "Note how it is present tense."

"What do you care?" Megan turned to me with a frown. "If I *was* with someone else it would take you off the hook."

She took a sip off her drink, read her lines off the bottom of the glass.

"You always close your eyes," she said softly. "I ask what you're thinking about and you always say you're just enjoying the moment--I know you're thinking about someone else. And then there's the history on your phone…"

She trailed off with a shake of her head. I just looked at her; my wife appeared sad, deeply hurt, and I felt guilty for that. *Why* didn't I get turned on by her anymore? Why did I have to look at porn to get aroused to fuck my beautiful wife? I had no idea, all I understood was that things couldn't go on as they were.

MEGAN GETS VICIOUS AGAIN

"What did you mean when you said we'd be taken care of?" I asked Chelsea.

"Money from our contestants goes to a place we call the Haven," She explained. "It's a place out in the country with a bunch of cabins; contestants can stay out there as long as they want but if it's full time they have to do work around the place."

Great. If we needed a place to live we got to stay on fucking *commune*.

"Sounds lovely," I said sarcastically.

"It kind of does," Megan slurred. "Just...relax."

Chelsea seemed pleased by that—

Maybe she has a big dick she can fuck my wife with, as well—

I am seriously losing my shit.

"It's a good way to reset," Chelsea nodded. "Clear your head, see what your priorities really are."

Something about that triggered something in Megan who looked up at the hostess with venom.

"We *had* what we wanted: We had a home, we had been saving money for our retirement; we provided for our kids---"

"This place sucks," Mara said.

"Then we will legally emancipate you and you can live in a fucking squalid art studio or whatever it is you want!" Megan shouted at her.

"Megan, *stop*," I said firmly. I grabbed her arm but she shook it off because I am the bad guy who doesn't send her pictures of his oversized dick.

And then I saw regret on my wife's face as if her words were a boomerang that had come back and struck her. It was a relief to see that, even if a lot of it was due to the alcohol; maybe my wife still did care about the kids. I know she loved them, would do anything for them, but she could be distant, *cavalier*, as Mara would say.

"Mara," My wife's voice was equally slurred and shaky as if she were on the verge of tears. "I don't...I don't know what to do with you. I love you so much but I don't know...we're so different."

That's all she got out; if she had tried to say anymore Megan would have cried and I know her well enough to understand she would never cry in front of Chelsea.

Noah walked back in with his phone in his hand, the female camera op took it from him.

"Sorry," Chelsea said. "No phones, no tablets, no laptops."

"Afraid we'll call the cops?" I asked

"No," Chelsea said with a tight smile. "So you can focus. This is important, the most important weekend of your lives."

"You're going to be here the whole weekend?" Megan whined.

"That's usually how long it takes," Chelsea replied.

A few minutes after midnight Mara was nodding off. I got her a blanket from the closet and Chelsea told us that we could sleep in our rooms with the caveat that cameras were in place. My daughter walked out of the living room followed by Noah a couple of minutes later. Megan poured another three fingers of whiskey; the bottle was now a little more than half full. I wanted to try to talk her into easing back but knew she would not take that well. If anything, it would make her drink more.

And I also understand she's drinking like this in part because all the talk about the texts reminds her of how neglected she feels, that she craves attention even from creeps like Rick.

I had the feeling that she didn't want to share a bed with me that night. Even though I was sleepy, I didn't go in our room because I wanted my wife to have the bed. There was a couch in my office, but if I went in there then maybe Megan would feel rejected—

I had no fucking idea what to do.

"Do you mind sleeping on the couch in your office?" Megan asked.

"No, that's fine."

I was relieved she had brought it up but it also hurt; I felt like I had lost her, the woman I loved. I understood my role, but why hadn't she agreed to marriage counseling? Maybe a professional could have saved our marriage.

SCOOBY DOO

I didn't sleep well and was the first one in the living room; the first member of our family, at least—two different ski mask people were there. They must have contacted Chelsea because fifteen minutes later the host of the show walked in the living room.

"Is there coffee?"She asked.

I went into the kitchen and started a pot. Megan never made coffee, had never bothered learning how. I made it and taught the kids how to once they started drinking coffee. When the coffee was done brewing, I got cups for Chelsea and I. The ski mask people didn't want it, maybe they thought I'd try to poison them or something.

"I remember Saturday morning when I was a kid," I said, not sure why the memory was coming back. "First thing I'd do was pour a bowl of cereal and then go into the living room to watch cartoons, sitting on the floor with my back against the couch and my legs under the coffee table."

"Did you have a favorite?" Chelsea asked with a smile.

I had to think about that for a few seconds.

"Scooby Doo."

"I liked Scooby Doo, as well," she replied with a nod. "Then they brought in a little dog---"

"Scrappy Doo---" I sighed.

"Yeah," Chelsea laughed a little. "*Scrappy Doo*, and it wasn't as good anymore."

"Scrappy Doo was the nadir of that cartoon," I agreed.

"Is there more coffee?" Mara asked, I hadn't even noticed her walking in.

"I don't know," I replied.

"A little," Chelsea nodded at my daughter. "Get it before it's gone."

When Mara was getting coffee more of my childhood memories came back. Chelsea seemed about the age of my wife and I so I asked if she remembered the old days before cable television and the internet. She seemed into the conversation; Chelsea seemed like a friend, someone I could see hanging out with—

She was also our jailor, the person who had destroyed us. Megan walked in and it was easy to see that she was hungover. And then my wife was looking at our daughter—the green cup, Mara had taken the green mug knowing it was Megan's favorite. After a couple of seconds, my wife walked into the kitchen.

"Where are the filters?" She called out.

Mara rolled her eyes and walked into the kitchen.

MEGAN

As I tuned into the Gamblers game, I could hear the microwave and smell popcorn cooking. Kyle always made popcorn for family game night as if his putting a couple of bags into a microwave could fix things. We were dealing with gushing wounds and there was my husband holding a band aid with a sheepish grin on his face. I've never liked popcorn, the smell reminds me of depressing office break rooms---that dislike has turned into passionate disgust; it has become a metaphor for half assed efforts, of people who pretend they care but don't actually.

My husband thinks I am a bitch. I have no idea how long this has gone on, he would certainly never be open enough to admit such a thing, but I can see it on his face. *Bitch.* Well…it has always been *the bitch* who gets things done because at least the bitch is proactive and is actively participating in our marriage.

That family game night was no different than any other family game night: All four of us doing things on our tablets or phones. Kyle occasionally looking over at me with that sick dog look of his:
Why do you seem upset? Why can't you ever give me a break, cut me some slack? Why do you have to be such a…
Bitch.
At the beginning of the fourth quarter the game changed, became exciting. I'm the only one in the family who has ever had even a remote interest in sports, even followed the LA Lakers for a few seasons. Mara, being a cynic, liked to say that I picked something we all hated for family game night. No, I never stopped enjoying basketball, it was just with the kids and then my career I stopped having time for it. That night, the Gamblers' forward,

Tyrell Dube, suddenly shifted into another gear, a gear none of the other players had. I got sucked in, it was like twenty years ago when I was in college and would scream when Kobe would make a play. Kyle and the kids were also drawn in. I was so into the game, I actually started shoving popcorn into my mouth.

"It's going to go into overtime," I said.

What do you mean?" Kyle asked.

"Watch."

Dube made a shot from behind the key and the announcers confirmed what I had seen coming.

"He loves it when they fall," My husband mumbled. "He likes it even more when they bleed."

"What?" Noah asked.

And then I sensed something, a sound, a key in the deadbolt—

All four people who were supposed to have a key were in the room---

The intruder was a superficial looking blonde woman in an expensive suit, I thought I recognized the brand. Behind her were a man and a woman, burly, the woman was built like a man though you could tell she had boobs. Both were wearing ski masks and carrying small cameras. Kyle got up to confront the strangers; dorky Kyle trying to look after us; it was as idiotic as it was endearing. The blonde woman just smiled at him like a timeshare salesperson as he tried to be all butch, demanding what she was doing in our house. Afraid he would get hurt, I jumped up and came around Kyle's side; the blonde didn't look hard but the way the people in ski masks moved alluded to a knowledge of some sort of martial art or military training. Sure enough, the blonde told me that both ski masks were a couple of levels ahead of me in Kuk Sool. It seemed like a weird coincidence; kuk sool is not as popular as judo or karate or jujitsu.

"What's happening here?" I asked.

"Reset," Mara said.

I turned to look at her and saw Kyle doing the same.

"Reset?" Kyle asked our daughter.

She looked at him in a funny way: *Ah, Dad, silly old Dad.* Her face seemed to say that.

"It's the Mayans," My daughter clarified.

The blonde asked us to sit back down and had one of the people in ski masks switch off the television. When the screen was black our guest told us that the Gamblers would win the game

"There's still two minutes eighteen seconds left," I pointed out.

The blonde just smiled at me: *You know, this timeshare arrangement is a great deal for you and your family.*

"It doesn't matter, Megan," the intruder smiled. "This is not about the NBA, this is about your family."

She took a small camera out of the bag, set it on top of the television, and aimed it at the couch where Noah and Mara were sitting. The blonde woman backed away and looked at the camera.

"Welcome to another chapter of Reset," She said. "Where you never see us coming…"

She turned towards the four of us.

"Or *three* of you didn't know this was coming, Shone family," The blonde added, looking over at me. "One of you contacted us, gave us the keys and alarm codes. We know everything, where you keep guns…we have accessed your bank accounts, car loans, the mortgage on this house, your 401ks—"

I kept my face neutral: This was happening, this was really happening—was this what we needed?

"Wait---you can't just get to our money like that," Kyle whined. "There are passwords, security measures."

"If having faith in that makes you happy," The blonde laughed at him. "Then...go with that!"

"What happens in this Reset, Noah?" It seemed a good thing for me to be asking.

"Our lives are over," my son said. "Our bank accounts have been cleaned out, 401ks, whatever. The SUVs will be dismantled and sold for parts, the boat taken to Mexico and sold. When this is over, the furniture will be removed from the house and sold."

Anxiety, I rarely feel anxiety….anxiety or guilt.

"So, this is a scam," Kyle said gruffly. "You just steal our money and stuff---"

"The money goes to charity," The blonde clarified.

"That money is so our kids can go to college," I replied.

"Relax, Megan," Kyle said, trying to be the man in charge. "There is no way they can get away with this."

The blonde intruder looked from Kyle to myself, still selling timeshare: *You have to admit, it's a great deal: For a tenth the cost of a house you have weeks in a vacation paradise.*

A woman wearing a ski mask, much smaller than the other two, walked in carrying a bag that she sat on the coffee table next to the *Money* magazines.

"What's in the box?" I asked.

"It will be tempting to cause trouble," the intruder said. "Inside the box is insurance so we can all be friends."

"The Diapers of Distress," Noah said.

"We prefer to call them *the Garment*," The blonde nodded to him.

She opened the box and pulled out what looked like a diaper.

"It's like a shock collar for your junk," Mara said, registering Kyle's confusion.

My husband made an ugly face and muttered an obscenity and how there was no way blah blah blah.

"Please, Kyle," The blonde said. "I won't hurt you or your family if you play along."

Mara and Noah's father told the blonde to get the hell out of our house and stepped towards her—

What do you think that will accomplish, Kyle? Do you really think---

And then the blonde reached in her purse and pulled out something, a taser. Kyle made a ridiculous noise, flopped some, and fell in front of a chair.

"It doesn't have to be like this," The blonde said, she almost looked as if she had regretted tasing Kyle. "Put on the Garment, play along, and no one gets hurt."

"You just take everything," I said.

Everyone had been distracted by Kyle's little show. He had made a show of "standing up for his family" and I understood that I had to as well when I broke and ran for the hall to the bedroom. A woman leapt from the kitchen. If you knew nothing about martial arts you would assume that we tried some martial arts moves on each other. Unfortunately, the woman on the ski mask connected and I saw stars. I staggered towards a chair and she helped me into it. Kyle looked over at me plaintively and I understood how weak and vulnerable he was and how the things that had been set in motion would hurt him.

Again, guilt. I looked away from him.

"I'm sorry, kids," he said, looking from Noah to Mara.

"It's okay, there's nothing we can do," Our daughter replied.

CHELSEA INTRODUCES HERSELF

Mara was the first one taken into her room to put in *the Garment*.

I could see that Kyle was worried so I reached over and squeezed his hand. It felt weird, comforting him, so I quickly let go. The children were taken to their rooms and then Kyle was taken to the master bedroom and I was taken to Kyle's office for whatever reason.

Kyle and I got back to the living room at the same time; I asked the blonde her name.

"I'm sorry," she laughed. "My name is Chelsea Seen; your kids have clearly watched our show but maybe that's a generational thing."

Kyle asked the blonde why, if they had already cleaned us out, why the intruders were still in our house.

"What's wrong, Kyle? Don't you like me?"

Kyle got all flustered, I was sure he'd jerk off later to some silly fantasy of the blonde woman.

"This isn't just about money," Chelsea said. "One of you told us all about the situation around here. We dug deeper---"

She paused and nodded at me, I felt exposed.

"---the Shone family is kind of a mess, isn't it?"

"You have no right to judge us," I said, keeping my voice (hopefully) unreadable. "You broke into our home, you assaulted us---"

"And I may be able to save you," Chelsea smiled.

"Save us?" Kyle laughed. "You took all our money. How the hell are we supposed to live? We were saving that for retirement, for the kids to go to college!"

"Noah and Mara will still be able to go to college," Chelsea said. "We would not deprive them of that. All the money we get goes in a pool, a chain of investments. You will not be homeless, your children will not be denied an education."

"I don't get this," I mumbled. "I need a drink."

Mara, Noah, and Kyle looked at me—wasn't this something they would expect me to do in a stressful situation?

"It's okay," I said. "This is kind of a special situation."

"You don't want us to call your sponsor?" Chelsea teased.

Was she really going there? I felt betrayed.

Kyle kept a six pack of beer in the fridge. When I was working through my drinking problem he had offered to stop drinking himself. I knew what he was up to: My husband was trying to win points, to be the *good guy*. That is one of Kyle's mantras when I bring up the issues we have: *Why are you being like this? I'm not a bad guy, I'm a good guy.*

He does these trivial things, like offer to give up beer or make popcorn, and thinks it will cause me to overlook how he has failed our marriage.

"If you want anything else we can get it," Chelsea said to me.

Why was she looking at me? Was she trying to turn my family against me?

"You must know that my wife has been fighting a drinking problem," Kyle said; you could hear the *judgey* in his voice.

"I was never a drunk," I pointed out. "I always took care of things, always brought money in."

"I'm not judging." Liar.

He gets this look on his face, this know it all passive aggressive little wince, it makes me see red—always.

"You don't have any place to judge," I yelled. "You can't even please your wife!"

I fucked up. I mean, I totally meant what I said, but it was over the top; the kids looked deeply embarrassed.

"I think I'll have a beer, too," Kyle said weakly.

Kyle went into the kitchen to get us beers. Knowing him he was probably looking at the cast iron skillet or the knives and having some macho daydream. Chelsea kept needling me to talk about what I had said to Kyle as if she didn't already know. When Kyle walked back in she pointed at me and I took it as a cue.

"I'm not talking about it on some fucking show!" I yelled.

With thanks, I took the bottle from Kyle and took a long drink. Kyle was watching me, it was supposed to be with concern but it just looked...judgey. I needed to numb myself to keep from yelling so I finished the beer and set it on the coffee table. Kyle decided to be bitchy and set the bottle on the Monet book so it didn't leave a ring even though I'd told him dozens of times that the table was okay....and the book cost seventy-five fucking dollars.

"Megan," Kyle said. "You don't want this, you really don't."

And I could hear by the tone of his voice that he was sincere, that he loved me. It wasn't enough; what good is a marriage if one spouse is leaving the other unfulfilled and feeling like they're doing all the work?

"We're not getting into this, Kyle," I said firmly. "Eventually these people will leave our house and I will call Rick---"

"Wait, Rick is still your sponsor?" You could hear an edge in his voice, a real edge, not that pretend macho stuff.

"Can we have drinks, too?" Mara asked. "Maybe white wine or something."

"No," Kyle barked before looking at me. "We talked about this, I thought you were getting another sponsor."

"We are not talking about this now," I said in a tone of voice that left no room for argument.

RICK'S PENIS

Rick was a good sponsor. The thing is, he was also a creep. He was tall, a little stooped over...I don't know, you could tell he liked to smoke weed and listen to jam bands. His smile, you just *knew* what really made him smile was seeing fifteen year old girls spilling out of bikinis. He had hair up to his neck; the hair just exploded out of the neckline of his shirts as if someone had set a hair bomb in there. Rick also always smelled like garlic, *always*, like he ate cloves of it. And his *shoes*...not even going there.

The thing is, it was clear Rick wanted me. He thought I was hot and it felt good to have a man look at me that way. When had Kyle last looked at me that way? Fifteen years? Longer? Rick's texts excited me at first. To be honest, I imagined they were from some other guy...Kyle, the man I used to love who had changed or maybe he was always this Kyle...

I imagined them coming from the man Kyle could be if he wanted. God...it is so frustrating, understanding what Kyle could be if he weren't so stubborn and lazy.

At first, Rick's texts were fun, playful, not creepy...

Then he started talking about my boobs, and then there was this description of how he imagined my nipples looked...

It was so gross—it was no longer fun, it was creepy, Rick was a fucking creep.

And then he sent a picture of his penis; it looked dirty, you *know* it probably reeked of garlic, just like the rest of him. His penis was ugly, just an ugly, splotchy piece of meat.

Kyle hacked into my phone and came at me with it, brandishing it like you hold a cross up to a vampire. We had a fight. Kyle wanted to report him but I needed Rick; I had other sponsors and they hadn't helped me, Rick the creep did. I texted Rick, told him that his texts were unacceptable and that he had violated my trust. Rick was the only sponsor who had worked but I just toughed it out and kept abstaining on my own.

In the present, Kyle was trying to get Noah to talk. He was always good with the kids, I know he loves them a lot; if our marriage ended it would have been logical to give custody of them to my husband. I went a little soft for K again, seeing him looking at our son sweetly, putting a hand on his shoulder. N looked unsure about the invaders and the cameras but still told us about some kittens he had found at school---

And then Mara walked in from the hallway.

"What is the situation with Rick?" She interrupted, looking from me to Kyle and then back to me.

"Noah was telling us about these kittens he found at school," Kyle said, giving her a stern look.

"Fuck the kittens," Mara said.

Rick might, I had to bite back a smile at that.

"Mara," I said quietly. "I know this is a weird situation, but we need to be nice to each other."

I looked up at Chelsea meaningfully.

"And we are not discussing private family business with strangers."

"Maybe they already know," Noah said softly.

"Yeah," My daughter agreed. "They've probably already interviewed Rick, if you guys were texting or whatever—"

For some reason, Kyle started laughing, chuckling at first, then really laughing. I shook my head at him.

"I texted him telling him to stop texting me," I pointed out. "I have been totally straight with you—"

"No," Kyle snapped. "Rick is still your sponsor therefore you have *not* been straight with me."

"What do you care?" I meant that—what did he care?

"It's going to be okay, guys," Kyle said with a weak smile. "Your mother and I still have good jobs---"

"Actually," Chelsea said. "You don't."

"What?" Kyle asked, the limp smile gone, a ragged edge to his voice.

I was smirking; maybe I looked amused but really it was a nervous smirk, a pained smirk—this was really happening, everything that *anchored us* was gone.

"Megan resigned with notice," Chelsea explained. "On Monday you, Kyle, will be called into a video conference with HR. They are going to have to let you go."

"And why is that?" K asked, actually holding his arms akimbo like a character in a play.

"They found a bunch of pornography on a work computer---"

"Of course they did!" My husband laughed.

The show's producers really *had* thought of everything.

I thought of how embarrassing that video conference would be for Kyle, a man with a lot of pride, and felt guilty. The moment the door had opened— The moment Chelsea used the key in the deadbolt, I understood there was no going back, no retracting things, no cancellation policy; the reset was happening.

Kyle said he was getting a beer and asked if our children wanted anything. Not me, just the children; it seemed passive aggressive.

Chelsea gave me a nod and I laid into her about how she ruined our lives and the negative effect it would have on our children. Kyle walked back from the kitchen in the middle of my tirade. Everything came naturally to me, maybe in my new life I could be a stage actress or something.

"Whatever," I scoffed. "When you leave we will just have to get new jobs and buy new cars and everything else."

I sat forward in the chair and looked meaningfully at Chelsea.

"All you've done is make our lives more difficult," I added. "Is this how your stupid show got so popular, ruining the lives of good people?"

"Maybe we need this," Mara said.

I knew my daughter would say something like that; Kyle likes to think he knows the children better, that he loves them more, but he *needs* to believe that—

There were words inside me, awful words, things that had been gone over and over. I really didn't want to say them, I knew they would put even more distance between my daughter and I, but it was part of the whole experience—that had been explained to me.

"Why do you have to be like this?" I barked at Mara.

She looked stunned, I didn't want to go on but I had to.

"It would be easier for you if you could be more like your brother," I continued, the words coming out my mouth hurting me as much as I knew they'd hurt my daughter. "He isn't into all this *dark shit*, he has friends and works hard in school, he befriends the mentally challenged kids, he even rescues kittens."

"Come on, Mom," Noah said. "Leave her alone."

"I love Mara," I finished, glad that part was nearly over. "But I just wish she was more like you, *for her sake*."

"You don't know anything," Noah said softly.

Kyle kept looking over at the glass of scotch meaningfully, a sick dog smile on his face. He probably thought I was getting sloppy because of the alcohol. It wasn't, it was my emotions, the pain of the terrible things I'd said to my child.

Noah wanted to go to his room. Chelsea went with him leaving the rest of us with the two intruders in ski masks.

"This is idiotic," Kyle pointed out. "Why are you filming us when she isn't here?"

"Why don't you just pretend she's here," the male cameraperson said, like the woman he had a gentle voice.

"This is just *ridiculous*," Kyle continued. "I'm guessing we will get kicked out of the house."

"That's part of it," the man with the camera said. "But there is a place for it if you want it. Chelsea will be able to explain it better."

"Why don't you talk about the text from Rick?" The woman camera operator asked, focusing on my husband and then myself.

"I am not talking about that with strangers," I said firmly but calmly.

"It's safe to assume that the Show has access to your text messages," Male Ski Mask said. "What would stop us from cutting to the texts from this discussion?"

"Uh, because we could sue you!" I pointed out. "Because those are private conversations and there are laws protecting people."

"We entered your house and are holding you against your will," Female Ski Mask said. "Do you really think the Show is concerned about *laws*?"

"Ah, you got to a good part without me!" Chelsea laughed as she walked back into the room.

"Is Noah okay?" Kyle asked.

"Yeah, he just got to talking about stuff and it got emotional," Chelsea smiled kindly. "He just needs a few to get it together."

She sat back down, looked from Megan to me and back to Megan again.

"You were about to talk about the texts, I can smell it!" Chelsea said.

"Rick and I were sexting, he did most of it," I said. "We never did anything."

Kyle snorted and shook his head.

"What do you care?" I asked him. "If I *was* with someone else it would take you off the hook."

"You always close your eyes," I continued, improvising. "I ask what you're thinking about and you always say you're just enjoying the moment--I know you're thinking about someone else. And then there's the history on your phone..."

Kyle had gone on and on about those texts, texts I had *not* initiated—what about the porn he looked at? I had asked him over and over not to look at porn without me, to make it part of things the two of us did together, and he'd nod and agree but it was just to shut me up and when he was in his office he'd look at porn again...and again. How was that not worse than a bunch of creepy texts I never asked for?

"What did you mean when you said we'd be taken care of?" Kyle asked Chelsea.

"Money from our contestants goes to a place we call the Haven," She explained. "It's a place out in the country with a bunch of cabins; contestants can stay out there as long as they want but if it's full time they have to do work around the place. It's actually a great place, we have all sorts of wildlife, I love the blue jays."

"Sounds lovely," Kyle said snidely.

"It kind of does," I said. "Just...relax."

Chelsea gave me a funny look—what was wrong with what I said? How much longer would I have to keep things to myself?

"It's a good way to reset," Chelsea nodded to my husband. "Clear your head, see what your priorities really are."

C reached up and touched her left ear, another cue. The scotch *was* affecting me, I was forgetting lines.

"We *had* what we wanted," I snarled. "We had a home, we had been saving money for our retirement; we provided for our kids---"

"This place sucks," Mara said.

"Then we will legally emancipate you and you can live in a fucking squalid art studio or whatever it is you want!" I shouted at her. She winced, I could feel it in my own muscles.

"Megan, *stop*," Kyle said.

"Mara," I continued, almost on the verge of tears. "I don't...I don't know what to do with you. I love you so much but I don't know...we're so different."

That was true, every word of it. How had normal people like Kyle and I created such a brilliant, artistic daughter? When she was a child it had been easy, she was simple and open then; my daughter even loved the same music as me and we'd have little dance parties. But then she was in the double digits and became…Mara, the real Mara. The child had just been an egg, a beautiful robin's egg or something, but then the egg cracked open and my real daughter emerged.

Noah walked back in with his phone in his hand, the female camera op took it from him.

"Sorry," Chelsea said. "No phones, no tablets, no laptops."

"Afraid we'll call the cops?" Kyle aske.d

"No," Chelsea said with a tight smile. "So you can focus. This is important, the most important weekend of your lives."

"You're going to be here the whole weekend?" I asked.

"That's usually how long it takes," Chelsea replied.

THE COUCH

A few minutes after midnight Mara was nodding off. Kyle went to get her a blanket from the closet and it touched me; after all the stuff I had been forced to say everything inside me was raw and Kyle's gesture got to me. He loves our kids so much, probably even loved *me* in a sweet, simple, but genuine way that nevertheless left me unfulfilled. Chelsea told us that we could sleep in our rooms but added that there would be cameras there. My daughter walked out of the living room followed by Noah a couple of minutes later. I poured more whiskey. Kyle, of course, watched grimly. I was feeling the alcohol; it was a relief. I had been at that job for years and we'd been in this house for a decade; soon it would all be gone. What then? All those filled up spaces, suddenly empty.

My husband was clearly nodding off. He looked anxious and I had a good idea why.
"Do you mind sleeping on the couch in your office?" I asked him.
"No, that's fine," he smiled.
Part of me wanted to be close to him, to be comforted, but things needed to change; neither of us could keep falling back on something neither of us wanted.

MAKING COFFEE

My body wasn't used to the alcohol and I had drank a lot. I slept badly.
When I walked into the living room Kyle looked happy; he was talking
about when he was a child and the joy he felt was apparent. Looking at him,
I understood that I still loved him deeply; in the same breath I also
understood that was no longer enough to justify our remaining married.

Mara was drinking coffee from my green mug, a little *fuck you, bitch* on her
part. How could I blame her after the things I said? Again, I wondered if I
had made a bad decision; I had thought about it for nearly a year but maybe
that wasn't long enough. Needing coffee, I went into the kitchen—Mara
had poured herself the last of it…into my cup. Normally Kyle or our
daughter makes the coffee---
"Where are the filters?" I called in the direction of the living room.
Mara walked into the kitchen. She did not look at me as she got the filters
and coffee and made a fresh pot.
"You have every right to be angry with me," I said.
That only made my daughter angrier, I could see her gritting her teeth.
"You make it strong, don't you?" I asked.
Mara froze, I could see her thinking, probably trying to figure out how
snide she wanted her reaction to be.
"You used to like it stronger," My daughter said. You could hear the tension
in her voice. "I learned to make coffee for someone who was usually
nursing a hangover."
I deserved that, especially after the day before—
What had I done? Why had I agreed to say such an awful thing to my
daughter?

"You knew I was going to come in here, Mara," I said gently. "You knew I was going to follow you in, part of you wants to talk to me."

The coffeemaker was burbling, Mara was glancing in my general direction but mostly averting her eyes.

Part of me *did* want to talk to her but that part had no idea what to say.

"You were just telling the truth," Mara said wearily. "It's what you feel...whatever."

Kyle would have taken a step forward to awkwardly put a hand on her shoulder—

No, he would have had no reason to because he would never say the things I said.

"I'm not upset with you, Mara, I just worry---"

"I'm okay," My daughter cut in. "Worry about Noah."

"I do," I replied. "But I worry about *you* because...who do you have who gets you? You're all about art...you see the world in a way your father and I don't—we have no idea how to guide you because our minds don't work like yours, we have never had similar experiences growing up."

Mara faced me, I could see how difficult it was for her. I wanted to hug her; I am not normally a hugger and in that moment I really wished I was.

"Maybe you're not supposed to," Mara said. "Maybe all I need is for you to be there for me."

And then she looked over, towards the streaming coffee maker.

"Sorry I took your cup," She added. "Coffee should be done in a minute."

Before I could say anything else my daughter walked out of the kitchen. The coffee appeared to be finished. I had grabbed a cup from my old college; the logo was nearly faded, I just stared at that stupid logo and understood why looking at the past made Kyle so happy; things were simpler back then. I was dating a great guy, a caring boy becoming a caring man. He had been a virgin and Kyle was the second guy I'd been with so we were generally equal in that area—

But 21 year old me was not 41 year old me; I have different needs, maybe I am a different person.

Chelsea walked into the kitchen. She took the cup from my hands, filled it two thirds of the way, and handed it back.

"You put a lot of milk in it, right?" Our guest asked.

By the way she was smiling, it was clear that was some sort of joke—

Of course she knew, it was all part of the paperwork.

"She'll forgive you," Chelsea added, getting a second cup for herself. "It may take awhile, but she's only sixteen, she'll be a different person in a few years and that person will be open to reconciling with you."

"I think Mara is who she is supposed to be," I said quietly. "I don't think she will ever change, just evolve."

Chelsea took a sip of her coffee and seemed to be studying me.

"You did this for your family," she said. "Remember that. Everything is going to be crazy for a while, you'll all feel displacement, but your new life….I have faith it is going to be so much better.

"I hope so."

LAUREL

CHAPTER FINALE

Chelsea and Megan walked out of the kitchen. Brad had gone out front for a smoke but neither of us were worried: I could handle the husband and the teenagers myself; we had been watching them closely, how they moved, how they reacted to things.

"Cool," Brad said after we agreed one of us could handle the Shones. "When you need a break, let me know."

"Yeah, I'll see how Big C calls things," I sighed; our boss tended to be over cautious. Brad and I are the security experts, I don't know why she couldn't just leave the security to us.

C nodded over at me, something was going to happen, maybe the *reveal*. This was the part of the show I still enjoyed even after five chapters: The anticipation of the family members to discover who had contacted the producers. Chelsea got into a conversation with the boy. The abortion hadn't come up which confused Brad and I because it seemed like a huge plot point, a big twist, engrossing to viewers to see the side of a character they never imagined.

"It seems like a cliche," C had said in the RV the night before. "This show is better than that."

My boss thinks Reset is the most revolutionary show ever: A huge statement about the uselessness of materialism or something like that. I liked my job but I had no idea what to believe about the boss; when she wasn't hosting a new season she was off at Haven dressing and living like a hippy. Viewers always ask why the boss always wears long sleeves even in summer and it can't be explained that it is to cover up all the tattoos. One of us had to remind her to wear deodorant; you wouldn't guess any of these things if you went by how she appears on the show—she plays the Host like a high dollar realtor or something.

"Kyle, do you know who contacted me about your family?" Chelsea asked the husband.

Kyle looked over at Mara; of course he suspected *her*, the daughter was the outsider in the family. Viewers would probably suspect Mara as well, Chelsea had said as much in the RV.

"Really, Dad?" Mara looked offended. "You think I want anything to do with some cheesy show?"

Her dad looked flustered. I felt sorry for the guy; he was kind of a pussy, not as direct and strong as he should be, but it was clear he loved his family. Did the others suspect *him*? Viewers might; he was stuck in a marriage he had no idea how to fix—if it ended he would be free of Megan and could get custody of the kids he clearly loved. All of us agreed that viewers would place lower odds on Noah; he seemed too earnest to throw a wrench in everything, and he would be afraid of his mother's reaction.

"And what will viewers think of Megan?"Chelsea asked me in the RV the previous night.

"She seems to have the most invested in the status quo," I replied after thinking about it for a few seconds. "She is the Alpha, she made this house happen, lowest odds will be on her."

My observation pleased the boss.

Back at the reveal, C went over and put a hand on Noah's shoulder.

"What about you, Noah? Who do you think contacted us?"

"I have no idea,"the teenager said quietly. It was clear he was lying both in his voice and his body language.

"It was Mom," Mara said out of nowhere.

That surprised Megan, caught her off guard enough that she didn't have time to pull a straight face. Her husband and children looked over at her. "You?"Kyle asked, genuinely surprised.

"I built all this," his wife said. "I could see that I had to destroy it."

The husband looked pissed. He was kind of a wuss, but even wimps sometimes *explode*. I took a step closer to the action, pressed a button to let Brad know his smoke break was over.

"Yeah, okay,"Kyle sighed.

He no longer looked pissed off, his expression revealed a few different things: Determination. Relief. Sadness.

"I want custody of the kids," he added firmly. "But we can work all this out after these people leave."

Megan looked stunned by that, she opened her mouth but no words came out. Kyle saw how distressed his wife was and softened, I was really hoping he wouldn't wimp out.

"Why couldn't you have gone to counseling with me?"He said sadly. Was he going to cry? That tended to turn viewers off, soft dudes crying. Oddly enough, a manly sort of man crying was actually a positive thing in the ratings—go figure.

Megan took a step forward and took her husband's hands in her own. Would they reconcile? It was kind of cheesy but people still bought into happy endings. Kyle looked down at their hands, squeezed his wife's, he was struggling not to cry.

"I'll always have love for you,"he said with a gentle smile. "But you broke it, and now it's broken."

The boss was in a good mood as we drove away. The Shones no longer had a house, cars, or jobs and the family had broken up; it seemed kind of cold to be so gleeful.

"You don't get it, Laurel," Chelsea said, leaning forward in her seat. "The Shones are dead, long live the Shones. Kyle wasn't happy, nor was Megan. She is at her peak sexually, Kyle…I don't know, it sounds like he got bored with her sexually….combine that with Megan being unwilling to go to marriage counseling—"

Chelsea lit a cigarette and opened the window behind her.

"They were just going to stay in that rut,"she continued. "Finally one of them just threw a bomb in the middle of everything."

"I wonder how they'll make out,"I said, mostly to myself.

"It will be hard at first,"C said, blowing smoke out her nostrils. "But Megan is tough and Kyle will do what he has to for those kids."

"Do you see them coming out to Haven?"

My boss had to think about that.

"No, none of them are the type. Megan might entertain the idea, but we're a hundred miles from the nearest Starbucks."

I had no response to that. It was pointless to talk about the Shones anymore, they were a closed chapter. In a couple of weeks we'd get the notes on a new family and a new chapter of *Reset* would begin.

Written between 20 February, 2021 and 21 August, 2022

Music listened to: "Year of the Cat" Al Stewart